LAST ORDERS

LAST ORDERS

GRAHAM SWIFT

ALFRED A. KNOPF   NEW YORK

1996

For Al

*But man is a Noble Animal, splendid in ashes,
and pompous in the grave.*

Sir Thomas Browne: *Urn Burial*

I do like to be beside the seaside.

John A. Glover-Kind

BERMONDSEY

It aint like your regular sort of day.

Bernie pulls me a pint and puts it in front of me. He looks at me, puzzled, with his loose, doggy face but he can tell I don't want no chit-chat. That's why I'm here, five minutes after opening, for a little silent pow-wow with a pint glass. He can see the black tie, though it's four days since the funeral. I hand him a fiver and he takes it to the till and brings back my change. He puts the coins, extra gently, eyeing me, on the bar beside my pint.

'Won't be the same, will it?' he says, shaking his head and looking a little way along the bar, like at unoccupied space. 'Won't be the same.'

I say, 'You aint seen the last of him yet.'

He says, 'You what?'

I sip the froth off my beer. 'I said you aint seen the last of him yet.'

He frowns, scratching his cheek, looking at me. 'Course, Ray,' he says and moves off down the bar.

I never meant to make no joke of it.

I suck an inch off my pint and light up a snout. There's maybe three or four other early-birds apart from me, and the place don't look its best. Chilly, a whiff of disinfectant, too much empty space. There's a shaft of sunlight coming through the window, full of specks. Makes you think of a church.

I sit there, watching the old clock, up behind the bar. *Thos. Slattery, Clockmaker, Southwark.* The bottles racked up like organ pipes.

Lenny's next to arrive. He's not wearing a black tie, he's not wearing a tie at all. He takes a quick shufty at what I'm wearing and we both feel we gauged it wrong.

'Let me, Lenny,' I say. 'Pint?'

He says, 'This is a turn-up.'

Bernie comes over. He says, 'New timetable, is it?'

'Morning,' Lenny says.

'Pint for Lenny,' I say.

'Retired now, have we, Lenny?' Bernie says.

'Past the age for it, aint I, Bern? I aint like Raysy here, man of leisure. Fruit and veg trade needs me.'

'But not today, eh?' Bernie says.

Bernie draws the pint and moves off to the till.

'You haven't told him?' Lenny says, looking at Bernie.

'No,' I say, looking at my beer, then at Lenny.

Lenny lifts his eyebrows. His face looks raw and flushed. It always does, like it's going to come out in a bruise. He tugs at his collar where his tie isn't.

'It's a turn-up,' he says. 'And Amy aint coming? I mean, she aint changed her mind?'

'No,' I say. 'Down to us, I reckon. The inner circle.'

'Her own husband,' he says.

He takes hold of his pint but he's slow to start drinking, as if there's different rules today even for drinking a pint of beer.

'We going to Vic's?' he says.

'No, Vic's coming here,' I say.

He nods, lifts his glass, then checks it, sudden, half-way to his mouth. His eyebrows go even higher.

I say, 'Vic's coming here. With Jack. Drink up, Lenny.'

Vic arrives about five minutes later. He's wearing a black tie but you'd expect that, seeing as he's an undertaker, seeing as he's just come from his premises. But he's not wearing his full rig. He's wearing a fawn raincoat, with a flat cap poking out of one of the pockets, as if he's aimed to pitch it right: he's just one of us, it aint official business, it's different.

'Morning,' he says.

I've been wondering what he'll have with him. So's Lenny, I dare say. Like I've had this picture of Vic opening the pub door and marching in, all solemn, with a little oak casket with brass fittings. But all he's carrying, under one arm, is a plain brown cardboard box, about a foot high and six inches square. He looks like a man who's been down the shops and bought a set of bathroom tiles.

He parks himself on the stool next to Lenny, putting the box on the bar, unbuttoning his raincoat.

'Fresh out,' he says.

'Is that it then?' Lenny says, looking. 'Is that him?'

'Yes,' Vic says. 'What are we drinking?'

'What's inside?' Lenny says.

'What do you think?' Vic says.

He twists the box round so we can see there's a white card sellotaped to one side. There's a date and a number and a name: JACK ARTHUR DODDS.

Lenny says, 'I mean, he aint just in a box, is he?'

By way of answering Vic picks up the box and flips open the flaps at the top with his thumb. 'Mine's a whisky,' he says, 'I think it's a whisky day.'

He feels inside the box and slowly pulls out a plastic container. It looks like a large instant-coffee jar, it's got the same kind of screw-on cap. But it's not glass, it's a bronzy-coloured, faintly shiny plastic. There's another label on the cap.

'Here,' Vic says and hands the jar to Lenny.

Lenny takes it, uncertain, as if he's not ready to take it

but he can't not take it, as if he ought to have washed his hands first. He don't seem prepared for the weight. He sits on his bar-stool, holding it, not knowing what to say, but I reckon he's thinking the same things I'm thinking. Whether it's all Jack in there or Jack mixed up with bits of others, the ones who were done before and the ones who were done after. So Lenny could be holding some of Jack and some of some other feller's wife, for example. And if it *is* Jack, whether it's really all of him or only what they could fit in the jar, him being a big bloke.

He says, 'Don't seem possible, does it?' Then he hands me the jar, all sort of getting-in-the-mood, like it's a party game. Guess the weight.

'Heavy,' I say.

'Packed solid,' Vic says.

I reckon I wouldn't fill it, being on the small side. I suppose it wouldn't do to unscrew the cap.

I pass it back to Lenny. Lenny passes it back to Vic.

Vic says, 'Where's Bern got to?'

Vic's a square-set, ready-and-steady sort of a bloke, the sort of bloke who rubs his hands together at the start of something. His hands are always clean. He looks at me holding the jar like he's just given me a present. It's a comfort to know your undertaker's your mate. It must have been a comfort to Jack. It's a comfort to know your own mate will lay you out and box you up and do the necessary. So Vic better last out.

It must have been a comfort to Jack that there was his shop, *Dodds & Son, Family Butcher*, and there was Vic's just across the street, with the wax flowers and the marble slabs and the angel with its head bowed in the window: *Tucker & Sons, Funeral Services*. A comfort and an incentive, and a sort of fittingness too, seeing as there was dead animals in the one and stiffs in the other.

Maybe that's why Jack never wanted to budge.

RAY

I'd said to Jack, 'It aint never gone nowhere,' and Jack'd
said, 'What's that, Raysy? Can't hear you.' He was leaning
over towards Vince.

It was coming up to last orders.

I said, 'They calls it the Coach and Horses but it aint
never gone nowhere.'

He said, 'What?'

We were perched by the bar, usual spot. Me, Lenny, Jack
and Vince. It was young Vince's birthday, so we were all well
oiled, Vince's fortieth. And it was the Coach's hundredth, if
you could go by the clock. I was staring at it – Coach and
Horses in brass letters round the top. *Slattery. 1884.* First
time I'd thought of it. And Vince was staring at Bernie
Skinner's new barmaid, Brenda, or was it Glenda? Or rather
at the skirt she was squeezed into, like she was sitting down
when she was standing up.

I wasn't just staring at the clock, either.

Jack said, 'Vince, your eyes'll pop out.'

Vince said, 'So will her arse.'

Jack laughed. You could see how we were all wishing we
were Vincey's age again.

I hadn't seen Jack so chummy with Vince for a long time.
Maybe he was having to be, on account of it being Vincey's
big day. That's if it was his big day, because Lenny says to
me, same evening, when we meet up in the pisser, 'Have
you ever wondered how he knows it's his birthday? Jack and
Amy weren't ever a witness, were they? They never got no
certificate. My Joan thinks Amy just picked March the third

6

out the air. April the first might've been a better bet, mightn't it?'

Lenny's a stirrer.

We stood there piddling and swaying and I said, 'No, I aint ever wondered that. All these years.'

Lenny said, 'Still, I forget my own birthday these days. It's been a while since the rest of us saw forty, aint it, Ray?'

I said, 'Fair while.'

Lenny said, 'Mustn't begrudge the tosser his turn.' He zipped up and lurched back into the bar and I stood there staring at the porcelain.

I said, 'Daft name to call a pub.'

Jack said, 'What's that?'

I said, 'The Coach. The Coach. I'm trying to tell you.'

Vince said, looking at Brenda, 'It's Ray's joke.'

'When it aint ever moved.'

Jack said, 'Well, you should put that right, Raysy. You're the one for the horses. You ought to tell old Bernie there to crack his whip.'

Vince said, 'She can crack my whip any day.'

Jack said, 'I'll crack your head. If Mandy don't.'

And he only said it in the nick of time because half a minute later Mandy herself walks in, come to fetch Vincey home. She's been round at Jack's place, nattering with Amy and Joan. Vincey don't see her, looking at other things, but Jack and me do but we don't let on, and she comes up behind Vince and spreads her hands over his face and says, 'Hello, big eyes, guess who?'

She aint built on Brenda's lines any more but she's not doing so bad for nearly forty herself, and there's the clobber, red leather jacket over a black lace top, for a start. She says,

'Come to get you, birthday boy,' and Vincey pulls down one of her hands and pretends to bite it. He's wearing one of his fancy ties, blue and yellow zig-zags, knot pulled loose. He nibbles Mandy's hand and she takes her other hand from his face and pretends to claw his chest. So when they get up to go and we watch them move to the door, Lenny says, 'Young love, eh?', his tongue in the corner of his mouth.

But before they go Jack says, 'Don't I get a kiss, then?' and Mandy says, 'Course you do, Jack,' smiling, and we all watch while she puts her arms round Jack's neck, like she means it, and gives him two big wet ones, one on each cheek, and we all see Jack's hand come round, while she hangs on, to pat her arse. It's a big hand. We all see one of Mandy's heels lift out of her shoe. I reckon she took a drop of something with her round to Amy's. Then Jack says, shaking loose, 'Go on, get on out of it. And get this clown out of it too,' pointing at Vince.

Then Jack and Vince look at each other and Jack says, 'Happy birthday, son. Good to see you,' as if he can't see him any day he chooses. Vince says, 'Night Jack,' grabbing his jacket from the hook under the bar, and just for a moment it's like he's going to hold out his hand for Jack to shake. Forgive and forget. He puts his hand on Jack's shoulder instead, like he needs the help-up, but I reckon, by Jack's face, he gives a quick squeeze.

Jack says, 'You've only got an hour of it left.'

Mandy says, 'Better make the most of it.'

Lenny says, 'Promises.'

Vince says, 'Never know your luck.'

Mandy tugs at Vince's arm while he picks up his glass and drains off what's left, not hurrying. He says, 'Keep 'em hungry, that's what I say.' He runs his wrist across his mouth. 'Needs must.'

Lenny says, 'You're an old man now, Big Boy. Home before closing, and you have to be carted.'

I say, 'Coach is leaving.'

Lenny says, 'Don't mind Ray, Mandy. Aint his day. Backed the wrong gee-gee. Sleep tight, won't you, Mandy.'

That red jacket's a bad clash with Lenny's face.

Mandy says, 'Night boys.'

Jack's smiling. 'Night kids.'

And everyone can see, as they slip out, Vincey with his hand just nudging Mandy's back, that they're the only ones in this pub with the jam. Nice motor parked outside, perk of the trade. Nice little daughter waiting up for them, fourteen years old. But that's like eighteen these days.

Lenny says, 'Turtle doves, eh?' pawing an empty glass. 'Who's in the chair?' And Jack says, 'I am,' looking like it's his birthday too.

It was coming up to last orders, to when Bernie bangs on his bell, like it isn't a coach, it's a fire-engine. Even then it don't move. There was smoke and noise and yak and cackle and Brenda bending and pools of spillage along the bar top. Saturday night. And I said, 'It's a hundred this year, aint anyone noticed?'

Jack said, 'What's a hundred?'

I said, 'Pub is, Coach is. Look at the clock.'

Jack said, 'It's ten to eleven.'

'But it aint ever gone nowhere, has it?'

'The clock?'

'The Coach, the Coach.'

And Jack said, 'Where d'you think it should be going, Raysy? Where d'you think we've all got to get to that the bleeding coach should be taking us?'

BERMONDSEY

Vic takes the jar and starts to ease it back in the box but it's a tricky business and the box slides from his lap on to the floor, so he puts the jar on the bar.

It's about the same size as a pint glass.

He says, 'Bern!'

Bernie's at the other end of the bar, usual drying-up towel over his shoulder. He turns and comes towards us. He's about to say something to Vic, then he sees the jar, by Lenny's pint. He checks himself and he says, 'What's that?' But as if he's already worked out the answer.

'It's Jack,' Vic says. 'It's Jack's ashes.'

Bernie looks at the jar, then he looks at Vic, then he gives a quick look round the whole of the bar. He looks like he looks when he's making up his mind to eject an unwanted customer, which he's good at. Like he's building up steam. Then his face goes quiet, it goes almost shy.

'That's Jack?' he says, leaning closer, as if the jar might answer back, it might say, 'Hello Bernie.'

'Jesus God,' Bernie says, 'what's he doing here?'

So Vic explains. It's best that Vic explains, being the professional. Coming from Lenny or me, it might sound like a load of hooey.

Then I say, 'So we thought he should have a last look-in at the Coach.'

'I see,' Bernie says, like he don't see.

'It's a turn-up,' Lenny says.

Vic says, 'Get me a large scotch, Bernie. Have one yourself.'

'I will, thank you, I will, Vic,' Bernie says, all considered and respectful, like a scotch is appropriate and it don't do to refuse a drink from an undertaker.

He takes two glasses from the rack and squeezes one up against the scotch bottle, two shots, then he takes just a single for himself. He turns and slides the double across to Vic. Vic pushes over a fiver, but Bernie holds up a hand. 'On the house, Vic, on the house,' he says. 'Aint every day, is it?' Then he raises his glass, eyes on the jar, as if he's going to say something speechy and grand but he says, 'Jesus God, he was only sitting there six weeks ago.'

We all look into our drinks.

Vic says, 'Well here's to him.'

We lift our glasses, mumbling. JackJackJack.

'And here's to you, Vic,' I say. 'You did a good job Thursday.'

'Went a treat,' Lenny says.

'Don't mention it,' Vic says. 'How's Amy?'

'Managing,' I say.

'She hasn't changed her mind about coming then?'

'No, she'll be seeing June, as per usual.'

Everyone's silent.

Vic says, 'Her decision, isn't it?'

Lenny sticks his nose in his glass like he's not going to say anything.

Bernie's looking at the jar and looking anxiously round the bar. He looks at Vic like he don't want to make a fuss but.

Vic says, 'Point taken, Bernie,' and takes the jar from where it's sitting. He reaches down for the fallen box. 'Not much good for business, is it?'

'Aint helping yours much either, Vic,' Lenny says.

Vic slides the jar carefully back into the box. It's eleven

twenty by Slattery's clock and it feels less churchy. There's more punters coming in. Someone's put on the music machine. *Going back some day, come what may, to Blue Bayou . . .* That's better, that's better.

First wet rings on the mahogany, first drifts of blue smoke.

Vic says, 'Well all we need now is our chauffeur.'

Lenny says, 'They're playing his tune. Wonder what he'll bring. Drives something different every week, these days, far as I can see.'

Bernie says, 'Same again all round?'

As he speaks there's a hooting and tooting outside in the street. A pause, then another burst.

Lenny says, 'Sounds like him now. Sounds like Vincey.'

There's a fresh round of hooting.

Vic says, 'Isn't he coming in?'

Lenny says, 'I reckon he wants us out there.'

We don't go out but we get up and go over to the window. Vic keeps hold of the box, like someone might pinch it. We raise ourselves up on our toes, heads close together, so we can see above the frosted half of the window. I can't quite, but I don't say.

'Jesus Christ,' Lenny says.

'It's a Merc,' Vic says.

'Trust Big Boy,' Lenny says.

I push down on the sill to give myself a second's extra lift. It's a royal blue Merc, cream seats, gleaming in the April sunshine.

'Jesus,' I say. 'A Merc.'

Lenny says, it's like a joke he's been saving up for fifty years, 'Rommel *would* be pleased.'

RAY

Amy eyes me as I look up from reading the letter.

She says, 'I suppose he thought he'd get there in the end, one way or the other.'

I say, 'When did he write it?'

She says, 'A couple of days before he—'

I look at her and I say, 'He could have just told you. Why'd he have to write a letter?'

She says, 'I suppose he thought I'd think he was joking. I suppose he thought it would make it proper.'

It's not a long letter, but it could be shorter, because of the way it's wrapped up in language like you see in the small print on the back of forms. It's not Jack's language at all. But I suppose a man can get all wordy, all official, when he knows his number's up.

But the gist of it's plain. It says he wants his ashes to be chucked off the end of Margate pier.

It don't even say, 'Dear Amy'. It says, 'To whom it may concern'.

She says, 'I've told Vic. He said it don't make any difference. It says in his will he's to be cremated but what gets done with the ashes is a free decision. You can throw them anywhere so long as it's not over someone else's property.'

'So?'

'So Vic says: "Amy, if you want to do it, do it. If you want me to do it, I'll do it. I'll see it doesn't add too much on the bill. But one thing's certain," he says, "if you don't do it, Jack won't ever know." '

'So?'

We're sitting out in the garden by St Thomas's, opposite Big Ben. She looks out across the river as if she's putting it to herself what she'd do if she had Jack's ashes now and he'd told her she should chuck him in the Thames, to the sound of Big Ben. But we haven't got Jack's ashes. All we've got is Jack's pyjamas, two pairs, and his toothbrush and his razor and his wristwatch and a few other odds and ends, which they give you in a plastic bag when you collect the forms. So we don't have to go there any more now, there aint no reason. No more walking down that squeaky corridor, no more hanging about drinking cups of tea. There'll be someone else in his bed now already, some other bleeder.

It's a mild grey day and the water's grey, and she keeps looking out over it without speaking, so I say, because I think maybe it's what she wants me to say: 'If you want to do it, Amy, I'll take you.'

'In the old camper?' she says, turning.

I say, 'Course.' I think she's going to smile and say yes. I think the day's going to brighten up.

She says, 'I can't do it, Ray. I mean – thank you. But I don't want to do it anyway.'

She looks out again at the river and I can't tell whether she thinks it's all a bad joke, on account of how Jack had been finally about to do what it was looking like he'd never do: sell up the shop, hang up his striped apron and look around for some other way to pass the time. On account of how she and Jack had found this nice little bungalow down in Margate. Westgate. It was all set up to go ahead. Then Jack goes down with a nasty touch of stomach cancer.

It's not for me to say it but I say it: 'A dying man's request, Amy.'

She looks at me. 'Will *you* do it, Ray?' Her face looks emptied out. 'That way it's done, isn't it? That way his wish gets carried out. He only says, "To whom it may concern", doesn't he?'

I pause for just a bit. 'Okay, I'll do it. Course I'll do it. But what about Vince?'

'I haven't told Vince. About this, I mean.' She nods at the letter. 'I'll tell him. Maybe you and him—'

I say, 'I'll talk to Vince.'

I hand back the letter. It's Jack's handwriting, but it's Jack's handwriting gone all wispy and weak and thin. It's not like the writing you used to see on that board at the front of the shop. *Pork Chops – Down in Price.*

I say, 'Could have been worse, Amy. You could already have bought that bungalow and be just about to move. Or you could have just been settling in and—'

She says, 'It's like he almost got his own way, anyway.'

I look at her.

'To work on till he dropped.' She folds the letter. 'In the end *I* was the problem. *I* was the obstacle. Didn't you know? When I knew he was serious, when I knew he really meant to pack it all in. I said, "What am I going to do about June?" He said, "That's just the point, girl. If I can give up being Jack Dodds, family butcher, then you can give up going on that fool's errand every week." That's what he called it: "fool's errand".'

She looks again at the water. 'You know how when he had a change of mind, the whole world had to change too. He said, we're going to be new people.' She gives another little snort. 'New people.'

I look away across the garden because I don't want her to see the thought that might be showing in my face: that it's a pretty poor starting-point, all said, for becoming new people, a bungalow in Margate. It's not exactly the promised land.

There's a nurse chomping a sandwich on a bench in the far corner. Pigeons waddling.

Maybe Amy's having the same thought, maybe she's had it. Not the promised land.

I say, 'You sure you wouldn't want to come?'

She shakes her head. 'Got my reasons, haven't I, Ray?' She looks at me.

'I suppose Jack had too,' I say, tapping the letter in her hand. I let my hand move up to give her arm a little squeeze.

'The seaside, eh Ray?' She looks again at the river. 'Yes, he had his reasons.' Then she clams up.

The nurse has blonde hair, tied up nurse-fashion. Black legs.

'Anyway,' she says, 'I don't think we could've done it. When you totted it all up. When you took away what Jack owed on the shop.' Her face goes just a touch bitter.

'We'd have been a fair bit short.'

The nurse finishes her sandwich, brushing down her skirt. The pigeons waddle quicker, pecking. They look like scatterings of ashes, bits of ashes with wings.

I say, 'How much short?'

OLD KENT ROAD

We head down past Albany Road and Trafalgar Avenue and the Rotherhithe turn. Green Man, Thomas à Becket, Lord Nelson. The sky's almost as blue as the car.

Vince says, 'Goes along sweet, don't it?' And he takes his hands off the wheel so we can get the feel of how the car takes care of itself. It seems to veer a shade to the left.

He said he thought he should do Jack proud, he thought he should give him a real treat. Since it had been sitting there in the showroom for nearly a month anyway, with a 'client' who couldn't make up his mind, and a bit more on the clock wouldn't signify and it don't do to let a car sit. He thought he should give Jack the best.

But it's not so bad for us too, for Vic and Lenny and me, sitting up, alive and breathing. The world looks pretty good when you're perched on cream leather and looking out at it through tinted electric windows, even the Old Kent Road looks good.

It veers a shade to the left. Lenny says, 'Don't go and give it a dent, will you, Big Boy? Don't want you to lose a sale.'

Vince says he don't dent cars, ever, least of all when he's driving extra steady and careful, on account of the special occasion.

Lenny says, 'With your hands off the wheel.'

Then Vince asks Vic what they do in a hearse when they have to go on a motorway.

Vic says, 'We step on it.'

Vince isn't wearing a black tie. It's just me and Vic. He's wearing a red and white jazzy tie and a dark blue suit. It's his showroom clobber, and he's come from the showroom, but he could have chosen some other tie. He's taken off his jacket, which is lying folded on the back seat between me and Lenny. Good-quality stuff. I reckon Vince is doing all right, he's not so badly placed after all. He says now they're feeling the pinch in the City they pop across in their lunch hours to do deals for cash.

Lenny says, 'Don't encourage him, Vic.'

Vic says, 'A hearse is different, everyone makes way for a hearse.'

Lenny says, 'You mean they don't make way for Vincey here?'

Vic sits in the front beside Vince, holding the box on his knees. I can see it's how it should be, Vic being the professional, but it don't seem right he should hold it all the time. Maybe we should take it in turns.

Vince looks across at Vic. He says, smiling, 'Busman's holiday, eh, Vic?'

Vince is wearing a white shirt with silver cuff-links, and pongy after-shave. His hair is all slicked back. It's a brand new suit.

We head on past the gas works, Ilderton Road, under the railway bridge. Prince of Windsor. The sun comes out from behind the tower blocks, bright in our faces, and Vince pulls out a pair of chunky sun-glasses from under the dashboard. Lenny starts singing, slyly, through his teeth, '*Blue bayooo. . .*' And we all feel it, what with the sunshine and the beer inside us and the journey ahead: like it's something Jack has done for us, so as to make us feel special, so as to give us a treat. Like we're off on a jaunt, a spree, and the world looks good, it looks like it's there just for us.

AMY

Well let 'em go, eh June? Let 'em do it, the whole bunch of 'em. Let 'em do without me. And you. Boys' outing. Do 'em good.

Jack should know that. All work and no play. Unless you count propping up the bar in the Coach.

That's what I told him all those years ago. We should give ourselves a break, a treat, we should give ourselves a holiday. His brave little Amy. When you fall off your horse you should get straight back on again. We should get ourselves out of ourselves. *New people.*

It might never have come to a choice between you and him.

My poor brave Jack.

Back on the merry-go-round, back on the swings. Seaside fun. All those things, June, you never knew. Donkey rides, bucket and spade, Punch and Judy. The waves coming in and the crowds on the beach and kids yelling, running, kids everywhere, and him looking at it like it was all a trick. Watch the birdie, kiss me quick, end of the pier.

But it wasn't the Pier, he even got that wrong. It was the Jetty. He ought to have remembered: the Pier and the Jetty, two different things, even if the Jetty looked more like a pier, and the Pier was only a harbour wall. Except there isn't no Jetty now, all swept away in a storm, years ago, and good riddance, I say, and amen. So maybe it wasn't his mistake, maybe it was his alternative arrangement. If he had to be chucked, if it was a case of chucking, if he had to be taken to the end of somewhere and chucked, but count me out, Jack, I won't be doing any chucking, then it had to be the Pier. Though it should have been the Jetty.

NEW CROSS

Vic says, 'Pam sends regards. She'll be thinking of us.'

Lenny says, 'Same goes for Joan.'

Vince says, 'And Mandy.'

I reckon if wives are being mentioned I should shut up.

Vince says, 'It was good to see Pam at the funeral, Vic. Aint often we get the pleasure.'

Vic says, 'Sad pleasure.'

Lenny says, 'Went a treat.'

We're coming up to the lights by New Cross Gate station and the traffic's slowing to a crawl.

I don't suppose Carol's even heard. I'd've got the shock of my life if she'd showed up at the funeral.

Lenny says, 'They might all've come along too. Joan was all set. But I suppose if Amy—'

I say, 'I don't know how we'd've squeezed in seven of us, Lenny, even into this thing.'

Vince says, 'Four of us is comfy. Maybe it's a blokes' job anyway.'

I say, 'Five.'

Vince says, 'Five.' Then he says, 'It aint a thing, Raysy, it's a Mercedes.'

Lenny looks at me then at the traffic all around us. 'Still, aint no car built yet that'll beat a jam, is there, Big Boy?'

Lenny's a stirrer.

Vic says, 'Pam was all for doing us sandwiches and a thermos but I said I thought we were old enough to take care of ourselves.' He's holding the box like it might be his lunch.

Vince says, 'She's a good 'un, Vic. It was good to see her.'

Lenny says, 'Joan was dead set.'

We creep forward five yards then stop. People are walking past us on the pavement, slipping into the station entrance like it's an ordinary day. We should have a flashing sign up: ASHES.

Lenny says, 'Every car's the same in a snarl-up, aint it?'

Vince drums his fingers on the steering wheel.

Vic says, 'Anyhow Pam says he's got a good guard-of-honour.'

We all straighten up, as if we've got to be different people, as if we're royalty and the people on the pavement ought to stop and wave.

VINCE

It's a 380 S-Class, that's what it is. V8, automatic. It's six
years old but it could do a hundred and thirty without a
wobble. Though not in the New Cross Road it won't.

Custom paintwork, all-leather upholstery.

So Hussein better buy it soon, cash, he better just. Otherwise I'm out of readies.

I'm not telling no one, not Amy, not Mandy, about Jack's
little last request, or about my little hand-out. I always said,
Don't come running to me, Jack, don't expect me to do any
shelling out.

Seems to me the only time a man can get what he asks is
when he's dying. Though he didn't ask for an S-Class Merc,
extra long wheelbase, walnut dash. So I hope he damn well
appreciates it, I hope he damn well does.

Hussein better damn well an' all.

It's got white-walled tyres. It needs some air in the front
near-side.

I said, 'Let me get you another, Jack, then I'm off home.
Family man now, aint I?' But he looks at me, holding up
his hand sudden like everyone should shut up, like it was
that last remark that did it, and I see Ray and Lenny start
peering into their beers.

But it was true. Me, Mand and little Kath. She was still
in short socks then.

He says, 'Excuse us, gents, Vince and me have got to have
a private word,' and he jostles me over to a table in the

corner. He says it's been a tough week and could I spare him a fiver, just so he can buy Ray and Lenny there a drink and not look a fool, but I knew it wasn't the five quid, I knew it wasn't why he'd asked me to call by in the first place. Five quid. Five large might be nearer the mark. If you're going to plead, plead straight.

But he don't go all humble and pleading. He looks at me like I'm the one who should be begging, as if it aint a loan he's after but more like I should be settling my dues. As if the least I owed him, and hasn't he let me know it, was to have teamed up with him years ago and acted like it was a real case of flesh and blood. Except it wasn't flesh and blood, it was meat. Meat or motors. That was the choice.

I say, 'Don't expect me to bail you out.'

But he stares at me like that's exactly what I'm required to do, like we struck a deal and now he's calling in my side of it. I should know about deals, shouldn't I, being a dealer myself, a used-car dealer? As if there was something wrong about used cars and something bleeding holy about meat.

I say, 'If you can't see what's under your nozzle. A new supermarket just up the road and they offer you first refusal as their meat manager. Aint got no choice, have you?'

He says, 'Haven't I?'

I say, 'Stay put if you want. It's your funeral.'

He says, 'At least I'd be my own man.'

I say, 'Your own man? You never were your own man. You were your old man's man, weren't you? What does it say over the shop?'

He looks at me as if he could knock me between the eyes.

He says, 'That cuts two ways, don't it?'

I say, 'Don't expect me to bail you out, that's all,' giving him a fiver. 'Don't expect nothing.' Slipping him another fiver.

I say, 'There's ten, Jack. Go and buy your mates a drink. Buy one for yourself an' all. Now I'm shoving off.'

And what did he ever do anyway? It was Amy. All he did was come home from winning the war and there I was – his welcome-home present – lying in that cot that was meant for June.

It's got cruise control, power steering.

And there he was, forty-odd years later, lying with the tubes in him, his own bleeding man all right, and he says, 'Come here, Vince. I want to ask you something.' He don't give it a rest.

It's a beautiful car.

And that surgeon – Strickland – looks at me like I'm his next victim, like it's me he's going to stick his knife in. I think, It's because he knows I'm not really next-of-kin. But then I think, No, it's because the old bastard's given him a hard time in the first place, and now this prick's passing it on. It would be like Jack to give a hard time even to the man who could save his life.

He starts to explain. He says, 'Do you know what your stomach looks like?' as if I'm a complete arsehole.

He says, 'And do you know where it is?'

It's the only way I could think of it. Like doing a repair job. A rebore or something, a decoke. I don't know how we work inside but I know a good motor when I see one, I know how to strip an engine. If you ask me, flesh and blood aint such a neat piece of work, not always, but a good motor is a good motor.

So Hussein better cough.

RAY

Jack would say, 'Bunch of ghosts, that's what you are in that office, Raysy. Bunch of bleeding zombies.' He'd say, 'You want to come up to Smithfield some time and see how real men make a living.'

And sometimes I did. In the early mornings, specially when it was all falling apart with me and Carol, when we weren't even speaking. I'd slip out early and get the 63 as usual but get off two stops later and walk up from Farringdon Road, up Charterhouse Street, in the half light. Breakfast at Smithfield. We'd go to that caff in Long Lane or to one of those pubs that serves beer and nosh at half past seven in the morning. There was Ted White from Peckham and Joe Malone from Rotherhithe and Jimmy Phelps from Camberwell. And of course, in the early days, there'd be Vince, being trained up. Before he joined up.

They'd say, what you need, Raysy, is a good feed-up, you're looking peaky. What you need is some meat on you. I'd say it was my natural build. Flyweight. Shovel it in, it don't make no difference.

Strange thing but you never see a thin butcher.

He used to give me all that old Smithfield guff, all that Smithfield blather. How Smithfield was the true centre, the true heart of London. Bleeding heart, of course, on account of the meat. How Smithfield wasn't just Smithfield, it was Life and Death. That's what it was: Life and Death. Because just across from the meat market there was St Bart's hospital, and just across from Bart's was your Old Bailey Central Criminal Court, on the site of old Newgate prison, where they used to string 'em up regular. So what you had in Smithfield was your three Ms: Meat, Medicine and Murders.

But it was Jimmy Phelps who told me that when he said all that, he was only saying what his old man used to say to him, Ronnie Dodds, word for word. And it was Jimmy Phelps who told me, when Jack was well out of earshot, when Jack and Vince were loaded up and on the way back to Bermondsey, that Jack had never wanted to be a butcher in the first place, never. It was only because the old man wouldn't have it otherwise. Dodds and Son, family butchers since 1903.

He says, 'Do you know what Jack wanted to be? Don't ever tell Jack I told you, will you?' And his face goes half smiling, half frightened, as if Jack's still there and might be creeping up behind him. 'When Jack was like Vince is now, being 'prenticed up, just like I was, he used to spend every spare minute eyeing up the nurses coming out of Bart's. I reckon it was the nurses that did it, he thought every doctor got a free couple of nurses to himself, but he says to me one day, and he aint joking, that he could chuck it all up and tell the old man to stew in his own stewing steak, because what he really wanted was to be a doctor.'

Jimmy creases up. He sits there in his smeared overalls, hands round a mug of tea, and he creases up. He says, 'He was serious. He said all it took was a change of white coats. Can you picture it? Doctor Dodds.'

But he sees I'm not laughing, so he sobers up.

'You won't tell Jack,' he says.

'No,' I say, sort of thoughtful, as if I might.

And I'm wondering if Jimmy Phelps always wanted to be a butcher. I'm remembering what Jack said, in the desert, that we're all the same underneath, officers and ranks, all the same material. Pips on a man's shoulders don't mean a tuppenny toss.

It wasn't out of wishing it that I became an insurance clerk.

But I never did tell Jack, and Jack never told me. Though you'd think when he was lying there in St Thomas's, with doctors and nurses all around him, it would have been a good time to let it slip. But all he said was, 'It should have been Bart's, eh Raysy? Bart's, by rights.'

And it seems to me that whether he ever wanted to be a doctor or not, all those years of being a butcher, all those years of going up to Smithfield stored him up a pretty good last laugh against the medical profession. Because he tells me that when the surgeon came to see him for the old heart-to-heart, the old word in the ear, he didn't want no flannel. No mumbo-jumbo.

'Raysy,' he says, 'I told him to give me the odds straight. He says he aint a betting man but I winkle it out of him. "Let's say two to one," he says. I say, "Sounds like I'm the bleeding favourite, don't it?" Then he starts up about how he can do this and he can do that, and I says, "Don't muck me about." I pulls open my pyjama top. I say, "Where d'you make the cut?" And he looks all sort of like his nose is out of joint and I aint playing according to the rules, so I say, "Professional interest, you understand. Professional interest." Then he looks at me puzzled, so I say, "Don't it say in that file of yours what I do for a living? Sorry, I mean 'did'." So he glances quickly down his notes – a bit sheepish now. Then he says, "Ah – I see that you were a butcher, Mr Dodds." And I says, "Master butcher." '

BLACKHEATH

'So anyone tell me?' Vic says. 'Why?'

'It's where we used to go,' Vince says. 'Sunday outings. In the old meat van.'

Lenny says, 'I know that, don't I, Big Boy? Think I don't remember? But this aint a Sunday outing.'

I say, 'It's where they went for their honeymoon.'

Lenny says, 'I thought they didn't have no honeymoon. I thought they were saving up for a pram at the time.'

'They had a honeymoon later,' I say. 'After June was born. They thought at least they should have their honeymoon.'

Lenny gives me a glance. 'Must have been some honeymoon.'

'It's true, though,' Vince says. 'Summer of '39.'

'You were there, were you, Big Boy?' Lenny says.

Everyone goes quiet.

'From a meat van to a Merc, eh?' Lenny says. 'Come to think of it, Raysy, you weren't around either.'

Vince is watching us in the driving mirror. You can't see his eyes behind those shades.

I say, 'Amy told me.'

Lenny says, 'Amy told you. She told you why she aint come along an' all?'

Everyone goes quiet.

Vic says, 'Makes no difference, does it? Jack's none the wiser, is he? As a matter of fact, I told her if she wanted to forget the whole thing he'd be none the wiser either. If they scattered the ashes in the cemetery garden, he wouldn't know, would he?'

'And you an undertaker,' Lenny says.

I say, 'She's seeing June. Today's her day for seeing June.'

'That aint the point,' Lenny says. 'If Amy didn't go to see June just for once, June'd be none the wiser either. June aint none the wiser about anything, is she? If Amy weren't up to it, she could have waited till she was ready, it didn't have to be done today.'

Vic says, 'You shouldn't judge.'

Lenny says, 'Ashes is ashes.'

Vic says, 'And best to do things prompt.'

Lenny says, 'And wishes is wishes.'

Vince says, 'How do we know he'd be none the wiser?'

Lenny says, 'Not that I'm saying I'd be such a fool as to make such a wish myself.'

'It wasn't specific,' I say.

Lenny says, 'What weren't specific?'

'What Jack wrote. About his wishes. It never said Amy should do it, just that he wanted it done.'

Lenny says, 'How d'you know that?'

'Amy showed me.'

'Amy showed you? Seems I'm the only one here who aint in the know.' He looks out the window. We're coming up on to Blackheath, past the back end of Greenwich Park. There are daffs out on the verges. 'And Raysy here's a mine of information.'

Vince is looking in the mirror.

Vic is getting all uncomfortable and tut-tutty, like it's time to change the subject. He says, 'It's like the horses. Have to prise it out of him these days.'

Vic's holding the box. I don't think he should hold the box all the time.

Lenny says, 'Even then, he gives you duff tips.'

I say, 'Last tip I gave came good.'

Vince is still looking.

Lenny says, 'Well it weren't for any of us.'

Vic says, 'Who, Raysy?' Vic'd make a good referee.

I say, 'Be telling, wouldn't it?'

I look out the window. Blackheath isn't black and it isn't a heath. It's all green grass under blue sky. If it weren't for the roads criss-crossing it, it would make a good gallop. Highwaymen here once. Coaches to Dover. Your money or your life.

Vic says, 'Well it's still a mystery. Why Margate?'

Lenny says, 'I reckon it was a try-on, just to see if we'd do it.'

Vince half turns in his seat. 'So you think he does know? You think he can see us?'

Lenny blinks and pauses a moment. He looks at me, then at Vic as if he needs some of that refereeing.

'Manner of speaking, Vincey, manner of speaking. Course he can't see us. He can't see nothing.'

Vic's hands move a little over the box.

Then Lenny chuckles. 'Mind you, Big Boy, if he can't see us, if he can't see nothing, why d'you go and borrow a Merc?'

Vince looks at the road ahead.

The sun's sparkling on the grass. Jack can't see it.

Vic says, slow and gentle, 'It's the gesture, Vince. It's a fine gesture. It's a beautiful car.'

Vince says, 'It aint a meat van.'

VINCE

Jack's eyes are shut, he looks asleep, and I think, I could just slip away, I could just sneak out, but if he's not asleep he'll know I've sneaked out, he'll have tested me. So I say, 'Jack?' and he opens his eyes, quick as you like.

There's that nurse on duty, Nurse Kelly, the one I fancy, black hair. I think, Given half the chance, I could try it on. Special circs, after all. Like when the world's about to end. How about it, Nursey, you and me? I could sneak out with Nurse Kelly.

I say, 'Amy said you wanted a word. Just you and me.'

He doesn't say nothing for a bit, then he says, 'I told Amy I wanted to see Ray. I told Amy to tell Ray to drop by.'

He looks at me.

I say, 'It's me, Jack. It's Vince.' Because you can't tell, what with the drugs. What with everything.

He says, 'I aint lost my marbles.' Staring at me.

I suppose he knows by now, really knows. Like it's sunk in proper and he's had time to live with it, *live with it*, and it's not someone's idea of a joke. Like someone tells you it's the finish, but you hadn't finished, you weren't even close to finishing.

He must know. But I don't know what it's like to know. Don't want to know either.

He says, 'I know it's you, Vince, and I know it's me. You want to swap?'

I smile, sort of stupid.

He says, 'Come here, Vince, I want to ask you something.'

It's a wild night out, wet and windy. On the window at the end of the unit you can see the drops fluttering and fanning. But I don't suppose it matters in here, what it's like out there, rain or shine, it aint a major talking-point.

I think of Nurse Kelly going off-shift, wind up her skirt.

'Come here, Vince.'

I reckon I'm close enough, but I shift up the bed a bit and I lean forward. His hand's lying there on the bedclothes, the fingers half curled, the tapes and stuff further up on his wrist where the tubes go in. I know he wants me to take his hand. It shouldn't be such a hard thing, to take his hand, but it's as though if I take it, he's got me, he won't ever let go.

He says, 'I told Amy I wanted a word with Ray, all alone.'

'That's good,' I say. 'Ray's a mate.'

'Ray's a mate,' he says.

He looks at me.

He says, 'Amy don't know what's happening, does she? Amy don't know if she's coming or going.'

I say, 'She's okay, she's managing. She'll manage.'

Knowing she isn't, even if she will. Knowing she'll come into the spare room again tonight, where Mandy and me are sleeping, and want me to hold her and hug her, right there in front of Mandy, like I'm her new husband, like I'm Jack.

He says, 'I've got the easier job.'

I look at him.

I say, 'Don't seem a doddle to me.'

He says, 'People panic.'

Nurse Kelly's bending over some other poor bastard. I used to say to him, when I first saw her, 'You'll be all right there, Jack, landed on your feet there.' But I don't now. I don't know if it would be a torture or a mercy to be tucked up by Nurse Kelly when you're pegging out.

Her name's Joy. Nurse Joy Kelly. It says so on her badge, on her left tit.

Jack's dying and I've got a cockstand.

He says, 'So what did that geezer Strickland tell you? Before the op. Sweet-talk, you, did he?'

I think a bit then I say, 'I can tell you now, makes no difference. He said you had a one-in-ten chance.'

He looks at me. 'Ten to one. And you didn't bet, did you? I bet you didn't bet.'

I can tell he knows that I've known all along, somehow, that I haven't wished or hoped.

Chips for you, Jack.

He says, 'Help me up a bit, Vince,' and he grabs my arm and I brace myself so he can pull himself up. It must hurt with that zip in his belly, there's a purply stain on the bandage, but he doesn't wince, he just hangs on while I shift the pillows with my free hand. He don't weigh so much now. Big Jack.

He says, 'That's better.' But as he says it I can see the spasm starting inside him, I can see his throat working. He's going to fetch up some more of that muck. I grab a bowl from the stack and I get the tissues all ready. It's like when Kath was little.

He settles back, wiping his mouth. I put the bowl on the cabinet. He ought to look less like himself but he doesn't, he looks more like himself. It's as if because his body's packed up, everything's gone into his face and though that's changed, though it's all hollow with the flesh hanging on it, it only makes the main thing show through better, like someone's turned on a little light inside.

I say, 'What did you want to see me about?' As if I'm a

busy man and I've got to be getting along. It came out wrong.

He looks at me. He looks right into my face like he's looking for a little light too, like he's looking for his own face in mine, and it goes right through me, like I'm hollow, like I'm empty, that I haven't got his eyes, his voice, his bones, his way of holding his jaw and looking straight at you without so much as a bleeding blink.

Then it wouldn't be finished, it wouldn't have to finish.

It's like I'm not real, I aint ever been real. But Jack's real, he's realler than ever. Though he aint going to be real much longer.

He says, 'I want you to lend me some cash.'

I say, 'Cash?'

He says, 'Cash.'

I say, 'You need cash?'

He touches the drawer of his bedside cabinet. 'I've got my wallet right here, next to my watch and my comb.' He half pulls open the drawer, sort of cautious and secretive. It's as though his whole life's in there.

I say, 'You need cash in here?'

He says, 'I need cash, son.'

But it's like I'm like his father now. Bedtime, Jack, no more larking about, I've come to say night-night.

I look at him and shrug and reach for my inside pocket but he grabs hold of my hand.

He says, 'I was thinking of a thousand pounds.'

I say, 'A thousand pounds? You want a thousand pounds?'

He says, 'By Friday, let's say. And not a dicky-bird.'

He looks at me, I look at him. He's holding my hand. He says, 'Don't ask me, Vince, don't ask me. It's a request, it aint an order.'

I look at him. There's the sign dangling over his head:
NIL BY MOUTH.

I say, 'Lend?'

RAY

He said, 'Take the reins, Ray boy. Go on, take 'em for your dad.'

It said 'Frank Johnson – Sites Cleared' up there on the board behind seat on the cart, and sometimes he used to let me sit there with him just for the ride. But he said I wasn't cut out for scrap. He said I should get myself a job behind a desk, with my brains, and I never knew if it was on account of my build or my brains or on account of a desk job being a higher calling anyway, to his mind. So that if I'd been born all muscle, it wouldn't have made no difference, he still wouldn't have let me unload the cart. He had Charlie Dixon for that.

He wasn't so beefy himself, just tall, with a body that hung all loose and dangly from his shoulders like a coat from a coat hanger, as if he could've done with being an inch or two nearer the ground. And I used to wonder, sometimes, how a tall man like him had produced a half-pint like me, and whether it was such a straight piece of production, not remembering my mother.

It wasn't that it was a trade to be ashamed of: scrap-metal merchant. He wasn't no rag-and-bone man. He didn't sit on that cart bellowing himself hoarse, couldn't have done anyway, what with his chest. He didn't tout, he did work by arrangement, contract. All the same.

So I got the job at the insurance house. He was proud of me being an office boy. And him his own boss. Boss of the scrap-heap. Then the war came and scrap metal was a full-swing industry and he could've done with my extra pair of hands, but I had to swap being an office boy for being a soldier. He said, 'A titch like you, they'll pass you over.' But they didn't. He said, 'Well, anyhow, it'll be easier for you to keep your head down. That's my advice to you, keep your head down.' I did. And after the war it wasn't me who wasn't there any more, it was him. It wasn't a bomb, it was his chest. But I went back to the office anyway. After camping out in the desert with Jack Dodds I went back to an office in Blackfriars. I had the yard and the two-up-two-down, no war damage. I was drawing rent on the one, from Charlie Dixon, to keep up the payments on the other. A man of property, you might say, but I went to work every day as a clerk. It was partly that I knew then that it didn't make no difference, what a man does and how he lives in his head are two different things. But it was partly the memory of him, as if he was watching.

He used to let me muck out and feed Duke and he used to let me sit beside him on that cart sometimes. But I wasn't to lift scrap. Clip-clop, clip-clop. The day came when he said I could take the reins and I took 'em and learnt the knack of driving a cart-horse. He said, 'Don't pull 'em, twitch 'em, and click your tongue more like you mean it.' And I never said to him, there's this job that little fellers can do, little fellers only. It's to do with horses.

This is Bermondsey, Ray boy. Where d'you think it is – Ascot?

I expect it was sitting there beside him, looking at Duke's backside, that I had my first dirty thoughts about women. It was what I had to go on. I suppose women might as well have been another kind of animal, for all the know-how I had of them. But it didn't work as a basis for proceeding, and when I took Daisy Dixon round to see Duke one Sunday, knowing that Duke wasn't there because the old man was on a special job, the smell of horse dung and horse piss didn't seem to rouse her animal nature. It didn't seem to have the desired effect. I'd put down clean straw specially. I said, 'Place all to ourselves.' And she says, going all short and shirty on me, 'So what am I going to do with these sugar lumps?'

Then ten years later, after Dad was long gone, along comes her younger sister Carol, wanting to know if I had it in mind to sell the yard, only her dad was worried, not knowing if he should buy that lorry, without the security of premises. I think, So why can't Charlie ask me this himself? And I think, Does she know I always fancied Daisy? What did Daisy tell her? I think, as she bends over to turn up the gas on the fire, She's got a good arse on her.

It was a horse-world, that's what it was. When I think of him sitting beside me up there on the cart I don't think of scrap metal, brass, copper, lead, cast-iron. I think of Duke. I think of the life of carters and pedlars. I see him lean forward, elbows on knees, after I've taken up the reins, and start to look around him as if he hadn't noticed the world passing by. I see him scratch his neck and reset his cap. I see him light up a snout, dicky chest or no dicky chest, and breathe out the first drag, bottom lip jutting, then rub his chin with the tip of his thumb, cigarette between his fingers, then run the ball of his thumb across his forehead, and I know I do all those things, without helping it, the same gestures, the same motions.

I should never have let Vince have that yard.

LENNY

Sunday outings in the meat van, as if I don't remember.

As if I don't remember them dropping our Sally off – half asleep she'd be sometimes – and my Joan saying, 'Won't you come in for a cuppa?' And Amy saying, 'Best not, we'd better get Vince home to bed.' As if I don't remember the sand between Sally's toes and that toy bucket full of shells and bits of seaweed and dead crabs, and the smell of the seaside on her, in her hair, in her clothes, and the pints of calamine lotion Joan and I got through for her sunburn.

We'd have taken her ourselves, only we didn't have the train fare, and we didn't have no motor, of course. No motor, no shop, no house to speak of, scratching a bleeding living, that's what we was doing. I was better off in the Army if you ask me. And I remember that look Amy'd give – but maybe I imagined it, it don't do credit to a woman like Amy – when she said, no, they wouldn't come in. Like it was because we lived in a prefab and they lived in bricks and mortar. Like Amy was getting above herself. She and Jack had been to the sea for the day and me and Joan had been to feed the ducks in Southwark Park.

Amy'd be standing there still holding on to Sally's hand and stroking her hair and stooping down to give her a kiss, so I'd feel like saying, 'That's one thing we've got that you aint got.' But I didn't. I just watched Amy kissing my daughter, and Joan would suck in her breath.

Well it wasn't our fault the bombs fell where they did. It wasn't my fault that all the old man left was three-and-six in the Post Office and a barrow in the Borough Market.

And you had to remember that Jack and Amy had their hard luck too, and little Vince, of course, poor little pillock. There's luck and there's luck. So maybe I did imagine it, maybe it was me just thinking: Amy looks pretty good on a day out and some sea air, she looks pretty good. She still looks a cracker, Jack.

Jack would say, 'Come on then, Ame.' And Vincey would be sitting up there in the front of the van, ready for being carted off to bed, but he wouldn't look so sleepy because he'd be watching Amy and Sally too while they hung around on our doorstep, hoping like hell Sally was going to turn round and wave goodbye to him.

We could have done with a day out ourselves. I said the last beach I paddled on was at Salerno, I aint so keen on beaches, but we could have done with a day out. I could have done with seeing Amy in her bathing-suit. But that's what parenthood is, I reckon, it's drawing the short straw deliberate. There wasn't no room for us too in the front of that van, it's a wonder the four of them managed to squeeze in. So it was all for Sally's sake. And for Jack and Amy's, of course, specially Amy. As if we didn't get the message.

Joan says, 'Them two kids are getting just like brother and sister, aren't they?'

But one day Sally comes in from school and says how they're starting to say things in the playground about Vince. How he aint all there in his head. Same as his *big sister.* How he ought to be in a Home too, a Barnardo's Home. Though when you think about it, it had to be one or the other, either the orphanage or the bin. She says Vince is getting into fight after fight and she don't know where she stands herself.

So we tell her. She must have been about ten years old. We tell her not to tell a living soul we've told her, but we tell her. It sounded half like a fairy-tale, after all, half like what you'd make up to tell a kid.

How years ago when they first got married Uncle Jack and Auntie Amy, who weren't her real aunt and uncle, of course, but she knew that, had this little baby girl called June. But it wasn't a proper baby, it wasn't born right, it had to be looked after special. It happens sometimes, not so often, hardly ever, but it happens. And Auntie Amy knew she couldn't have another baby, at least not without running the same risk, so she wasn't a happy woman. Jack wasn't too chuffed either.

Then there was the war. Bombs dropping on Bermondsey and one of 'em drops on your ma and pa's old home, but that's a different story, because there's another bomb which drops on the house where the Pritchett family has just had a new arrival, called Vince. Vincent Ian Pritchett, if you want to know: V.I.P. Blame his parents. This was in Powell Road, where the flats are now, just round the corner from Wheeler Street where Auntie Amy lived then. It was June '44 – a flying-bomb. Another week and Mrs Pritchett and Vince would have been evacuated – taken somewhere safe. And it was five years to the month since June was born. That's how she got *her* name. Mr Pritchett was home on leave, which was bad luck, or perhaps not, depending how you look at it. And your dad and Uncle Jack were both away fighting Germans, though we hadn't even set eyes on each other then.

Well, there aint much left of the Pritchett family. Except Vince, who, being a little bouncy baby, bounces clear away without a scratch. And, if you haven't worked it out, it was Amy who took Vince in and looked after him and started to bring him up just like her own baby. Maybe you can work it out too, or you will one day, that she had more than one reason.

There's rules, there's laws about how you should bring up an orphaned baby, but this was wartime, remember, when rules get forgotten. So when the war's over a year or so later and Uncle Jack comes home, no one argues over the fact that he and Amy have got themselves an adopted child and Vince has found himself a new mum and dad. So you could say it all ended up neat and happy ever after. Except there's still June, who shouldn't be a baby any more but she is. You still following this? And Amy'd always wanted, she'd specially wanted, a girl.

'You aint to breathe a word of this,' we say.

But it was only a little while after that she tells us they'll be off again to Margate next Sunday but they don't want her to come with them. Joan says, 'What you gone and said?' getting all in a panic. And Sally says she aint said nothing, only it was getting to be a tight fit in that van, even with Vince travelling now in the back. I say, 'They put Vince in the back?' She says, 'Yes.' And a little while after that she comes home from school, tears in her eyes, and says that Vince knew now, anyway. They'd gone and told him themselves.

Well it had to happen sooner or later, and search me how you pick your time.

So now Vince has got some real beef to chew. He says to Sally so now he knew what they said in the playground was true, and she says it didn't matter, he was still Vince, she'd stick by him. So Vince goes and knocks her down.

I reckon every generation wants the next one to make it all come better, to make it seem like there's a second chance.

I should have known she was the type to get more trampled on the keener she got. Fact is, she was soft on Vincey, sweet as sugar, and I reckon she'd have made a good wife for him, it wasn't every woman would have taken him on, knowing the score. She could've done worse, too, than hitch up to Dodds and Son, all things being as they were. You could say it wasn't much to set your sights on, a butcher's shop, but when all your old man had was a fruit-and-veg stall, it was a notch up. Except Vince had his own ideas about Dodds and Son, like not having nothing to do with it, and I suppose if I'd have known how he'd turn out in the end, I might have said, 'Get your hooks in deeper, girl.' Or I might have said, 'Back off him, he aint for you.'

But then it was my dream too once, it was every poor bleeder's dream. A flash suit, a flash tie, a flash car, a wad of oncers always in your pocket. When I went down to Scobie's gym every evening, that was the promise. And all the crackling you could ask. The war put paid to that. A boxer, eh, a fighter? Good show, good man. Though I never saw how having a good left hook helped you dig a recoil pit.

And look who got in there first. Little Miss Mandy. Fucking lassie from Lancashire.

I reckon every generation makes a fool of itself for the next one. Vince had his own ideas about Dodds and Son, but it was stretching it, even so, to do what he did, to sign up for five years just to keep out of Jack's reach, just at the time when every kid his age was thanking sweet Jesus there wasn't no call-up any more. I reckon a tour in the Middle East was a hard price to pay for not being a butcher's apprentice and for learning how to fix a jeep. Lad might even have had his arse shot off. I wouldn't have minded if he had.

And don't give me that tosh, my girl, about how he'd come back and see you right. About how he'd run off to join the Foreign Legion to make a better man of himself.

I said, 'Well, Jack, you can't say he aint following in your footsteps. You were a soldier once, as well as a butcher.'

He looks at me like he's saying, I aint in no mood for jokes.

He says, 'I was a butcher by choice.'

But I knew a bit of conscripting had gone on there too. Like I'd been having a few private chats with Raysy.

He says, 'Soldier – bleeding defaulter I'd call him. Bleeding deserter. That's what I'd call him.'

I think, And you'd be right.

I say, 'It wasn't the only reason. What you think was his reason – it wasn't his only reason.'

But he doesn't listen. Hears me but he doesn't listen. Like there's only one reason in the world and that's Jack Dodds, family butcher.

I say, 'You don't own him, Jack. We don't own 'em, do we?'

He says, 'Talk sense.'

He looks at me and I think, You ought to be glad you don't own him, when you finally listen to what I'm saying, because you may be a big feller and it may be fifteen years since I stepped into a ring, but.

I say, 'We don't own 'em, do we? Even when we own 'em, we don't own 'em.'

He says, 'You're talking bollocks.'

So I say, 'The other reason was Sally. He left her a little leaving present. I'd say she's going to have to get rid of it.'

DARTFORD

Lenny says, 'So how's your Kath?'

Vince don't answer for a long time. It's as though he hasn't heard or he's concentrating on the road. I see him looking in the mirror.

'Still working for you at the garage?' Lenny says.

Lenny knows she isn't, and Lenny knows Vince doesn't like 'garage'. It's 'showroom' these days. It was Lenny who said one night in the Coach, 'Showroom, he calls it, well we all know what's on show.'

'No,' Vince says. 'Packed it in, didn't she?'

Lenny says, 'Aint out of a job, I hope.'

Vince don't answer.

Lenny says, answering for him, 'No, I heard she aint out of a job.'

Vince says, 'So why you asking then?'

Vince puts his foot down just a bit. We all hear the extra revs.

Vic says, 'What d'you say we all stop somewhere for lunch, take a break?'

Lenny says, 'Curious, that's all. Can't always trust what you hear.'

I say, 'Good idea, Vic.'

Vic's still holding the box. He shouldn't keep hogging it.

Lenny says, 'Only it's a shame she never went to see Jack, in the hospital. When he was— Jack would've appreciated that. Time was she used to call him Grandad.'

Vince says, 'But he wasn't.'

Vic says, 'I'd say somewhere around Rochester way.'

Lenny says, 'Daughters. Who'd have 'em?'

We're coming up to the M25 junction. The traffic's busy.

Lenny looks at me. He says, 'You hear much from your Susie these days?'

I say, 'Odd letter.'

He says, 'You reckon she'd come, if you was— I mean, d'you think she'd show up?'

Vic says, 'What a question.'

Lenny says, 'It's a fair one.'

I say, 'I aint thought about it.' But I have.

Lenny says, 'It's a fair question.'

Vic says, 'Jack would've reckoned on us taking a break for lunch.' Vince looks at him.

Lenny says, 'And how's your brood, Vic? I reckon you did the right thing – get yourself a couple of sons, set 'em up in the firm, so you can bow out easy. Passing on the torch. All that.'

Vic says, 'Can't complain.'

Lenny says, ' "Tucker and Sons" – sounds all right, don't it, Vince?'

Vince doesn't answer.

'Don't it, Vince?'

Vince says, all fierce and hissy, 'I'm here. I came.'

He moves out to overtake a truck.

Lenny says, 'Daughters.'

The sky's clear and blue and clean with just a few wisps of cloud. There's a breeze stirring the trees at the side of the road. The signs say 'Sevenoaks, Dartford Tunnel'. We're clear of London but the view either side can't make up its mind whether it's town or country. It's like we're travelling but it's all the same place.

I say, 'That box must be getting heavy, Vic, you want to pass it back here?'

Lenny says, 'So when you going to put yourself out to grass, Vic? When you going to let them boys take over?'

I look at Lenny. I think, Don't quit yet, Vic, there's the two of us.

Vic says, 'No rush. There's a few customers I should stick around for yet.'

I can't see Vic's face but he isn't chuckling and he hasn't turned round and winked.

'And the lads aren't kicking me out yet. You hungry, Lenny?'

'I'm thirsty.'

Vince says, 'You could swan it, Vic. You could do better than Margate.'

Lenny says, 'Big Boy here's aiming at the Bahamas.'

Vince says, 'At best part of a grand a throw.'

Lenny says, 'Jack cost that? Joan better start saving.'

Vince says, 'That's what I'd guess.'

Vic's keeping quiet.

Lenny says, 'You aint picking up the tab, Big Boy?'

I say, 'So if you want to pass him over here, Vic.'

Vic says, 'Sorry, Raysy,' like he'd forgotten. 'You want to hold him for a bit then?' He turns and smiles gently, as if he don't want to upset any feelings.

Lenny says, 'Still, Vic, if you ever pegged out on the job, it'd be handy.'

Vic says, 'I'd thought of that. Here.'

He passes me the box.

'Dick and Trev do the business?' Lenny says.

'Course.'

'Neat that,' Lenny says, 'sweet that. Daughters, eh Raysy? Nothing but trouble.'

I'm holding the box now, Jack's on my knees. We all

watch what's passing by for a bit, then Lenny says, 'Still, you should retire, Vic. If young Kath can, I reckon you can.'

Vince says, 'She aint retired.'

Lenny says, 'No? So it's true she aint having to scrounge? You know, you lost quite an asset there, Big Boy, I reckon she pulled in the punters.'

Vince don't say anything.

'I reckon one of her skirts was worth six of your ties.'

Vince don't say nothing, but his shoulders sort of winch up.

'What I hear, she's pulling in punters of her own now.'

Lenny's face is all rough and hot. I've never known if it was the fights, years ago, or if his face was always like that, it was never smoothed off at the start. He looks at me, quick, with the box on my lap, and I feel a fool now for asking for it, for sitting holding it like a kid needing its toy.

Vince says, 'Yeh, maybe we should stop off for a break.'

Lenny says, 'Maybe it was just as well she never went to see Jack. That way, he never had to know his granddaughter was a—'

Vince says, 'She weren't his granddaughter.'

'And the other bit?'

Vic says, 'Gents – remember who's on board.' He ought to have a whistle.

Lenny says, 'He can't hear nothing, no more than he can see. Unless you believe Big Boy here.'

I lift the box off my knees. I mean to put it on the seat between Lenny and me but there's Vince's jacket there.

Lenny says, 'Funny that, since if you asked me if Vincey had a motto, I'd say it was "Out of sight, out of mind".'

Lenny looks at me juggling with the box. He says, 'Jack in a box, eh Raysy?'

I put the box down on the jacket and give the cloth a

little pat like I don't want to so much as wrinkle it. Vince angles the mirror a bit to see what I'm doing but I can tell somehow he doesn't mind, it's not his jacket he's thinking of. He doesn't shift back the mirror.

We drive on in silence, though it feels like Vince is working up to saying something. He keeps looking at the box on his jacket. At last he lifts his head and tilts it as though to say he aint talking to anyone in particular but if he is, it's Lenny. There's an odd pitch to his voice.

He says, 'I used to think they could see me. I used to think, I couldn't see them but they could see me.'

RAY

Susie puts the dryer down and gives her head a couple of brisk, stern shakes to loosen the hair and I think, I can't deny it, she's better-looking than Carol ever was, even Carol at her age. It's a kind of disrespect and unfairness to Carol to think it but that don't matter because she's a part of Carol, there's a part of Carol in her, we're all part of each other. It's not as if, given a second chance, I could choose Sue not Carol, because without Carol there couldn't have been no Sue. But it's still true that if I were a different man, a younger one, if my name was Andy and I came from Sydney, Australia, then I'd fancy Sue, like I fancied Carol, only more. I'd fancy my own daughter.

And another thing's still true, that they have it better now, better, easier, quicker. When I was her age it was time to get your kit and get fell in. Should've been born later perhaps, like Vincey. But I aint like Vincey. And then there wouldn't have been no Susie alive and eighteen now.

Her transistor radio's going. *Round, round, get around, I get around* . . . She moves her shoulders to the beat like she's dancing but sitting down. I knock again on the half-open door. She didn't hear me the first time, what with the dryer going and the radio, so I've stood there for maybe half a minute, holding the mug of coffee.

Carol's down the shops, Sue's washing her hair. Saturday morning. And any second I'll be off myself. The regular run: the baccy shop, the betting shop, the boozer. The cup of coffee's a way of smoothing my exit, but it's also a way of spying on my daughter.

She looks round, smiles, tosses her hair again, this time just for the sake of tossing it, and I say to myself as I said for the first time years ago when she was hardly out of her pram, She's a flirt, she damn well knows how to flirt. She flirts with her own father, she knows when she's doing it and it means she wants something.

She says, 'Thanks,' turning down the radio, and curls her fingers round the mug and takes a quick sip, blowing first across the top. Then she puts down the mug and starts combing her hair and looks at me, suspicious, like I'm up to no good, and says, 'Off down the Coach?' It's not a question that needs asking since I'm off down the Coach most Saturdays, but she asks it anyway to catch me off balance, which is another reason why I know she's after something. And when I make the old joke – 'The Coach won't come to me' – she smiles but she frowns at the same time, there's a little hard pucker just above her nose, which makes me think it's not something small.

She drops the smile and sips her coffee again. 'Well don't go just yet.' She takes a deep slow breath. She holds the coffee in her lap and looks into it, hair tumbling, like she's making a wish, like she's saying her prayers, and I think, *Christ.* I almost say it aloud. Remembering Sally, remembering how Lenny came to me: 'Raysy, I need a winner, quick.' Remembering the name of the horse that won at Kempton: Bold Buccaneer, eleven to two. She looks up. She can read my face like a results board. 'No, it isn't *that*,' she says, almost with a laugh, almost with relief. 'It's not that, it's something else.'

Then she pats the bed for me to sit down, the little narrow single bed she's slept in since she was six years old.

*

She said, 'He's looking for his roots.'

Carol said, 'What are they when they're at home?'

She said, 'His ancestors, his origins. He wants to trace his family, he wants to go to where they came from. A lot of them do it, if they're over here for a bit.'

All looking for their roots.

And it was a handy thing that his lot started out from some village at the far end of Somerset, because that way it made a neat holiday, it made a neat little jaunt to the West Country. They could take in Stonehenge, Salisbury Cathedral, Cheddar Gorge, and all those other sights an Aussie over here might care to see. With a tent and an old Ford Anglia he'd cadged off a mate. It was a handy thing that it was summer, her first summer in college, and times were changing, long hair, short skirts and short odds. Don't tell me that wasn't why he was here in the first place, origins my arse, and I don't suppose it would have mattered if they'd never found Little Dunghole, or whatever it was called, so long as they found a few fields of long grass to roll around in together.

We'd never have said yes if it wasn't for his bleeding roots.

But you had to give permission on account of it was the permissive age, never mind what your own folks might have said, your own ancestors.

Can't all have it all, can we, Ray boy? Gee-up! I see Daisy Dixon's getting spliced.

But when they were gone I wished them well. I wished I was them. I thought of them travelling across England. Hampshire, Wiltshire, Somerset, over the hills and far away. I pictured them putting up their tent and curling up together with the smell of grass and only a thin fold of fabric between them and the night. I could tell you some things, girl, about camping out under the stars, desert nights'd freeze your bollocks off. And, whether they ever did or not, I couldn't help imagining them finding some tucked-away churchyard, green and quiet, and looking at the names on the gravestones.

It took a war to make me travel, to make me see the world, if that's what you could call it. But there was him having hopped all the way from Sydney to Somerset, and there was her sharing the journey with him, out on the road, and there was me, still living in Bermondsey, still sitting on the old man's yard to keep Charlie Dixon happy. The boozer, the betting shop, the bus to Blackfriars. And in over fifteen years I hadn't taken Carol anywhere.

I said, 'What's the betting that car packs up on them?'

She said, 'What's the betting she comes back pregnant?'

Her face was all fixed and hard, like it would be all my fault, all my doing because it wasn't her who ever said yes in the first place.

Yes, you two, why don't you just go and run off together?

I don't know which came first: whether it was her daughter growing up and having a whole lot of things she never had that made her act like a woman who'd made a wrong choice, or whether she'd been thinking that, anyway, for years, but shoved it to the back of her mind for the sake of bringing up Sue. She was forty years old, knocking forty-one. She hadn't wanted another kid, one was plenty. Sometimes I'd think she'd never wanted Sue. Susie was for me. Sometimes I'd think, It aint a fair world, when you think of Amy.

She said, 'So what's the betting, Lucky Johnson? Why don't you put your money on that?'

*

She takes another gulp of coffee and there's still that pucker in her forehead, and I think, If she hasn't got one in the oven then what's the problem and why's she having so much trouble finding words? Then it's as though I kick myself inside, a big kick, so I almost give a jolt right there on the bed, because I see what's coming, plain as day, and I should have seen it coming long before, more fool me, and I think she sees that I see it, because it's then that she starts in, as if I've given her the all-clear. She flashes those brown eyes she knows how to flash and says, 'Dad.'

She says Andy's going back to Sydney in the winter and she wants to go with him too, to live with him there. She wants to go and live in Australia.

More fool me. Give 'em an inch. First they drive to Somerset, then they want to fly to Sydney. I think, This is one Saturday I aint going to get down the Coach.

She puts her hand on my arm and gives it a squeeze as if she's trying to say that, just for the moment, it's something between me and her only – Andy boy don't come into it – it's something she and I have got to work out. Like if I said no, she'd accept.

But the one thing I don't say, like Carol would've said if it'd been just up to her, is 'No. No, girl. No again.'

I say, 'Aint you got a home here?' But I know that's a poor start even as I say it because all she has to say, if put to it, is 'I'm eighteen and you don't own me.' But she don't say it, she just gives me the look of someone who could say it.

I say, 'What about college?'

Which isn't such a small point, it's not such a small point that Ray Johnson's daughter is going to college and means to be a teacher. The old man would have been proud.

She says, 'There's colleges in Australia, there's teachers in

Australia.' She looks at me as if she's ready and waiting if I want to go further down this line of argument, because she knows it aint exactly through my example that she's done what she's done. It's always been a sore point with her, though she doesn't bring it up any more, like she's started to give her own dad up for lost, that I could've found a better use for those brains I'm supposed to have.

'Got it up here,' Jack would say, 'got it up here, Raysy has.'

You could do something better, Dad, than go to that boring office.

But I do, I go to the bookie's. I work, I play the nags.

I say, 'You don't know nothing about Australia.'

She says, 'I'll find out, won't I? And Andy'll show me.' She winces because she's been trying not to mention his name.

I say, 'I bet he will. I bet I could show him the back of my hand.'

She looks all surprised and hurt and furious at the same time, because it's unfair, it's unworthy, it aint me. Fighting talk. With my brains, with my physique. And I never said I never liked Andy. I do, I like him, I like the toe-rag.

Her face flames up, her eyes glare but then she switches tack – she's not stupid either – and goes all soft and imploring.

And I think, It's only right that she should look better than her mother ever did when she was eighteen, because the world gets better, yes it does, it's meant to get better, it's no one's fault they're born too soon. Except I never saw Carol when she was eighteen, I was still getting fell in. So how do I know? And, anyhow, the fact is, I've never told Sue this, maybe now's the time, I fancied her mum's big sister.

I always fancied your Auntie Daisy.

I say, 'So what's Andy got to offer you then? What's he got to offer?'

I see them crossing Australia in a jeep.

But then Carol comes in from the shops. We hear the front door and the sound of bags being dumped. I ought to be down at the Coach by now, first pint on the go, having put on a treble at the turfie's. Then the sparks start really flying, then I cop it as much as Sue. Because it's all my fault, Carol says, all my doing, she hopes I understand that, same as if Sue *had* got herself pregnant. So I have to take Sue's side, to defend myself, I have to argue for the thing I don't want. I suppose that's just what Sue's reckoned on. But it don't cut much ice either way, what I say, because it's between the two of them, I see that, it's a fight between the two of them. I'm just the man in the middle they each try to dodge behind. They go at it all weekend like two cats, and there comes a point when I'm dazed and baffled and I can't think straight, and I think, I've lived with two of them for over eighteen years and I still don't understand them. There comes a point when I'm not seeing Sue or Carol, I'm seeing Duke's arse.

I put thirty quid on a horse called Silver Lord, outsider of five. Thirty quid, in '65. I don't tell no one. I think, If he wins, it means she goes, and it means she'll have the fare too. Wasn't no other way of settling it. But I suppose you could say I'd already settled it, because I wasn't intending to lose thirty quid. And there are times when you go by the form and the going and every last little thing you know about a nag, but there are times when you just get the feeling, you just see the signs.

It aint everyone who sees signs, but they call me Lucky Johnson.

And sometimes I'm wrong.

I think, I'm putting money on Susie's life, I'm putting money against the thing I want, but at the back of my mind is a little chink of another thought, I don't want to think it, but I think it, and I reckon Sue's thought it too, I reckon even Carol's thought it. That if Sue wasn't here, if she was far away where we couldn't see her, that that might be a way of me and Carol having another bash at it.

He comes in by half a length, twelve to one, and when her mother's not around, I slip her the money, three hundred and sixty smackers. I say, 'Don't breathe a word.' I say, 'Here's your fare. Use it when you need to. If you need to.' I wasn't going to tell her how I got it but I suppose it wasn't a hard guess. So I said, 'Silver Lord, Chepstow. Half a length.'

Then Handy Andy comes round to say his piece, with Sue sitting beside him, hands clasped round her knees. He says they've decided, there's no two ways about it, and he'll look after Sue. He says he's feeling so much more in tune now – now he's tapped into his origins – which is hard to believe with him wearing that Afghan jacket. He says he's feeling so much more 'together' now because of everything, because of Sue. He's got this crinkle in his face, like he's used to peering into sunshine. I want to kick him. I want to squeeze the bugger's shoulder.

Carol walks out the room. We hear the kitchen door slam. There's a pause and he says, 'Thanks, Mr Johnson. Some horse, eh?' I look at Sue who bites her lip and looks down. Andy's smiling like a berk. Then I get up and go to Carol.

She isn't angry any more, she's crying, she's got a hand

to her face. It's like that kitchen door was her last round of ammo. She leans over the sink, crying. She says, 'If she goes, I don't want to see her ever again, understand that?' But it's not said in anger, it's said like she's pleading.

I put my arms around her. She's still pretty trim for a woman of forty, I can feel her ribs. If I was taller, she'd have tucked her head under my chin and I'd've kissed her hair. It's like she's become another daughter. She was always her daddy's girl, Charlie's girl. Married me for him.

I say, 'You can't stop her. She's eighteen.'

She says, 'And I'm not.'

And that's when I realized that it wasn't that she didn't want Sue setting off for a new life across the world. It was that she was jealous.

I tried to make it better, I tried to make us a better life. I even gave up the betting. I learnt to go without.

But it didn't work. Or maybe it might have worked if that December her father hadn't died, sudden. Never rains but. Has a fall, out on a job, cast-iron guttering, and cracks his head. Instant. Charlie Dixon, Scrap Metal Merchant, Sites Cleared.

It wasn't like I had a feeling, it wasn't like I saw a sign, but it wasn't like it set her free either. Opposite.

I slept in Sue's old bed, or didn't sleep. Left for work early. Breakfasts at Smithfield.

Then one day that April it came to me, I saw the signs. Or maybe you could say I'd had enough of going without, all senses. If I could do it once I could do it again. £100. All that I might have staked in a good three months' betting. And one Saturday it was me who went down the shops. When I came back I was humming a tune. *If I am fancy-*

free and love to wander . . . I looked her in the face like spring had sprung and I was the bringer of joy. I said, 'There's something I want you to see – out on the street.'

She looked out the window and I pointed.

Rockabilly, Uttoxeter, hundred to eight.

She said, 'What is it?'

I said, 'It's a dormobile. A camper-van, deluxe model. A travelling home for two.'

She said, 'That's the last straw.'

VINCE

It wasn't like it is now, a quick race down the motorway and the taste of London still in your mouth half-way through Kent. It was like a voyage, only the other way round. So that instead of the waiting and hoping to sight land, you were moving over land in the first place, all impatient, all ready for that first glimpse. The seaside. The sea.

I watched Sally's legs. I watched the fields and the woods and the hills and the cows and sheep and farms and I watched the road, grey and hot, like elephant skin, coming towards us, always coming towards us, like something we were scooping up, eating up, but then I'd watch Sally's legs, resting on top of Amy's. Or not so much resting, because they were always moving, shifting, sliding, and when we got near the sea they'd start to jiggle up and down, her feet going under the dashboard, the way they did when she won at the spotting game, 'O' for orchard, 'P' for petrol station, or when Amy asked her if she needed to stop and have a pee, 'P' for pee. Then she and Amy would go off together, separate, behind a hedge, so I knew it wasn't just a case of pulling out your widdler, it was something different.

It wasn't so much the way they moved or even the way her cotton skirt would ride up sometimes so Amy would flip it down again if Sally didn't. It was their smoothness and bareness, their sticky-without-being-stickiness, and it was that they had a smell which you couldn't smell above the smells of going along the road but I knew it was there and I knew it was how Sally must smell all over, the bits you couldn't see. It was like the smell of the seaside, it was like the differentness of the seaside before you got there.

Sally on Amy's lap, me in the middle, Jack. We could've swapped round, I could've gone on Amy's lap, I wasn't so heavy. *Sally could've gone on my lap.* But that was how Amy wanted it. I saw that.

And one day he said anyway, 'You'll have to go in the back. You aint getting smaller, either of you. If you want Sally to come, you'll have to go in the back.'

So I went in the back where I couldn't watch Sally's legs, and all you could smell was the sweet, stale, stick-in-your-throat smell of meat.

It wouldn't be there at first. There was the picnic bag and the bag of beach things and the rug they put down for me and the soapy smell of whatever he used to scrub it all out with. But after a while the meat smell would come through, like something that had been hiding, and after a while more the sick feeling would start and you'd have to fight it.

But I never said, I never said, and I don't suppose they even guessed, what with the windows down in front and the air rushing in, I never banged on the metal and said, 'Let me out, I wanna be sick.' Because I was doing it for Sally's sake, so she could be there. She was in the front where I couldn't see or smell her, I could only smell meat, but her being there where I couldn't see or smell her was better than her not being there at all, and when we got out at the other end she'd be there, really, and so would the seaside. The meat smell and the sick feeling would get blown away by the smell of the seaside, and though you knew it was still there in the van and there was the journey back, you didn't think about that till it happened. When something's one thing, it aint another. And when I got back in the van to go home, I'd think, It evens out, because in one direction there's what's ahead and in another there's the memory, and maybe there's nothing more or less to it than that, it's nothing more or less than what you should expect, a good thing between two bad things. Air and sunshine and, either side, being in a box.

I reckon she should've been impressed, that I did it for her sake. So I never said. But maybe she wasn't impressed, maybe she never guessed either, maybe she even thought it was something to laugh at, me being in the back like an animal in a cage, and maybe the real reason why they wanted me in the back was because they preferred Sally to me.

June aint my sister. I aint got no sister.

I'd get in and he'd close the doors behind me, the one that said *Dodds* and the one that said *& Son*. Then he'd go round and start the engine and I'd start to hate him. I'd hate him and hate the meat smell till they were one and the same. It was better than anything for fighting the sick feeling, better than thinking of good things, the seaside and Sally, because there wasn't no fight in those feelings. I'd lie there on the rug hating him and I'd think, I aint going to be a butcher never, it aint what I'm going to be. And as I lay there hating him I discovered something else, beyond and beneath the meat smell, something that made those journeys bearable. I'd put my ear to the rug. I'd feel the metal throbbing underneath, I'd hear the grind and grip of the transmission, the thrum of the shafts taking the power to the wheels, and I'd think, This is how a motor works, I'm lying on the workings of this van. I aint me, I'm part of this van.

But one day I sick up anyway. All over the rug and the beach bag and the picnic an' all. I never said, I just sicked up. So there aint the smell of meat, there's the smell of sick.

The next time, he says Sally aint coming so I can get in the front. So I think, I've done it now, Sally aint coming now ever again, and I say, 'I don't mind, I don't mind going in the back. I won't be sick again, honest.' But he says, 'She aint coming anyway, not this time. So hop in the front.'

Neither of them says much. It's like when I was in the back it was a sort of punishment but now I'm in the front again it's a punishment too. But then I think, It's not me who's sorry, I aint sorry, it's them who's sorry. They're sorry because they made me go in the back. They're sorry because they've been playing at being Sally's parents but now they've got me again. Then he takes a turn off the main road as if we aren't going to the seaside at all.

We stop near the top of a hill, with fields sloping away. It's all green. I think, I aint saying nothing, I aint saying, 'Why are we here?' There's an old windmill on the top of the hill, I remember that, and there's a view below: fields and woods and hedges and orchards, a farmhouse, a church tower, a village. It's spread out in different patches like someone's pieced it together.

We sit for a bit with the engine ticking and the breeze outside. Then they look at each other and he says, 'See down there. That's where your mum and me first met. Hop-picking.' But that don't mean much to me, because I know what it means to hop and I know what it means when he says 'hop in the van' but I don't have the foggiest what hop-picking is. So I say, 'What's hop-picking?' and he tries to explain, like he hadn't planned on that bit. And I aint much the wiser. And Amy says, 'They call Kent the Garden of England.' She's smiling at me funny. Then he says, like he hadn't planned on this bit either and he's only saying it so as not to say something else, 'It's like you've got to have the country to have the town. See them orchards. Uncle Lenny couldn't have no apples to sell, could he? See them sheep . . .' Then he stops and goes quiet, looking at me. Then he looks at Amy and Amy nods and he says, 'Come with me.'

We get out and walk into the fields and I'm scared. There are sheep bleating and staring. He stands and looks at the view. I think, It's because the sheep get killed. It's because the sheep get chopped up and eaten. The view's all far-off and little and it's as though we're far-off and little too and someone could be looking at us like we're looking at the view. He looks at me, and I know the reason I'm scared is because he is. And my dad Jack aint never scared. He doesn't look like my dad Jack, he looks as if he could be anyone. He takes a deep breath, then another one, quick, and I reckon he wanted to change his mind, but he was already teetering, toppling, on top of that hill, and he couldn't stop himself.

LENNY

So Vincey comes home, in his new civvies, and parks himself on a stool in the Coach, drinks all round, and after loosening me up with a large scotch I should never have accepted, he says, cool as Christmas, 'How's Sally?'

You couldn't tell from looking at him whether it was bare-faced cheek or whether there really was some dumb part of him that thought he could carry on again where he left off, that reckoned he'd done due penance, courtesy of the regular Army, and now here he was to ask for my daughter.

I suppose he pulled the same wool over Jack's eyes because you'd think by the way Jack behaves that Vince had had a change of heart, he'd gone and seen the error of his ways. You'd think Jack would have more sense than to believe that the only reason why Vince had bunked off for five years was so he could come back and ask to be forgiven and pick things up just as they were.

It takes the Army to put a finish on a man.

Good to have you back, lad. Take your time, rest up, have fun. Always a place for you in the old shop, you know that.

But he doesn't rest up and have fun, he gets to work pretty damn fast. He puts a tidy slice of his saved-up soldier's pay on one of Ray Johnson's special recommendations, and Ray, as he's been doing of late, comes good. Witness, one camper-van. Except that's a touchy subject, we don't talk about that, same as we don't talk about how Raysy came good when Lenny Tate needed a special job done for his daughter.

And Vince don't buy a camper-van, he buys a '59 Jaguar, so you might think he's letting the world know how he means to live. Takes the Army to turn out a true spiv. But he parks the Jag in Charlie Dixon's old yard, courtesy of Ray. Charlie Dixon having passed on to the scrapyard in the sky. Then he gets himself a set of tools and a trolley-jack and spends most of his days tinkering with the engine and taking it apart and putting it together again, then he touches up the bodywork and sells it. Then he buys another car and does the same, and before the year's out there are two cars standing there in Ray's yard, apart from the camper, that is, and I say to Jack, 'You can't kid yourself any longer, it aint just the lad's hobby. He might want nothing better than to lie under a car all day but he aint just doing it for the love of it. It don't stop there.'

He says, 'It's Ray's fault.'

I say, 'Maybe. But Ray's got troubles of his own, aint he?'

But Jack don't give up easy. He makes one last bid to win Vince over. It's about as half-baked and cock-eyed as they come and it takes the form of Mandy Black, from Blackburn.

The story goes she turned up at Smithfield early one morning in a meat lorry, a long way from home and so far as she was concerned the further the better, but tired and lost and hungry. So Jack and his mates get her a decent breakfast. But Jack goes one step further and offers her a roof over her head for the night. Anyone else would have pointed her back in the direction she came and saved himself some sniggers and some trouble, but not Jack. And you'd think Amy might've had a thing or two to say about it. You could say it was plain kindness or you could say he was just following the old family tradition the Dodds' had of picking up strays. Anyhow, Mandy turns up in Bermondsey, in Jack's van, and my guess is that Jack wasn't thinking of Vince at all at this stage. He was thinking of June for once. He was thinking of Amy. Poor berk.

Snag is that with Vince back home there aint no spare bed. But that's no problem, Vincey says, he'll see if he can't kip down in Ray's camper. It's only for one night and he's used to living in a bivvy, even if it is the middle of November. And he'll be nearer to his precious cars. But one night turns into the best part of a week, she's begging them not to let on about her and they haven't got the heart to turf her out, and I reckon it was only when they were getting used to her being a sort of permanent lodger that Jack got it into his head that he could use her somehow as a bribe for Vince. Though why he should've thought that, I don't know. Like he was expecting Vince to say, 'Thanks, Jack, now I'll start coming to Smithfield again. Seems like a good spot.' As if Vince couldn't make his own moves and that wasn't just what he was doing. As if Mandy was Jack's to dispose of anyway. Fact is that there's Miss Lancashire Hotpot using Vince's room, and there's Vince using Ray's camper, and sooner or later she goes down to the yard to thank him for his trouble and see what he gets up to all day long. And there's the two of them and there's the camper and Vincey's got the key. So blow you, Jack.

Joke of it all is that Mandy didn't know how lucky she was, or else she was cleverer than anyone thought, an eye for the long shot. Because, though no one knew it, Vincey was already on his way to being Dodds Motors and later Dodds Auto Showroom. Garage, I call it. And though it always seemed to me a touch-and-go operation and not what you'd hold up as a shining example of a fine career for a man, it worked for him, it's brought in more dosh than

Dodds and Son ever did. *Look at that suit.* It's kept her in frocks and hairdos and holidays in the sun. Sometimes I wish my Sally had got back together again with Big Boy, sod him, I do. Because she couldn't have done much worse than what she did, and I remember them trips to Margate Joan and I never went on, I do.

He says, 'How's Sally?'

I say, 'Wouldn't you like to know.'

He says, 'I would like to know, Lenny. Have another one.' Face don't crack.

I say, 'She got married, didn't she?'

I think, The pillock's got a nerve, I'll give him that, the tosser's got a way about him. It takes the Army. He aint got such an ugly mug on him either, more's the pity, he's filled out fine. I can see why they'd let him walk all over them, what with the little-orphan act as a standby. I suppose he'll've had a few in the last five years, camp trollops, bints. And why should he be sitting there, standing drinks, like he's the conquering hero, when all he's done is have the honour of being one of the last troops to clear out of Aden, and learnt how to use a spanner and a grease gun? It was different for Jack, Ray and me. Bleeding desert.

I say, She got married, didn't she? But I don't say she's not living with her husband, seeing as her husband's living in Pentonville Prison. Because he'll've heard that anyway. Four counts of larceny and one of assault. What the country needs is to bring back military service, eh Vincey?

And I don't say how she's making ends meet. Odd jobs for cash. Taking in lodgers. It's do as you like now. Ask Raysy.

I don't say she aint got no kids. Still, that's one less load on her mind, aint it?

He says, 'I heard. I heard she got married.' Not a flicker. 'So how's the fruit-and-veg trade, Lenny?'

VINCE

But a good motor aint just a good motor.

A good motor is a comfort and companion and an asset to a man, as well as getting him from A to B. I can't speak for women. Mandy drives like it's nothing special, like a car is a handbag. But a good motor deserves respect, treat it right and it treats you right. And if needs be you can take it apart and see how it works. It aint no mystery.

People curse 'em. They say, curse of our time. But I say, aint it amazing? Aint it amazing there's this thing that exists so everyone can jump in and travel where they please? Can't imagine a world without motors. There's nothing finer, if you ask me, there's nothing that shows better that you're alive and humming and living in this present day and age than when you squeeze the juice and burn up road and there are the signs and the lights and the white lines all so it can happen and everything's moving, going. Where are we? Gravesend, 3 miles. We're coming up to Gravesend. Or when you're cruising through town on a hot day with your shades on and your arm dangling out the window and a ciggy dangling from the end of your arm and some skirt to clock on the pavement. *Ridin' along in my automobeeel . . .*

And I always say it aint the motor by itself, it's the combination of man and motor, it's the intercombustion. A motor aint nothing without a man to tweak its buttons. And sometimes a man aint nothing without a motor, I see that. Motorvation, I call it. Fit the car to the customer, that's what I say. I aint just a car dealer, I'm a car *tailor.* I'm an ace mechanic too, as it happens, I know engines like you know your wife's fanny, but I've moved on from them days. A good motor's like a good suit.

He said, 'I'm sorry, Mr Dodds, I'm very sorry to hear it.'

Oily twat.

I said, 'Business as usual, Mr Hussein. Want to run it round the block?'

So we got in the Merc.

He said, 'When's the funeral?'

I said, 'Thursday. Engine's good as new. Paintwork and trim's all custom.'

He said, 'A sad blow, Mr Dodds, the worst, losing a father.'

I said, 'Front suspension needs a peek, I'll see to that. Shift's smooth as cream, aint it?'

He thinks, Jack's dead so I'm an easy touch.

I said, 'Usual guarantees.'

We went along Jamaica Road, doubling back at the Rotherhithe roundabout.

He said, 'Let me think about it.'

Which means he might not buy. Which means he's getting tired of Kath. Which means I aint got no hold and I don't get no extra.

And I'm already a grand under.

We came back down Abbey Street and parked by the kerb and we sat there for a bit. But you always let the punter think about it.

I said, 'I've had lots of inquiries, Mr H, but – you know me – your first pickings.'

He said, 'Say – till Friday. Kathy'll go to the funeral of course.'

I said, 'You asking or telling?'

Puts a dampener on it, does it, if your doxy has to wear a long face? Has to traipse off and pay respects.

He said, 'Asking.'

I said, 'It's up to her.' Which means it's up to him. 'It's a beautiful motor, Mr H. And it's you all over. I don't even know if I'll go myself.'

He looks at me all confused. He thinks, Jack's dead so I'm a pushover.

I said, 'You mean Kath aint ever told you? She aint ever said?'

It's the best thing that's ever been invented. If it hadn't been invented we'd've had to invent it. And it aint just a seat on wheels. It's a workmate. It's a mate. It won't ask no questions, it won't tell no lies. It's somewhere you can be and be who you are. If you aint got no place to call your own, you're okay in a motor.

GRAVESEND

Vic settles down in the front, now he's not holding the box, trying out the seat position with the control on the door panel.

'You quite comfy there, Vic?' Lenny says.

'Fine,' Vic says.

'All seats power-adjustable,' Vince says. 'Upholstery's custom.'

'But Vic aint no customer,' Lenny says.

'Don't be so sure,' Vic says. 'How much you asking, Vince?' And Vince turns his head sudden, falling for it, before Vic chuckles and winks. Straight face has Vic.

I'd say Vic's looking the best of us all, by a long chalk. I'd say if you took Lenny, Vic and me, any one'd give Vic a five-year advantage. It's a fair bet he'll be the last of us to go. Excluding Vince, that is, and he aint no spring chicken. And the first of us to go, the next of us to go, will be—

'Just testing,' Vic says.

Neat, straight, toned-up sort of a face, and I reckon he's a once-a-fortnight haircut man. Maybe it's working with stiffs, keeps a man in the pink, by contrast. Maybe it's all them preservatives. Or maybe it's having been in the Navy. Fresh air and briny. It was me, Jack and Lenny got the dust and the flies.

But it's not just the way he looks, it's the way he is. Like no one's going to catch Vic Tucker out. Like no one's arguing that he should be sitting there in the front seat, box or no box, as if he's the leader of this little expedition. Steady as she goes, Vincey. Aye aye, skipper. I reckon that must come from the job too. It puts things in perspective, keeps a man on an even keel. And of course it wouldn't do in his line of business to be short on dignity.

Dignity, that's the word, dignity.

Vic Tucker, at your disposal.

He sinks back in the seat and half shuts his eyes.

Lenny says, 'You aint said yet, Raysy.'

'Said what?'

'If you think Sue'd show up. To see you off.'

I say, 'It's immaterial, aint it? It's immaterial.'

'Even so.' Lenny's talking softly, like he thinks Vic might be nodding off. 'You've got to have someone.'

He means: not having Carol. Or anyone.

I say, 'Australia's a long way.'

'Aint as far as from here to the next world.'

I look at Lenny.

'What next world?' Vince says.

'Manner of speaking, Big Boy,' Lenny says.

Vince says, 'It's further than Sydenham though.'

Because that's where Carol lives now, where she moved in. Barry Stokes, Household and Electrical.

Lenny says, 'Suppose,' like he hasn't heard Vincey.

Vince says, 'We could pop in on the way back, eh Raysy? On the South Circular.'

Vince is perking up, like he's remembering he's the nipper of the party.

Lenny says, 'Suppose. Suppose you had some special request, suppose you had some special daft request like Jack here. Who's going to do it?'

'I aint going to have no daft request.'

'Who knows?'

I think: Amy aint here.

'Well,' I say, looking at Lenny, 'there's you.'

Lenny looks at me. His face is all squashy. Must be working with fruit and veg. You can tell it's the answer he wanted to hear, but then he shakes his head, gently, smiling. 'You want to think twice about that? Or you planning on something quick?'

Vince says, 'Don't worry, Raysy, I'll be around. What do you want – Merc or Rolls?'

Mr Tact.

Lenny says, 'Eyes on the road, or none of us'll be around.'

Vince says, 'And where do you want to be chucked?'

Vic coughs and stirs in his seat, he aint kipped off. He says, 'You can go there now, can't you, Raysy? Go to Australia, see Sue. See those grandchildren you're supposed to have. What's stopping you? You're a free man.'

He turns round and looks at me. Like he's got me out of one corner just to steer me into another.

'Small matter of the fare, Vic,' I say.

Vic says, 'Put one of your bets on. I seem to recall it working before.'

I look at Vic. It's a straight face. What's he mean: free man?

'That's right,' Vince says. 'You could see a bit of the world. Live a little. Stop off in Bangkok.'

Vince's head is cocked towards the driving mirror.

He says, 'But just out of interest, where d'you want to be chucked?'

It's like he's a taxi-driver. So where to, guv?

'I aint particular. I'll leave that to Vic.'

But Vic doesn't say anything. He doesn't say, 'Whenever you're ready, Ray,' then give his little one-finger, undertaker's salute. And I get this sudden picture of me in a car, in a cardboard box, in a big car, with just Vince driving, just Vince in his tie and cuff-links and dark glasses.

I sold him the yard, for peanuts. And he sold it for a packet.

Then I think, But I aint going to see. It doesn't matter, it's immaterial, because I aint going to see. Unless it's true, like Vincey seems to think, that they're watching, the dead 'uns, so when I'm dead I'll be able to watch my own funeral. And they're all watching us, even now, the old man, and Charlie Dixon and Vince's mum and dad, and Duke, and Jack here, peeping through the cardboard, and all the dead 'uns me and Jack and Lenny left behind in the war, lying in the desert, because we were lucky and it wasn't our turn.

So I'd be able to see if Susie comes.

Lenny says, 'I reckon they should chuck you over Tatten-ham Corner.'

I look at Lenny. It aint a straight face.

Vince says, 'It'd firm up the going.' Vince is all sparky, like he's found a new game. 'How about the rest of us? How about you, Lenny?'

'Oh I'm with Ray, I aint choosy. It aint – material.'

The box is lying between us, like an armrest.

Vince says, 'Ashes is material.'

Lenny looks at Vince.

'And what about you, Vic?'

Vic lifts up his head as though he might have dozed off again.

'Oh,' he says, 'that's all arranged.'

Vince says, 'What's arranged?'

Vic says, 'I bought a plot, years ago, when plots were cheap. For me and Pam. Camberwell New Cemetery.'

Everyone goes quiet. We drive along. It's anyone's guess what each of us is thinking but Vic's guess is better than most, I'd say. I reckon Vic knows more than he shows. Maybe that comes from working with stiffs too.

VIC

It's a good trade. It doesn't exist to buy cheap and sell dear, or to palm off on the nearest mug something he doesn't need. No one wants it, everyone requires it. There's shysters in any trade, and they're the worst kind of shysters who will take advantage of another person's misfortune. There's those I know will fleece a widow of less than a week for a solid oak coffin, satin lining, solid brass handles, the lot, when a plain veneer will do the job. I haven't heard a corpse complain yet. There's them that will flog coffins like Vincey here flogs cars. But the trade itself is a good trade, a steady trade. It won't ever run short of custom.

And it's a privilege, to my mind, an education. You see humankind at its weakest and its strongest. You see it stripped bare of its everyday concerns when it can't help but take itself serious, when it needs a little wrapping up in solemnness and ceremony. But it doesn't do for an undertaker to get too solemn. That's why a joke's not out of place. That's why I say: Vic Tucker, at your disposal.

It's not a trade many will choose. You have to be raised to it, father to son. It runs in a family, like death itself runs in the human race, and there's comfort in that. The passing on. It's not what you'd call a favoured occupation. But there's satisfaction and pride to it. You can't run a funeral without pride. When you step out and slow-pace in front of the hearse, in your coat and hat and gloves, you can't do it like you're apologizing. You have to make happen at that moment what the bereaved and bereft want to happen. You have to make the whole world stop and take notice. There's times when an undertaker wields more clout than a copper. But you can't run a funeral without authority. When people don't know what to do they have to be told, and most people don't know left from right, they don't know back from front, it's a fact, in the face of death. It was the same at Jack's do as at a thousand others. When those curtains come across and the music plays nobody knows when to turn round and go. There's no one to say, 'Show's over.' So there was Raysy, beside Amy, in the front pew, next to the aisle, looking straight ahead, and I go up to him and touch his arm and whisper in his ear, as I've whispered similar in I don't know how many ears, 'You can go now, Raysy. They'll all follow. Amy'll follow.' And just for that moment Ray Johnson, known to those who know him as Lucky, was like putty in my hands, like a sleepy child I was sending off to bed.

I watched Jack clear off the meat trays, picking up the little sprigs of imitation greenery, then wash down the display counter, smoothly, without pausing, like he could do it all with his eyes closed, but carefully and deliberately, taking his time, it being a hot day. And I thought, He's early, and it's a while since I've seen him do that himself, it's usually that lad, the one he said couldn't tell chuck from chine and couldn't keep a price in his head. Unless he's gone and paid him off too. And that red and white awning's looking tattier, it won't last the year out.

It's an old habit at the end of the day, to watch the other shops shutting up. A shop is meant to be looked at, that's why it's built round a window. You can eye the goods and watch the shopkeeper, like a fish in a tank, except that doesn't apply in the case of an undertaker's. A coffin shop's the one shop no one wants to peer into. They're laid out according, no pun intended. Curtains, screens. No one wants to see an FD going about his business.

So I stood where I've often stood of a quiet evening, behind the lace curtain which runs the width of the window, above the half-partition of dark panelling. It's a habit that comes with the trade too. Secrecy, seeing and not being seen.

Trev had the half day off, Dick was on a pick-up from Maidstone, and the rest of the crew had slipped off, the hearses parked round the back, all waxed and polished for tomorrow. So I was alone on the premises. Excepting Mr Connolly, that is, who was waiting for his wife to come and view him.

I watched Jack step outside to wind up the awning, a few twists of the handle, then go back inside, then reappear to lock up and pull down the grilles. And all that must cost a bit too, though I've never had the bother of it myself, because I haven't heard of an undertaker's being broken into lately. Not favoured in that respect either. Though I dare say there's more in my cash safe than there is in Jack's.

I thought, Now he'll turn right, pat his pockets, look at his watch, wave at Des there in the dry-cleaner's, and head for the Coach, where I might well join him in an hour or so, if Vera Connolly isn't late. Thirsty weather. But I saw him walk instead to the kerb and look across, as if he could see me behind the lace curtain, as if I'd beckoned. Then he waited for the traffic and crossed over, so I stepped back inside quickly. Then I heard him rattle the door.

He said, 'Evening, Vic. You coming to the Coach?' And that was strange, because either he'd see me at the Coach or he wouldn't, I could find my own way there. He knew if I turned up it was usually later, since I seldom finished the day like he did, five thirty on the button.

I said, 'I was thinking of it.'

He said, 'Thirsty weather. Beautiful day.'

I said, 'Beautiful day. You come to tell me that?'

He said, 'First of June, Vic. Know what day it is?'

I looked at him. He looked around.

He said, 'You all on your tod?'

I nodded. I said, 'Why don't you sit down?' He glances at me, uncertain, as if it isn't plain as pie he's come for a purpose, but he sits down, where my clients sit, where the bereaved sit and discuss their requirements. Then he says, 'Moment's come, Vic. First of June. I'm going to sell up the shop.'

He says it like he's confessing to a crime. Like he's come to arrange his own funeral.

I say, 'Well then I'll definitely come and have that drink, as there's something to celebrate. You buying?' And he looks at me, narrow-eyed for a moment, as if he wasn't asking to be made fun of, and maybe I'm not so different from all the rest of them. Scoffers.

He says, 'I'm telling you, Vic. I aint telling no one else. Not yet.'

I say, 'My privilege. Mum's the word.'

But I think, But what's the big secret, and what's the big shame? That he's going to quit when he's sixty-eight, which is not before time by most people's reckoning. That he said he'd go on till he dropped, but he hasn't dropped, though he's gone on. That he's going to do what even Vincey said he ought to do years ago: cut his losses before they cut him. Maybe that's the nub of it, that Vincey told him. And there's Amy who nigh on gave up on him. Though he hasn't even guessed that, or how.

81

I think, Pride's a queer thing. It puffs a small man up but that's nothing to a big man who's afraid of looking small.

He says, 'What's a butcher's shop, anyway?'

And I think, You tell me, Jack, since your whole face is saying it's everything, and it hurts to be admitting otherwise. You wouldn't think it was such a tragedy, taking your nose from the grindstone. I think, Cheer up, Jack. In my book butchers used to be jolly bastards, big fellers with big arms and big grins, like you once used to be. I'm supposed to be Mister Sad. It's retirement, not defeat. And it's only the nature of the trade that keeps me hanging on here, same age as you, lingering in the office, when I could be handing over to the boys. Because it's the age when most people start to have need of an undertaker, the age of widows in the making, and I know Mrs Connolly will appreciate it.

He says, 'There's more to life than bacon, aint there?' as if he's not sure what that is. 'And it's only fair to Amy.'

I say, 'You told her?'

He lifts up his eyes, taken aback. He says, 'Hold on, Vic, I only made me mind up five minutes ago, swabbing down the trays.'

I thought, Well that's more like the Jack Dodds I know. So I was witness, without knowing it, to the great Decision. There must be something that makes you look where you look when you look.

He says, 'So I thought I better tell someone fast, I better tell Vic fast, otherwise I'll go back on myself before I can tell Amy.'

That's more like the Jack I know.

I say, 'That puts me on the spot though, doesn't it? If you don't tell her.'

He says, 'I'll tell her,' indignant, but his face drops again, as though he hasn't worked out how he's going to cross that bridge, as if there's nothing harder in the world than telling good news.

There's an old clock in my office that ticks steady. It's a comfort.

He says, 'Boys okay, Vic?'

I think, Boys, they're both over forty. But it's what I call them: boys.

I say, 'I'm keeping them busy.'

He looks round at the deserted office and then at me, as though to say, 'Looks like they're keeping you busy, Vic.' But I know what that glint in his eye means, I've seen it before. It means, It's easy for you, Vic, isn't it, to give up, let go. With Dick and Trev. So it's still there anyway. It would be easy for me.

It means Vince.

Well you've scuppered your chances there, Jack. Not even help me outs there.

He says, 'You know what today is? First of June.'

I shake my head.

He says, 'June's birthday. June's fiftieth birthday. First of June 1939. You know where Amy is right now?'

I say, 'Seeing June.'

He nods, then looks at his hands. 'She didn't say nothing but I knew what she was thinking. That I could make an exception. Fifty years is either special or it aint. A chance to do what I aint ever done before. She said, "I'm going to see June. It's my normal day but today's special, isn't it?" She said, "I've bought her a present, a bracelet." She didn't have to say nothing else, just look. She don't give up. So I said, "I'll see, I'll see." Cost me a load, Vic, just to say that.'

I think, A load of what?

'I said I could shut the shop early, maybe, and see you there. She said, "You sure you know where it is?" I didn't say nothing definite, but it was like a promise. But when the time came – half an hour ago – I knew I couldn't do it, I couldn't change, not like that. Fifty years. June don't know how old she is, does she? June don't know what a bracelet's for. So then I thought, But I can change another way. She won't see me turning up at that hospital but I can have something to tell her. Something to compensate.'

I think, You might have done both.

He says, 'Amy don't give up.'

I think, Who's talking?

He says, 'June aint ever going to change, is she? Still a baby, aint she, a fifty-year-old baby? But maybe I can.'

I don't think anything.

He looks at me and at the thought I'm not thinking. He looks round the office again, cagily, as if he's half forgotten where he is and that I'm Vic Tucker, undertaker, and not the parish priest.

He cocks his head towards the door at the back of the office. He says, 'Any lodgers?' Usual question.

I say, 'Just the one.'

And I can almost see him remembering it, that time when it was me who went running across to him. All on my own then too, short-staffed, and as luck would have it I had two in storage and one of them needed seeing to badly. It can be a two-man job. A hot day then too. So I thought of Jack across the road. I thought, Maybe a butcher. I said, 'Jack, can you do me a favour?' I had to steer him round to the back of the shop, out of earshot of a customer, to explain. He looked at me then he said, 'No problem, Vic,' as if I'd asked him if he could help me shift a piece of furniture. He said, 'Will I need this?' wiping his hands on his apron. We crossed back over, and I said before we went in, 'You sure about this?' and he says, looking at me sharply,

'I've seen bodies.' I thought, I saw them too, yours wasn't the only war. Heads bobbing in the oil. I said, 'Yes, but not women.' But he didn't turn a hair, didn't bat an eyelid, as if a seventy-four-year-old woman who'd died crossing the road wasn't any different from a joint of beef. I said, 'Thank you, Jack. It's not everyone.' He said, 'Any time, Vic. I aint everyone.'

And when the eldest son came to view I thought, You'll never know your mum was tidied up by the butcher across the road.

I suppose you'd expect a butcher not to be squeamish, you'd expect a man like Jack not to hold back. Jack Dodds was only ever squeamish about going to see his daughter. His own flesh and blood.

I say, 'Just the one. I've got someone coming to view.'

He says, 'Then I better hop it.' But he doesn't move. 'I suppose a man can change at the last minute.'

He looks at me and I look at him, as though I'm measuring him up. I think of Amy going to see June. Like Mrs Connolly.

I say, 'You sure you're going to tell Amy? I'm your witness now, Jack.'

I think, I'm a witness, all right. Shall I tell him?

'I'll tell her,' he says, like he's still got a trick up his sleeve. 'Or you can keep this.' And he dredges in his pocket and brings out a handful of crumpled notes. It can't have been much more than fifty quid.

'Day's takings,' he says. 'Double pledge. My word and my money. Now you can see how I can't afford to keep on the shop.'

He shoves the bunch of notes towards me. I don't refuse to take it.

Then he says, 'Do you know, Vic, what I once wanted to be?'

I look at him.

'A doctor.'

It's a good trade.

RAY

I said, 'I fancy seeing the Pyramids.'

He said, 'I fancy seeing the inside of the nearest knocking shop.'

It was Jack who first called me Lucky. It didn't have to do with the nags, that was later.

He said, 'Small fellers have the advantage, small fellers have the luck, hope you understand that. Less of a target for the enemy, less weight to carry in this fucking frying-pan. Mind you, doesn't take away my advantage. I could knock your block off any time I like. Hope you understand that.'

Then he smiled, held out his hand, clenched it for a moment, grinning, then opened it again.

'Jack Dodds.'

I said, 'Ray Johnson.'

He said, 'Hello Ray. Hello Lucky. How d'you get so small anyway? Someone shrink you in the wash?'

It was out of consideration, that's what I think. It was out of wanting to make me feel easier, on account of I was new draft and he'd had six months already. But he didn't have to pick on me. I reckon he decided, for some reason I'll never know, to choose me. All that luck stuff was eyewash. But if you say something and think it and mean it enough then, sometimes, it becomes the case. Same when you pick out a horse. It's not luck, it's confidence. Which is something I'd say that, except in the rarefied business of backing a gee-gee, Ray Johnson's always had precious little of. But so far as Jack was concerned, I reckon I was like a horse. He picked me. That's how I became Lucky Johnson.

He said, 'Where you from, Ray?'

I said, 'Bermondsey.'

He said, 'You're never.'

And I suppose that settled it.

I said, 'You know Valetta Street? You know the scrap merchant's, Frank Johnson's?'

He said, 'You know Dodds' butcher shop in Spring Road? I bet your ma buys her meat there.'

I never said I didn't have no ma. I reckon that would have made him reassess my luckiness.

He said, 'Best bangers in Bermondsey. And, talking of bangers, I suppose you could say we're as safe out here as there.'

He said it was because I was lucky that he ought to stick with me, but it was the other way round. It was Jack who underwrote me. It wasn't that I was small so the bullets would miss me, it was that he was big, like a wall, like a boulder. And the bullets missed him anyway, they missed him so they missed me, except that once. It was because a small man needs speaking up for, like the old man saying I'd got brains and I ought to use 'em. I never knew I had 'em till he insisted on it, and till Jack went and made it a selling point. 'This is Ray, got it up here has Ray.' Except one way I knew I had it up here was in sticking with Jack.

I thought, Stick with this man and you'll be okay, stick with this man and you'll get through this war.

He passed me a ciggy.

He said, 'Tell you what, Ray, we could give the Pyramids a miss.' Then he took a crumpled card with an address scrawled on it from his wallet. 'Mate gave me this. Personal recommendation.'

I said, 'Maybe I could—'

He said, 'Pyramids are tombs, aren't they, Ray? Pyramids are for dead people. Whereas a tart's tackle.'

Then he got something else out of his breast pocket, pushed it across the table to me. He said, 'It's be-kind-to-your-pecker day.'

I said, 'Maybe—'

He said, 'What's up? Not so long since you saw the missis?'

I said I didn't have no missis.

He said, 'So, then.' Then he said, blowing out a big cloud of smoke, as if that was about as much as anything meant to him, 'I have.' And he took something else from his wallet and passed it to me.

I looked, and I thought, I want one of those. I want one like that.

I looked at him and he looked back as if he hadn't noticed the question in my look or he wasn't going to answer it.

He said, 'Different place, different rules, eh?'

I said, 'Lucky man,' passing back the photo.

He said, 'No, that's you, remember? Drink up.'

Then he led me out into the noise and the glare and the stink, and I never said – I wasn't that much of a dummy – 'I aint ever been to a —. I aint ever.' Nearest I got was when Lily Foster tossed me off in the air-raid shelter, in the days when the only raids shelters saw were internal. I put my hand down her knickers, like I was rummaging in a bag of All-sorts, but she said, 'I aint letting you in there.' And I came so quick and sudden I messed up her skirt, must be hard for a girl to explain. Messed up my chances of any seconds an' all.

But as we dodged the touts and beggars he said, 'Tell you

what, Raysy, we'll go and see the Pyramids after.' So maybe he knew.

And so there's a photo of Jack and me, taken that afternoon, sitting on a camel, with the Pyramids behind us. There must be a thousand bloody photos of old desert campaigners sitting on camels with the Pyramids behind them, but this was Jack and me. And that camel was the nearest I ever got to being a jockey. He said, 'You sure about this?' I said, 'It's all right, I used to drive the old man's horse and cart.' He said, 'Yes, but this aint a horse and cart, it's a camel.' You wouldn't have thought it would've bothered him, of all things, a camel. I said, 'Trust me,' and he said, 'I trust you, I aint got no choice.'

So there we are, sitting on a camel, in the brass frame on Jack's sideboard, beside the fruit bowl. I'm laughing fit to bust. Jack's trying to laugh. The camel aint even cracking its face. And Amy never knew, and she still don't, what we were doing just hours before that photo was taken. 'Second ride of the day, eh Raysy?' Or that that was the day I first saw a photo of her.

I said, 'Amazing though, aint it, Jack? Ancient Egypt. One of the sights.'

He said, 'You'll see some sights.'

And so I did, so we both did. Just as well I was in insurance, and Jack was in butchery. It seems amazing now, like ancient history, that I was ever there, with Jack, in the desert. That I advanced with Jack from Egypt into Libya and retreated with him to Egypt and advanced again into Libya. A small man at big history. And somewhere in the same desert Lenny Tate was advancing and retreating, though we never knew him then. And Micky Dennis was killed at Belhamed and Bill Kennedy at Matruh, and Jack said it was unfair that a pharaoh got a whole pyramid when there was a good half of Bill that wasn't even in that grave. Then on to Tripoli, and never a scratch, never a scratch. Save that once. And it wasn't me, it was Jack. Clipped him on the left shoulder, went crack over my own head. But he always said if I hadn't been there to pull him down smart off of those sandbags, he'd've copped it worse. He'd've been like Bill Kennedy. Smack in the wife's-best-friend.

I saw it when he was lying there after his op. The new scar on his stomach, the old scar on his shoulder.

See this, Nursey? Come a bit closer. Got it in North Africa. If it wasn't for my mate Lucky there I wouldn't be here.

He said, 'Your first choice, Ray. As long as you don't pick the one with the big diddies on the right.'

But it wasn't easy, because I'd never seen five girls together before, leaning on a wooden balcony, naked except for some beads and frillies. Like looking at a row of iced buns. And all of them giggling.

I said, 'They're laughing, Jack.'

He said, 'What do you want 'em to do, cry?'

So I chose the smallest. No saying why, but it was a good choice as it turned out. I reckon I needed someone who could show me how to do what I'd never done before, so I could do it without help next time, and who wouldn't let on. No matter that Jack must have guessed anyway. I bet he did.

'Good choice, Ray. Your size.'

And when she got me into her little bivvy – about fifteen flies and a gallon of perfume – the problem wasn't so much in the actions as in the words. Like when she said, 'You lick me?' This was after she'd dropped everything, turned round, wiggled and turned round again, all of a bobble. And I had my tongue half out, like I was at the doc's, before I thought, She means 'like me', she means 'like me'. Though I suppose I'll never know. Or when, after I'd shot my jollop, quick as spit, same problem as with Lily Foster but at least I got inside, at least I was on target, and I'd got up to go, hoisting up my khakis, because I thought that was it, short and sweet, best not dwelt on, she said, 'You got ten mints. Look at cluck. What your fren think, you go now?'

And when we went back on to the balcony it was Jack who was already there, waiting, leaning on the balcony, smoking, telling the other girls, who were still giggling, things they didn't understand and trading lip with two sappers who were haggling with the madam in the yard below, like he could do them a better price.

He says, 'Well how was it, Ray? Madam Yashmak here was just about to come and prise you apart.'

But I didn't have to answer because my one was right behind me and she answers for me. She says, 'Very good, very good. Little man, big cuck.'

Jack says, 'Cuck? *Cuck!*' Then everyone starts laughing and I go red as ketchup.

'*Cuck?*' Jack's laughing and the girls are giggling and the sappers in the yard are looking up and laughing too, and we're in Cairo, in Egypt, in Africa, in the middle of a war.

'Well, Raysy, that sounds like just about everything rolled into one.'

Including luck.

VINCE

So I hit her. I hit Sally Tate.

Because I said, 'Do you know where babies come from?' and she said, 'No.' I said, 'I do.' Then I didn't say nothing, so she said, 'Well tell me, tell me where babies come from.' So I said, 'Hops. They come from hops,' and she looked at me like she was going to laugh.

She said, 'What are hops?'

I said I wasn't too sure but they were the things. You had to do something with them, called hop-picking.

She was looking at me with this laugh in her face, like she knew all along how babies got made. It must have been her who started the joke. You should never share your secrets. A little joke on top of the big joke, but it stuck. So Lenny would say, years after, 'Have another beer, Vince, have some more baby juice.'

But it wasn't why I was asking her, or telling her. It wasn't the hops or how you picked them, it was *who*. It was who picked them.

So then I said what I was meaning to say. It wasn't Jack and Amy who picked my hops, they picked someone else's hops. She was called June. So it was true what the other kids said, the ones I hit. *Vincey's got a sister.* But it wasn't true as well, because my hops were picked by someone else, they were picked by—

And she said she knew, she knew that already.

So I hit her. She wasn't laughing but I hit her like I hit those other kids.

And I didn't stop hitting those other kids, I carried on

hitting them, more and harder. Because I knew now it was true what they said, and not true. Because she wasn't my sister. *June aint my sister, I aint got no sister.* And though it was true she wasn't my sister, I hit all the harder because of her, I hit on behalf of her, because she couldn't hit for herself. Because before, when I never knew about June, I didn't have no one to hit on behalf of, I just hit.

I thought, It's one thing I can do for her. Because though she wasn't my sister I reckoned I was like her anyhow. Not like her like they said, funny in the head, but like her for having been played a trick on. So I hit.

The boys I hit. Alec Clarke I hit, Freddy Newman I hit. The girls I didn't hit, except Sally. You aint supposed to hit girls, they're different. But they know about hitting, they aint so different. So when one or two or a whole pack of 'em started up at me, same stuff as the boys only worse sometimes, I wouldn't hit them, I'd say, 'Show us your knickers.'

That was when Sally joined in, I noticed that, when it got like a game, when they'd start skipping and jigging and hopping in front of me, 'Look, Vince, look at all these hops,' trying to make me get to the point where I wouldn't be able to hit them.

Because up to then she'd kept her distance, we weren't speaking. Because I'd hit her.

But she didn't just give me a quick flash and run off screaming and shrieking like the others then sneak back for more. She said, 'Come with me, Vince.' We were picking our way through the bomb-site, through the weeds and bricks and rubbish and I aint ever thought what a bomb-site was before, it was just a word. Then she stopped and stood and looked at me and lifted up her skirt with both hands so the hem was touching her nose, like a veil. And it wasn't so much her knickers. They were dark blue, they weren't so interesting. It was the fact that she was standing there in front of me with her skirt held up like she was folding a tablecloth, all ready for inspection. So I said, 'Show me your pisshole.'

It was all different now with Sally.

She said, 'No.' So I said, 'Or I'll hit you.' So she said, 'If you show me yours.'

I said, 'I aint got a pisshole, I got a willy.'

She said, 'You piss through it, don't you?' So I didn't say nothing and she said, 'Well?'

Her face was all big and serious. I thought, She aint like a girl now, she's like a woman, with a life.

So I hoisted up a leg of my shorts, quick, maybe half a second's worth, but she said, 'Again,' like she was in charge. She looked, then she put her hand on it. She put her hand on it and felt, like she was feeling something she might want to buy, a tomato or something, like it was something her dad sold. Don't Squeeze Me Till I'm Yours.

So I hit her.

She was the only girl I hit. She must have known she was special. But the boys I hit unselective. I hit Terry Spencer. I hit Dave Croft. So the headmaster hauls me in for a talking-to. He was called Mr Snow and he used to breathe heavy and slow through his nose whenever he was angry, so we called him Snorter. I suppose it wasn't so simple for him, if he knew that I knew what I knew. Which I think he did. He said, Could I tell him the meaning of the word 'bully'? When you're that age there's a whole lot of things you can't find no words for, but what I said to him, one way or another, after he'd snorted a bit, was could he tell me the meaning of the word 'orphan'?

And I'd say that was a good answer, I'd say that was one of the best answers I ever give.

So he leans back in his chair and snorts and twiddles his pen. When I went in to see that surgeon I thought of Mr Snow. Life's a process of going before geezers who want to see you crawl.

He says, 'What do you want to be, Vince? What are you going to be?'

I think, That's a daft question because I'm something already. He looks at me, twiddling his pen. But the point is I aint even sure what I am in the first place. So I don't say nothing but I ruffle up and he can see it. There's playground noises coming from outside. I'd like to be Gary Cooper but I can't. I'd like to be all kinds of people, I'd even like to be Mr Snow putting some other poor kid on the mat, but I can't because I'm me. I think, This is what it must be like for June. There are all these people around her who aren't like June, because she's different, and if June thinks at all then she must think, I don't want to be like me, I want to be like them but I can't I can't I can't.

But maybe June doesn't think at all, she aint got a thought in her head, and supposing what you want to be is not like anything. Supposing what you want to be is a drive-shaft.

They said a flying-bomb killed them all so I was lucky.

He says, 'What I mean is, what do you want to *do*?' He smiles, like he don't mean no harm really. 'What job do you want to do?'

And I see them all hanging up before me, like clothes on a rack, all the jobs, tinker, tailor, soldier, and you have to pick one and then you have to pretend for the rest of your life that that's what you *are*. So they aint no different really from accidents of birth. I didn't know that phrase then but I learnt it later. It's a good phrase.

I think, He wants me to say 'butcher' but I aint going to say it. I aint going to say 'butcher'.

I said to Amy, 'Take me to see her, take me to see June.' I did something *he* never did, even if it was only once. *Vincey's got a sister, face like a blister.* And it was Amy who told me that he never wanted to tell me, never at all. Though how he thought he could keep me fooled beats me. It was Amy who told me that June was an accident, an accident of birth. She didn't mean the way June turned out, she meant that they'd never meant to have her.

So June was their accident and I was their choice, tinker, tailor.

He says, 'Well, how do you see yourself?'

He looks at me, knowing I've only got one answer. The whistle goes outside for play to end and the room goes quiet as cotton wool, except for his breathing. It was times like this I'd think, If they can see me, they must be watching me now.

No one ever kissed her, no one ever missed her.

I don't say nothing, and maybe he knows what I'd like to do is hit him.

Then I say, 'What I'd like to do, sir, what I'd like to be, is a hop-picker.'

RAY

It was Amy's voice but what I heard, just for a moment, was Carol's.

She said, 'There's nothing they can do, Ray.' I heard the bravery in her voice, just like Carol's.

She said he hadn't come round proper from the op yet and Strickland wasn't going to spell it out to him till he had. But he'd spelled it out to her, and to Vince, loud and clear. Nothing doing. Opened him up just to sew him back together again. Then, while she was there by his bed afterwards, he'd come round anyway just for a bit and she hadn't said nothing and he hadn't asked but he'd looked at her and all he'd said was, 'I want to see Lucky.'

I said, 'So do you think he knows?' And what I meant was: do you think he knows it's all over? But I thought, and maybe Amy was thinking it too, how you could take it another way, and maybe that's why he wanted to see me, because why do people get called to bedsides? I'd been going in to see him anyway, most days, but now he was asking: I want to see Lucky. What you never know won't hurt, but it's different when someone's dying, because it's not like you can say least said soonest mended, because there aint going to be no soonest or latest and you won't ever get the chance again to tell or not tell nothing.

Maybe that's what she was thinking too because she went all silent and choked.

So I said, 'You don't think he thinks that because I'm called Lucky—?'

Make a fool comment.

Then she started crying. I could hear the noise of people in corridors.

I said, 'Do you want – someone with you?'

She said, 'It's all right. I'm with Vince and Mandy. They'll stay the night.'

I said, 'I'll be there first thing tomorrow. Soon as they let in visitors.'

Then she said, 'Goodbye Ray,' as if she was setting out on some long journey, as if I might not see her again, not the same Amy. But it was Jack who was leaving, not Amy, and that's when her voice went like Carol's.

'I mean it, Ray, I'm not coming back. You listening to me? I'm not coming back.'

She couldn't tell me to my face.

I pressed the receiver to my ear as if I couldn't hear properly and I remembered when Sue first called from Sydney and I hunched right up to the phone as if you had to do that when someone was speaking from the other side of the world, but Sue had sounded like she was just round the corner. I said, 'You sound like you're just round the corner, sweetheart.' And now Carol was sounding like she was the other side of the world, but I knew where she was phoning from.

Not Sydney, Sydenham.

'I couldn't tell you to your face but I'm telling you now.'

But I could see her face, I could see it down the phone, trying to say her last words to me. I can still see it.

'I'm with him, Ray. I'm with him now and I'm not coming back. Goodbye Ray.'

I didn't say, 'Goodbye Carol.' Goodbye Mrs Johnson. I didn't give her that satisfaction, or me that shame. That was all, my one cheap come-back, I never said goodbye. I put down the receiver. I sat in the silence, with the evening coming on outside. I thought, I won't go to the Coach, I can't go to the Coach. I couldn't imagine her with another man, even when I knew she had one. Barry Stokes. As daft as imagining me with— But if she had to have another man she might at least have found some rich ponce, or some flash ponce, or some handy-between-the-sheets ponce, if that was it. Instead of the sub-manager at the domestic-appliance centre where she worked part-time.

If I'd been another man I wouldn't have just sat there with it getting dark, but not bothering to put the lights on, as if, if I sat very still, I might fade away altogether. Another man would've kicked in a cupboard or two or swept every knick-knack off the mantelpiece with one swing of his arm. Another man would've put on his coat and gone straight round to where she was and bust open the door if needs be, then bust open his face.

But I aint another man, I'm a little bloke.

I thought, First my daughter buggers off to Sydney and stops writing, now my wife goes and bunks it. And they call me Lucky.

I thought, It don't help you much, having been at the battle of El Alamein.

Another man would've acted different. But what I did was to sit there in the dark, not moving, not budging, till I wasn't sitting there any more, I was curled up with all my clothes still on and it was six in the morning. Then I got up and washed and shaved and changed my clothes and put two slices of toast under the grill and made tea like I wasn't thinking of anything. I washed up what was in the sink. I checked what was in my wallet and put some things in a bag. Then I went round to the yard, where the old stable had been turned by Charlie Dixon into a lock-up. I bought a *Sporting Life* on the way and twenty Player's and thought, I'm alive on this Wednesday morning. It was late April. I backed out the camper and wiped the dust off the windscreen with the engine still running. I looked at the tyres and thought of opening the engine compartment, but what was there to fuss over when the thing had hardly been driven? I checked all was okay in the back: the gas burners and cylinder, water carrier, the standby box with the kettle and mugs and tea-towel and stuff. *Guide to Places of Interest in England and Wales.* I drove out through the gates, stopped, got out and closed the gates, Chas. Dixon, Sites Cleared, and did the bolts and the padlock. It was a bright, clear morning. Then I jumped back in and drove to Newmarket.

VINCE

And passion wagons.

If you want to get your oats, get a car.

I said, 'Hop in, Mand.'

I used to drive her out along the old A20, or the Sevenoaks road or where we're driving right now. Turn off somewhere before Rochester. Badger's Mount, Shoreham Valley, Brand's Hatch, all that part of Kent. But I never took her further – down Memory Lane. I could've stopped, just like Jack did, and said, This is where. But it didn't need no mystery tours, because I told her straight out anyway, the time we first had it off in the back of Ray's camper, the whole story, the complete Jack and Amy set-up. June an' all.

She said, 'So Jack and Amy took you in, just like me. They were good to you like they were good to me.' Like she was speaking up on their behalf.

I said, 'I never asked 'em no favours.'

But we were two of a kind, all the same, Mandy and me.

You'd hit the country sooner, them days, driving out, and the traffic wasn't so thick, so it served two purposes. I could test my handiwork on the latest motor, I could see if it didn't go a lot better for having been given a going-over by me. Then we could test our handiwork on each other. In them early days we saw a fair range of back seats.

It's true we could've got out and walked and spread a rug down somewhere on some cosy patch of grass and done it like the bunny rabbits. Sometimes we did. But the ground aint always dry and the air aint always warm and I suppose she cottoned on anyhow soon enough that I liked doing it in cars, I did. An old black cracked leather seat the best. I liked it cramped and squashed and hasty, as if that was how you really had to do it, seeing as you had nowhere proper to do it, and I reckon that's how she liked it too, because it didn't take much coaxing, a look, a nod, and there she'd be with her legs round my neck. I said, 'You sure you aint done it in cars before?' and she said she never had no boyfriends in Blackburn with *cars*. I said, 'Boyfriends? What are they? You must have done it somewhere though.' She said, 'How d'you work that out?'

She'd sit on my cock, then she'd reach up to the roof of the camper, which was just about at the right height, and push.

I know it wasn't what she'd reckoned on, what she'd pictured, but people adapt quick, they adjust quick. They shove aside the pie-in-the-sky. I know she'd seen herself swinging away in Swinging London, wherever that was, or tooling around, making love not war with some long-haired tossers. Instead of which she gets scooped up off the streets, no questions asked, by Jack and Amy on her first night in town, as if she's run away from one mum and dad just to find another. And she aint so ungrateful, all things considered, she aint so disappointed. I said, They've done this before, you know, a long time ago. I said, spelling it out, 'It's because you're *supposed to be the sister I aint got.*' Which is when she could've done another runner, smart, if she'd wanted, but she didn't.

Instead of what she'd reckoned on, she got me: Vince Dodds, son of a doodlebug, fresh back from the arsehole of Arabia. Lying under a motor most of the time, when he wasn't lying on top of her.

I said I ran away an' all. I ran away to the Army. Most

people run away from the Army but I ran away to it. Because I wasn't going to be no butcher's boy, just for him.

She said, 'So why did you come back?'

I said it was different now, wasn't it? I had my own set-up now, thanks to Uncle Ray, and thanks to the Royal Electrical and Mechanicals. If Jack thought I was going to give up mucking around with motors and put on a white apron again, he had another think coming.

She said, 'If you hate him so much, why haven't you moved out?'

I said, 'I have, sweetheart, aint you noticed? It's you that's moved in.'

She said, 'I meant permanent.'

I said I was biding my time. Step by step, little by little. First my business had to take off, then I'd get a place of my own.

She said, 'Your business?'

I said, 'Yeh.'

She used to lick my tattoos, like she might lick 'em off.

She said, 'When you get a place of your own, will there be room for me?'

I said, 'Might be, if you ask nice. This aint bad for now.'

Came in handy, that camper.

Two of a kind, though we didn't look it. She was eighteen, I was twenty-three. I suppose I must have seemed to her at times like I belonged with some other bunch, some older bunch, like I was her bleeding uncle. She used to say now and then I ought to change, get with it, switch on. Roy Orbison had shot his bolt. I said I changed a long time ago, I switched right over, didn't I? Became a different person, didn't I? And 'with it'? Did she think I aint been around? I'd been on the hippie trail to Aden. Had she ever seen someone with their head sliced off? Well then.

She looked at me, blinking.

The world was changing all right, I knew that. I aint unaware. But I said I'll tell you what the big change is, the change underneath all the change. It aint the Beatles and it aint the Rolling Stones and it aint long hair or short skirts or free milk and baby-stoppers on the National Health. It's mobility, it's being mobile. How did you get to here from Blackburn? How did you get to shake off your ma and pa? Time was when the only way you got to travel was in the Army, though not everywhere's worth the trip, I'm telling you. But watch 'em all on the move now, watch 'em all going places. You listening? Ten years from now the Beatles and the Stones will be old-time music but what they'll still want is wheels. Wheels. More and more wheels. And I'll be there to sell 'em, Vince Dodds'll be right there to sell 'em. I'm in the right trade, the travel trade. So don't tell me I aint with it.

She looked at me as if she was doing a bit of trading of her own in her head.

She said, 'Course you are, lover.'

She'd twist the ends of her hair and suck 'em, like a schoolgirl.

I said, 'If it weren't for Hitler, Jack would never've budged from that shop. But one day Jack'll come crawling to me, you see.'

She said, 'Course he will, pet.'

We'd hit the road and head out through the suburbs, like we'd robbed a bank and were on the run. *Just runnin' scared! Du-du-du-dum!* There was a lay-by out beyond Swanley with a mobile caff where they'd sizzle up bacon waddies and brew tea like it had to be stirred with a dipstick. The cars would whack by and the slipstreams would tug the steam from our mugs and flip her long hair. I'll always see her standing by a road. Then we'd find our own little private lay-by somewhere. It was like the car joined in with us. Crazy for it, we'd be. Slippery with it, have to mop down afterwards. Then we'd go for a walk in the woods, across the fields, listen to the birdies, take the air, clock the view. I said – I thought it would impress her, coming from Blackburn, I thought she'd be impressed, it coming from me – 'They call Kent the Garden of England.'

ROCHESTER

We come up to the start of the M2 but Vince stays on the A2, through Strood to Rochester. We cross the Medway by the old road bridge, beside the railway bridge. It comes as a surprise, the sudden wide view of the river, like it's a whole look-out on the world you hadn't been thinking of, you'd forgotten it was there. Boats, jetties, moorings, mud banks.

Vic says, 'Tide's out,' and looks at his watch. 'It'll be coming in at Margate.'

Lenny says, 'Good thing, I suppose. Considering.'

You can see the castle and the cathedral spire ahead, standing out, like toy buildings set down special.

Vince says, 'So, anyone know any good pubs in Rochester?'

Vic says, 'No, but I knew a few once in Chatham.' Navy man.

Vince says, 'Memory Lane, eh Vic?'

The weather's changing, clouds brewing.

We overshoot on the main road then double back, getting lost in the side-streets and the one-way systems. Then we slip into a car park at the foot of the castle hill. Lenny says, 'I never knew this was a sight-seeing tour.' Vince says, 'Everybody out.' He takes off his shades and pats his hair. I lift up the box so he can get his jacket and he turns and reaches for it. He looks at Lenny as if Lenny might hand it to him but Lenny don't, then I put the box back on the seat. Then we all get out, stretching and putting on our clobber. It's nippy after being in the car. The castle looks dry and bony in the sunshine. Vince opens the boot and takes out a coat. Camel hair.

Then we should all move off but we stay put, loitering, looking at each other, sheepish.

I say, 'It don't seem right just to leave him there on the back seat, does it?'

Lenny says, 'Where d'you think he should go, in the boot?'

I say, 'I mean, it don't seem right us going off and just leaving him on his own.'

Lenny shrugs.

Vic don't say nothing, like it's not his business any more, it's not his say-so, now he's handed over the goods. He gives me a quick sharp look, settling his cap, then he squints up at the clouds in the sky.

Vince says, 'You're right, Ray. He should come with us, shouldn't he?'

He leans in and picks up the box. It's the first time he's held it. He tucks it under his arm while he locks the car, then he straightens up with it hugged against his chest. Now he's holding it, now he's standing there in that coat with the box, it's as though he's in charge, it's as though he's got his badge of authority. It was Vic who was in charge, in charge but sort of neutral at the same time, but now it's Vince.

He says, 'Okay men, follow me,' like he's leading a patrol of marines, and he marches off across the car park. I see Lenny turn his head as if he's going to spit.

We come out on the high street. It's not big and bustling like your normal high street. It's narrow and quiet and crooked and historical and full of lop-sided old buildings. There are people ambling up and down it, aimless, the way tourists walk. It looks like a high street in a picture book, like you shouldn't be here, walking in it, or like it shouldn't be here itself, with the traffic belting along on the A2 close by. Except it was here first.

There's a fancy grocer's opposite, the Rochester Food Fayre, the sort that sells funny teas and posh tins of biscuits, and Vince ducks in sudden, leaving us standing. Then he comes out again with a plastic carrier-bag. He's slipping the box into it but there's something else already in there, by the look of it. He says, 'Mandy said we were out of coffee.' Then we look this way and that and Vince scoots off again as if he can't abide ditherers. There's a sign up ahead saying 'Bull Hotel' and he heads straight for it, like he's been meaning to all along. He says, 'There, gents, this should do us.' It's a big old rambling place, with a Carvery and a Grill and a regular bar with snacks. I can see Vince considering the Carvery, like he's thinking of lashing out special and making us feel like we owe him. Then he back-tracks along the pavement, settling on the bar and snacks. You can see the bridge over the river from the hotel entrance. The high street dips down towards it and the main road, and if you shut your eyes and open them again you can picture how a stage-coach might once have rattled across and up the slope and swung into the yard of the Bull, with the castle looking down just like a Christmas card.

It's an old coaching inn, tarted up and buggered about. But I don't make no jokes.

It's warm and glinty and chattery inside. Vince says, 'I'll get 'em,' before we're hardly through the door. 'You take this, Ray.' He hands me the carrier bag. 'Grab that table over there. Pints all round and a shortie for you, Vic?'

He pulls out his wallet and steps up to the bar, like everyone round here knows Vince Dodds.

There's a barmaid with a white blouse and cherry red lipstick.

We go to the table. We hear Vince say, 'Any grub going, darling?' He wasn't ever one for speaking soft but maybe he means us to hear. He cocks his head in our direction. 'Three old codgers to look after, and one extra who aint eating.' The barmaid looks our way, puzzled, then back at Vince, as if she's not sure whether to smile or what. I can't see Vince's face but I know he's looking at her with that special look he has, like he knows he might seem just a bit ridiculous but he's daring her to make the mistake of thinking he really is.

Like when he said, 'Wanna do a deal on the yard?'

She reaches over for some menu cards, her face a bit pink. I can hear Vince thinking, 'Nice jubbies.'

We start on our drinks, then we order our nosh. Then Vic gets in another round. Then the food arrives: jumbo sausage, beans and chips for me and Lenny, steak and chips for Vince, quiche of the day for Vic. I reckon today he should eat meat. The barmaid brings over the plates and stretches across and Vince says, 'Looks a treat, sweetheart,' with his face in her armpit, and none of us says a thing. There's a strand of blonde hair that falls down her cheek like it's not meant to but it's meant to at the same time. Then we eat up and drink up and Lenny and I light up ciggies and Lenny gets in a round and it seems like we've always known the Bull in Rochester and it's always known us, and we're all thinking the same thing, that it's a pity we can't just carry on sitting here getting slowly pickled and at peace with the world, it's a pity we're obliged to take Jack on to Margate. Because Jack wouldn't have minded, it's even what he would've wanted for us, to get sweetly slewed on his account. *You carry on, lads, don't you worry about me.* If he was here now he'd be recommending it, he'd be doing the same as us. *Forget them ashes, fellers.* Except if he were here now there wouldn't be no problem, there wouldn't be no obligation. There wouldn't be no ashes. We wouldn't even be here in the first place, half-way down the Dover road.

Lenny says, 'It's a crying shame he aint here,' like Jack was planning on it but something else came up.

'He'd've appreciated it,' Vince says.

'He shouldn't've hurried off like he did,' I say, entering the spirit.

'Daft of him,' Lenny says.

Vic's gone quiet.

'Crying shame,' Lenny says.

It's as though, if we keep talking this way, Jack really will come through the door, any second now, unbuttoning his coat. 'Well, had you all fooled, didn't I?'

Then Vic says, like it's a truth we're not up to grasping, that has to be broke gently, 'If he was here, we wouldn't be, would we? It's because he's not that we are.'

'All the same,' Lenny says.

'He'd've appreciated it,' Vince says.

Lenny looks at Vince.

'If it weren't for him we wouldn't be here,' Vince says. 'We wouldn't be here without him,' and he looks sort of snagged up by his own words. We're all looking snagged up, like everything means one thing and something else at the same time.

I say, 'I've got to take a leak.'

But it's not just to take a leak. I find the Gents and I unzip, then I feel my eyes go hot and gluey, so I'm leaking at both ends. It's cold and damp and tangy in the Gents. There's two condom machines, one says 'Glowdom' and one says 'Fruit Cocktail'. *It's be-kind-to-your-pecker day.* There's a frosted window with a quarter-light half open so I get a peek of a bit of wall, a bit of roof, a bit of tree and a bit of sky, which isn't blue any more, and I think for some reason of all the pissers I've ever pissed in, porcelain, stainless steel, tarred-over cement, in pubs and car parks and market squares up and down the country, wherever there's a race-course to hand. There's always a frosted quarter-light, chinked open, with a view of the back end of somewhere, innyards, alleyways, with some little peephole out on life. Racecourse towns. It's when you stand up to piss you can tell how pissed you are. A drink or two helps for putting on a bet. A drink or three buggers your judgement. When I can't get to sleep I tick off in my head all the racetracks I've been to, in alphabetical order, and I see the map of England with the roads criss-crossing. AscotBrightonCheltenham-DoncasterEpsom.

I shake myself out and zip myself up again. I sniff and I run my sleeve across my face. Some other punter comes in, a young feller, but I don't reckon he sees, or thinks twice if he does. Old men get pissy eyes. He gets out his plonker like a young feller does, like it's a fully operational piece of machinery.

Well, that's that over with. Crying's like pissing. You don't want to get caught short, specially on a car journey.

But as I head back into the bar and I see them at the table, with the barmaid collecting glasses, nice arse an' all, and all the bar-room clobber, brass rails, pictures on the wall, of a pub I've never been in before and won't ever be in again, it's as though I'm looking at them like I'm not here. Like it's not Jack, it's me and I'm looking on, after-wards, and they're all talking about me. HaydockKempton. Like I'm not here but it's still all there, going on without me, and all it is is the scene, the place you pass through, like coachload after coachload passing through a coaching inn. NewburyPontefract.

I say, 'Same again, fellers?'

Vic's looking at me. He looks like he's thinking.

Vince says, 'Not me, Raysy,' holding up a flat palm, all strict. 'Unless you want to find another driver. You could get me a coffee. And a half-corona.'

Lenny looks at Vince like he's going to give a mock salute. He says, 'And I'll have a knickerbocker glory.'

It's always the third drink with Lenny.

I order the drinks and ferry over the pints and Vic's whisky.

Vic says, 'Just as well Amy didn't come, she wouldn't have planned on a piss-up.'

Lenny says, 'Is that whisky or tea you're drinking there then, Viccy?' He slurps some beer. 'Jack wouldn't begrudge us.' Then he says, 'All the same.'

Vince says, 'All the same what?'

Lenny says, 'He'd've appreciated it if his missis had carried out requirements.'

I say, 'That's been settled. We're doing it for her.'

They all look at me as if they're expecting a speech.

I glug some beer.

The barmaid brings over Vince's coffee. He looks up and says, smiling, 'Old ones are the worst, eh gorgeous?'

' "For" aint the point,' Lenny says. ' "For" don't apply. Some things is direct. None of us is next of kin, is we? None of us is close relative. Even Vincey aint close relative.' And he looks at Vince like he wouldn't look if he hadn't had three pints of heavy. Vince is lighting his cigar. 'Even Big

Boy here aint next of kin, is he? Vincey here aint got no more claim to be here than any of us, have you, Big Boy? Specially as, if you ask me, there wasn't no love lost in any case, not till Jack was on his last legs. There wasn't ever no love lost, was there?' Lenny's face is all knotted up.

Vince puffs on his cigar. He doesn't look at Lenny. He pours the milk from the plastic thingummy into his coffee, then he tears the sugar sachet and tips out the sugar, slow and careful, concentrating, stirring all the while with his free hand. It's like he doesn't intend talking to any of us again.

Lenny opens his mouth, as if there's more to come, but something sort of clicks shut in his throat. 'I've got to take a leak an' all,' he says. He gets up, sudden, looking around like he's dizzy. I jerk my thumb in the direction he should take.

Vic says, 'I was wondering—'

You can trust Vic to do his peace-keeping act.

Lenny slouches to the Gents. I wonder if he's going to do some blubbing too.

Vince shakes the sachet even though it's empty, then screws it up. He looks up. 'What was you wondering, Vic?' He smiles, calm and polite, and sips his coffee.

'I was wondering, as we're close, if we could pop over to Chatham and see the memorial. I've never—'

Vince looks at Vic. He raises his eyebrows slightly, he puffs his cigar. Vic's face is serious and steady. You can't ever tell with Vic.

'Don't see why not,' Vince says. 'Do you, Raysy?' He could be chairing a committee. He gives a quick glance to me then back again to Vic. It's like he's forgotten all about Lenny. 'If a man in your line don't get enough of memorials.' He smiles, then wipes off the smile quick, as if it wasn't anything to smile over. "That's why we're here, aint we? To remember the dead.'

'It means a detour,' Vic says.

Vince blows out smoke, thinking. 'We can do detours.'

Lenny comes back from the Gents. His face looks like it's been having a fight with itself, like it don't know what expression it should wear.

He says, 'My round, aint it? Same again, Vic? Ray? Vince? Another coffee? Something to go with it?'

I reckon Lenny'll need to do better than that.

Vince glances up quick at Lenny but he don't say nothing. He puffs his cigar, eyes narrowed, then he takes the stub from his mouth, there's still a few puffs left, and crushes it in the ashtray. He says, 'I don't know about you, Lenny, but I'm here to take something to Margate, that's what we're all here to do. And Vic here would like us to pay a little extra call on the way, which I aint against, considering. We're here to remember the dead.' He looks at his watch. 'Gone two fifteen. Now if you want to stay here drinking all afternoon' – he sweeps his gaze round the table as if we're all suddenly included in some plot against him, it's not just Lenny – 'that's your business. But I'm going to the car right now and I'm driving to Margate. If you don't want to come too, you better find out where the station is.'

He takes a last sip of coffee. Then he gets up, unhurried, putting on his coat, rolling his shoulders so the cloth sits, tugging at the lapels. Then he walks out, not looking back, the door swinging to behind him. When Vince was a nipper his hero was Gary Cooper.

We look at each other, not moving, though it's plain we don't have no choice.

Vic gets up first, then I get up.

Lenny says, 'Tosshead,' under his breath, not moving.

Vic says, 'You shouldn't judge.'

Then we notice the plastic bag, *Rochester Food Fayre*, lying on the seat and it's as though a new spark comes into Lenny's face, there's a new look in his eye. He picks up the bag and grabs his coat. He's the first of us to reach the door, though he pauses for a moment in front of it, waiting, as if he's thought for a moment that Vince might be about to step back in. Then he pushes it open and we follow.

Vince is walking back the way we came. The high street looks like a model. He isn't looking back but it doesn't seem like he's keen to make too much ground. We follow him, Lenny scuttling on ahead with the bag.

'Hey, Big Boy!'

Vince don't look back but his pace quickens and he hitches himself up a peg.

'Hey, Big Boy!' Lenny's moving at a fair old lick, you wouldn't think it. 'You forgot something, didn't you? You forgot something!'

Then it's as though Vince's shoulders sag just as quickly as they perked up and though he keeps on walking it's as if he can't make no more headway, as if his leg's tied to the end of a rope. He don't look round, like his neck's stuck. Then Lenny catches up with him and Vince turns his head slowly like someone else is having to wrench it round for him.

'Forgot this, didn't you? Forgot your coffee. You might think you can do without us but you'd look a bloody fool going to Margate without this.'

RAY

He says, 'If it wasn't for my mate Lucky there.'

It's that dark-haired nurse, the tasty one, Nurse Kelly. She's come to change his drip. She holds the glucose pack like it's something you throw in a game. Here, catch this. She has this gleam in her eye like she's used to warding off remarks.

He pulls the bed-shirt back over his shoulder where he's shown her the old scar. He says, 'I aint ever introduced you proper to my mate Lucky, have I?'

She shoots me a smile.

'We calls him Lucky but his real name's Ray. Ray Johnson.'

She says, 'Hello Ray, hello Lucky. I've seen you around.'

'Hear that, Ray? And, Ray, this is Joy. Joy Kelly.'

It's like we're in his home and we're his guests.

'Joy by name and Joy by nature.'

She smiles, like she hasn't heard it a hundred times before.

'Me and Raysy go back donkey's, before you was a twinkle. Fighting Rommel. Lucky here saved my life, more than once.'

'Aint true,' I say. 'Other way round.'

'Owe my life to Lucky,' he says.

She reaches up to change the drip.

'We calls him Lucky because he's lucky to be with, and on account of if you want to put a bet on, he's your man.'

She hangs up the new drip.

'It's like me and Ray have got this bet on that them's stockings you're wearing, not tights.'

She don't say nothing, fiddling with the drip. Then she says, 'That'd be telling, wouldn't it?'

'Wasn't telling I was thinking of.'

'How are your pillows? Want propping?'

She leans over him again and he says, 'You must get some suggestions, working in this place,' as though he hasn't just made one.

She says, 'A girl knows when she's safe.'

'And a man knows when he aint no danger.' He lifts the arm with the tubes going in it, like he's surrendering. 'But that don't apply to Ray here, now. You'd be okay with Ray, Ray's lucky. And he aint attached, like me.' He lifts the arm again. 'Nice pair of names that, nice pair. Ray and Joy.'

She straightens herself up.

'He's a little man but—'

'That's you done,' she says. 'I'll take this.'

It's his bottle of piss. It's all dark and bloody.

'You see, Ray. All she does is take the piss.'

'I'll see you later,' she says, moving off. She gives me another, head-shaking smile.

He says, 'I reckon you're on there, Raysy, I reckon you're on. Don't say I don't know how to fix you up.'

CHATHAM

Lenny says, panting, 'He never said it was up no bleeding hill.'

He never did, and he never said he didn't know where it was. When we stop and ask, they say, There it is, on top of that hill, see, you can't miss it, naval memorial, white tower. It's sticking up like a lighthouse for all to see, with a green ball on top instead of a beacon, it's a landmark. Except no one says how you get there and there aren't no signs. It's a funny memorial that no one remembers the way to.

So we trundle round half Chatham town and half Chatham dockyard with this hill in between, and Vince is fuming, though he was fuming in the first place, on account of Lenny. He's trying not to fume extra at Vic, he's trying to look the soul of patience for Vic, out of compensation for Lenny. Lenny says to Vic, 'Didn't they teach you no navigation in the Navy then?' And Vic's sitting there in the front again because this was his idea, all his idea, and it's looking as though he's sorry he ever spoke. But I reckon even that could be serving Vic's purpose: diversionary tactics, the blame on him for once, taking the heat away from Vince and Lenny. Except Vince is fuming like a grill pan. I reckon Vic is making a sacrifice, he makes a good martyr, and anyhow there must be some old lost mates of his with their names chalked up on that memorial for having made their own sacrifice, as they call it, once, so it don't do to deny them. If we ever get there.

We finally find this car park, half-way up the hill, just the other side of the Town Hall. But though it's just the other side of the Town Hall, it's as though Chatham stops and the wilderness begins. It's as though Chatham wasn't ever nothing more than a camp. There's just a low, scrubby wood with a muddy path leading up through it to where the memorial ought to be, except you can't see it because of the trees, no signs, no nothing. And the only advantage of the trees and of the fact that it looks like somewhere no one ever goes unless they're up to no good, is that, what with the beer we've drunk and the to-ing and fro-ing in a state of agitation round Chatham, Lenny and I need to piss again badly. So, soon as we're out of sight of the car park, we strike off the path to get the benefit.

He says, 'He never said it was up no bleeding hill,' panting and pissing at the same time. 'And I know we're doing Jack a turn, but I never knew it was Remembrance Day either.'

I say, 'Okay for Vic. It'd take a bit more doing, wouldn't it, for us to pay respects to our lot?'

He says, 'I aint so sure, way things are going.'

He breathes hard, though we haven't come so far. His face looks like strawberry jam. Vic's up ahead, walking on all by himself, determined, as if he's trying to put on a proper show. I don't suppose it helps when he looks round and sees Lenny and me taking a slash in the undergrowth. Whisky puts you at an advantage. He turns and presses on, though you can see him puffing too, and Vince is way on ahead of Vic, all in a huff of his own, not looking back, like he's team leader and he's not going to wait for a bunch of walking wounded, he just wants to get to the top quick and get it over with.

He's carrying the bag, *Rochester Food Fayre*, but he took out the coffee.

There's buds on the trees. Sunlight's trickling through the branches.

Lenny says, 'Wavy Navy. Frigging frigates.'

We move on and the path gets steeper. You can see where it comes out of the wood and there's just long grass, pale and wintry, with a scraggy bush or two shaking in the wind. We can't see no memorial. We see Vince stop and look around, a hand on his hip, like he's taking in a view. His coat flaps in the wind. Vic's getting nearer to Vince. We see Vince say something to Vic, though we can't hear it. Then Vince looks down at us as though he's enjoying watching us suffer.

Lenny stops, coughs and spits. He looks up at Vince. 'He aint letting go of it now, is he?' We stumble on, then Lenny stops again, his chest going like a pair of bellows. He leans over with his hands on his knees. It's as though he might be going to say, 'Raysy, you better go on without me.' There's a touch of froth in the corner of his mouth. I think, It wouldn't do for Lenny to peg out before we've said our last goodbye to Jack. It wouldn't do for any of us. I don't feel so A-1 myself.

But he levers himself up slowly. He puts a hand for a moment on my shoulder, leaning. Vince is looking. Then he gives me a soft nudge with his knuckles in the back. 'Do or die, eh Raysy?' like he's read my thoughts.

We carry on, not speaking, breathing too hard to speak. Then we come out of the trees and we can see the memorial all of a sudden, like it's been waiting for us all along, expecting us, sticking up tall and white against the sky, though the base of it's hidden behind the brow. There's a word for it. We can see the view spread out below, with the hill sloping down. Chatham merging into Rochester, the bend of the river with cranes sticking up, the cathedral like some big old bird sitting on a nest. You can see how a town gets set down where it is, in the folds of a valley by a river, by a bridge, and you can see where the river goes twisting on by the shape of the hills. You can see the sparkle of light on windows and cars. The sun's shining from under a bank of cloud across the pale grass and it's as if, though we're still climbing, we've entered an easier, kinder, cleaner zone. It's as though the tower of the memorial is pulling us up towards it. It's an obelisk, that's the word, obelisk. The sun's shining on it. It's white and tall. It looks like it's floating, because you can't see what it's attached to, like when you get near to it, it might shift off somewhere else. There's still no signs up to tell you, just the rough grass, ruffled by the wind, and a ragged path, and there aren't any people except us. It's like it got built then forgotten. Vince is going on ahead, getting closer, Vic's following behind. It's like it was only half meant to be here and so were we, but here we are, together, on top of this hill. It's like an effort at dignity, that's what it is, it's like a big tall effort at dignity.

VIC

. . . we therefore commit their bodies to the deep.

It would rear up howling and hissing, ice like marzipan on the forward deck, the bows plunging and whacking, so it seemed you didn't need another enemy to fire off shells and torpedoes at you, the sea was enough. Or it would stretch out broad and big and quiet as the moonlit night up above, the convoy spread like ducks on a lake. Floating coffins. Which was worse, a calm or an angry sea? Or you wouldn't see it, only feel it, through the swing and judder of steel. You joined the Navy to see the sea but what you saw were the giddy innards of a ship, and what you smelt wasn't the salt sea air but the smell of a ship's queasy stomach, oil and mess-fug and cook's latest apology and wet duffel and balaclavas and ether and rum and cordite and vomit, as if you were already there, where you might be, any moment, for ever, in the great heaving guts of the oggin.

He leant over me and I knew he was hoping I'd be asleep but my eyes were open and I said, 'Gramps died, didn't he?' Because I knew. His cheek was cold from the wet night air and his hair was damp but his clothes still had the hospital smell, the smell of Gramps. It wasn't so different from the usual smell, the smell on his skin of other people's dead skin, and you'd think if it was his daily business and had been Gramps's too that it would be a way of making it not matter so much when it was Gramps.

He said, 'Yes, Gramps died.' I knew he'd wanted to save it till morning. I might have pretended, for his sake. Now he would know he would have to leave me alone soon to face the whole of the night, in this strange room, with the rain at the window, with the knowledge that Gramps had died. But I wanted him to know I could do it, I could take it. Like when he told me what he did. He put people in boxes, because people died. But this wasn't people, it was Gramps.

I said, 'Will you tuck Gramps up yourself?'

He said, 'Course.'

He leant over me. He said, 'Night night. God bless.'

The rain made a noise like needles on the window, the wind swished. It would have been raining when Gramps died, it had rained all day. But I don't suppose he knew, or that it mattered, where he was, the weather outside. Whether it was sunny or wet, cold or warm. Or if you could see the sea, which you could if you went to the big window at the end of the ward, shiny and smooth, crinkly and grey. Though Gramps couldn't.

That's why they'd come here, Grandma and Gramps, to be by the sea. Bexhill-on-Sea. That's where people go when.

On a night like this you could think of all the people out at sea and how you were warm and safe and cosy, and how the people out at sea must be wishing they were warm and safe too, but Gramps couldn't think like that, not any more.

I could hear them talking downstairs, not the words, only the voices. Later when I woke in the night I could hear them being awake too. There were no voices, just the wind and the rain, but I could hear them being awake. I could hear how we were all lying awake in this dark, wind-rattled house, so each of us was like Gramps lying awake in that strange ward with all those other men around him, but alone, and all those other men alone too, like we were all together in this house but alone really, each of us in our beds, tucked up like we would be one day for ever and ever.

We're Tuckers, we fix up dead people. It's what we do for a living. We tuck 'em up.

Civilian occupation: undertaker's assistant.

It would spread, quick as fire, as things do in a ship. ''Ere, Buffer, we've got a gravedigger on board.' Like in the school playground: 'We know what your dad does,' except that then I'd never touched a corpse, and I wasn't at sea, or at war. Don't go on Tucker's watch, not if you can help it, don't be on Tucker's fire party. As if it were a way of altering your chances.

I wanted to say, I know about this, in a small way, I know about what you fear. I don't know much about ships and signals and bearings and soundings, any more than a Chatham rating learns in two months. But I know about the dead, I know about dead people, and I know that the sea is all around us anyway. Even on land we're all at sea, even on this hill high above Chatham where I can read the names. All in our berths going to our deaths.

Floating coffins.

So when the *Lothian* was hit, forward, and I was forward fire party but got sent aft for more hoses and then the second shell came in, killing Dempsey and Richards and Stone and Macleod, I knew, sharper than most, the pain of survival. It wasn't Tucker, notice. It was Dempsey and Richards, not Tucker. As if you could alter your chances.

He said he wouldn't hold me to it, I should choose my own life. Just because he and Gramps, just because the name of Tucker. But at least I shouldn't decide without knowing, and seeing, at least I shouldn't decide against out of unfounded fears. So I said yes, like it was my test. So he showed me, explaining, and I saw that there was, really, nothing to fear, nothing to be afraid of. It even made you feel a little calmer, surer. I was fourteen years old, the two of us together in the parlour. Three of us. So later I said, 'Yes, all right.' Your life cut out for you, your chances altered. And then it was too late to have any other foolish notions, like running away to sea.

They said, Here's a job for you, one you're equipped for, one no one else will volunteer for. Men at sea get foolish notions, like mermaids and monsters and that this convoy will be their last. So when we stopped engines, four days out of Iceland, to pick up survivors, they were all thinking, Here's work for Tucker, Tucker'll be busy. Though why pick them up, coughing up their last and half frozen-through, if it's only to crowd the mess deck and tip them back in a little while? Out of the sea they come and back they go, hardly making a splash in the grey swell. Tucker'll see to 'em, it's what he's good for. After a while I even earned respect, consideration. You shouldn't judge your fellow men, you shouldn't hold things against them. It even turned the other way round: You want to keep on the right side of Tucker, you want to keep in with Tucker. Yes, I'll be ship's bogey-man, someone has to do it. Tucker's here, have no fear. Tucker. Rhymes with. First name, Victor, good name in a war. Tucker'll do it, Tucker'll see to it. It's a tradition of the service to make use of the landsman's craft, like carpenter, ropemaker, surgeon. And the service has its own traditions for disposing of the dead. Out of the sea. A fold of canvas, a sinker of shot, and the last stitch, just in case and by custom, through the poor unfortunate frigging jolly Jack Tar's nose.

RAY

I reckon Vic's not going to tell us which are the names that matter, he's just going to look and keep quiet.

The obelisk is in the middle, it's for '14–'18, and there's a high white stone wall in a big half-circle with an iron gate in the centre where we've come in, and they're listed up on the wall on the inside of the curve in panel after panel, '39 onwards, like runners on a card. There's Captains and Lieutenants and Midshipmen and Petty Officers and Able and Ordinary Seamen, even some Boys. But there's also Stokers and Signalmen and Cooks and Telegraphists and Engine Room Artificers and Sick Berth Attendants, like there's a whole world on a ship.

And you can't tell nothing by looking at the lists because there aren't no odds quoted, there aren't no SPs. You can run your eyes down a card, when you're used to it, and work it out in your head that the bookies won't suffer, that the punter's going to lose. Like the insurance houses can do their sums and know they aren't going to come off worse in the long run, no matter what bad luck hits Joe Average Insured. There's always the gamble to make you think you're in with a chance and there's always the larger mathematics to make you think you should've saved your money and kept up your premiums. It depends on your underlying attitude.

But it's hard to have an attitude when there aren't no odds given and you can't see no larger mathematics. All you can tell by looking down the lists, and it don't matter that they're set in bronze on a white wall on top of a hill with an obelisk stuck in front an' all, is that a man is just a name. Which means something to him it attaches to, and to anyone who deals, same way, in the span of a human life, but it don't mean a monkey's beyond that. It don't mean a monkey's to things that live longer, like armies and navies and insurance houses and the Horserace Totalisator Board, it all goes on when you're gone and you don't make a blip. There's only one sensible attitude to take, looking at the lists, there's only one word of wisdom, like when Micky Dennis and Bill Kennedy copped it: 'It aint me, it wasn't me, it aint ever going to be me.' And there's only one lesson to be drawn, it's as cheery as it's not cheery, and that's that it aint living you're doing, they call it living, it's surviving.

But I reckon I could do it, I could still turn it into living again. I could forget the larger mathematics and take the gamble. Live a little, live again. See them grandchildren of mine, if there are any, the ones who'll survive me. In the surviving years of my life.

I could see the world. I could go to Bangkok.

I could say to Amy, 'About that shortfall.'

He stands there, looking, not telling. His face is all neat and straight, like a list itself. He's taken off his cap and shoved it in his pocket. The breeze lifts the hair on the top of his head. It's hard to picture Vic in a sailor suit, dancing a hornpipe, climbing the rigging, ship ahoy. Lenny's standing, stooped, just inside the gates, like he'll get round in a moment to seeing what's what, if he can just get his breath back first from coming up that hill. He shoots me a glance as though to say this is a place for sailor-boys but maybe us old soldiers should keep our end up. I reckon it's a toss-up, the sea, the desert. Vince has mooched off towards the obelisk. The sun's dazzling on the white stone. Either side of the gates there's a stone sailor, in duffel-coat and sea boots, at the ready, staring into space, so it looks like Lenny's shirking, it looks like he's a real sloucher. The gates are painted blue. Over the top it says, 'All These Were Honoured In Their Generations And Were The Glory Of Their Times.'

VINCE

Old buggers.

LENNY

All the same, I'd like to think my Joan would show up for me, though I wouldn't ever put her to such foolishness. I'd do the same for her, if it was that way round. Which it won't be.

Bleeding hill nearly finished me.

It's a question of duty, that's what it is.

Vic's standing there, looking, and Ray's gone over to chat to Vincey, at the foot of that tower thing. They're gazing up at it like a couple of tourists peering at Nelson's Column. 'Heligoland' it says on it, wherever that is, 'Heligoland. Jutland. Dogger Bank.' But it don't look like they're talking about the tower, it looks like they're talking about something else, strictly between the two of them.

Well I suppose I'm the odd man out here, I'm the odd man out on this whole caper, just along for the ride and the beer, and the hill-climbing. There's Vic there with his lists of dead, as if he don't get enough of that on a daily basis, and them two thick as thieves at the foot of the tower. I never understood how Raysy could get pally with that pillock. I suppose he never had no daughter up the spout by him, though he might've done, if Susie hadn't been whisked off to Australia first.

There's Ray and Jack who go back to the desert, same desert as me, Gunner Tate, except I never knew either of them then. There's Vic and Jack who had pitches opposite for the best part of fifty years, Dodds and Tucker, steaks and stiffs. And there's Jack and Vince, one in a bag and one off his rag.

The only reason I'm here, if you don't count being his regular boozing partner for close on forty years, is because of Sally. Is because Jack took her to the seaside when we couldn't take her ourselves. It was a kindness, one of the few that girl ever got. And now I'm taking Jack.

It's a question of duty. There's a soldier's duty, a sailor's duty. Heligoland. Jutland. But if you ask me, that aint duty so much as orders. Doing your duty in the ordinary course of life is another thing, it's harder. It's like Ray always said that Jack was a fine soldier, Jack should've got a medal, but when it came to being back in Civvy Street, he didn't know nothing better, like most of us, than to stick like glue to what he knew, like there was an order sent down from High Command that he couldn't ever be nothing else but a butcher. That shop was his bleeding billet, it's a fact.

Then he fancies going to the seaside.

They look like two spies on a rendezvous, standing there by that tower. One of 'em's got a bag, look, a suspicious-looking bag.

It's like Sally done wrong, for all I don't blame her, for all her having married that nutter on the rebound from Big Boy. Tommy Tyson, care of Pentonville Prison. She should've stuck with him, it'll be worse when he gets out, she should've kept going to see him. Like Amy sees June.

It's a question of paying your dues.

It's like Ray should patch things up with Susie, like Carol should never've run out on Ray. There shouldn't ever be no running off, deserting. Like Vincey should've knuckled down and done what was wanted of him, because he owed Jack and Amy for nigh on everything, and Jack was that lad's father to all intents and purposes.

And Jack shouldn't ever've given up on his own.

Nor should I.

Joan might show up, but not Sally.

They're moving round behind the tower.

So you could say it was Amy who always done her duty, her duty and a half, year in, year out. Never a squeak in return, for all I've heard. You could say she's doing it now, if she's going to see June. Except she could see June tomorrow or she could've seen her yesterday. You'd think she could spare the one day for Jack.

RAY

Vince looks up at the obelisk, all intent, as if it might do something sudden and he don't want to take his eyes off it, as if he's glad he don't have to look at me. It's the first time we've slipped away from Vic and Lenny. The sun and the view are behind us. He's got his hands in his pockets, his left wrist stuck through the handles of the carrier bag. It must be getting heavy, the plastic cutting into him, but he don't seem to mind. It's like he don't want to be separated from it.

. . . who have no other grave than the sea.

He looks up at the obelisk and I look up at him. It's hard when you've got the years without the height. But this obelisk must be having a littling effect on Vince, because though he doesn't turn to look at me I can see his face going all sort of boyish and outranked.

It's like when he was pumping me about the yard and he wasn't sure how I'd stand. 'Uncle Ray', he went and called me.

He squints at the white stone, forgot to bring his shades. He should've worn a different tie.

He says, 'I was wondering, Raysy.'

I say, 'Wondering?'

He says, 'Jack never said nothing to you about no money, did he? I mean, when he was— He never mentioned no sum of money?'

There's a stone lion crouching at each corner of the obelisk.

I say, 'What sum of money?'

He says, 'Don't matter,' shifting on his feet. He's got his head up, looking, but it's as though he might be begging. He says, 'Say about a thousand pounds.'

RedcarRiponSandownThirsk.

'No,' I say. 'He never mentioned no sum of money.'

He looks at me now, a quick flicker of a look, then away again. The sun goes in and the white stone goes grey, the breeze is cold on our necks.

'Only,' he says, like he's become the head of the family, 'we've got to see Amy right, aint we? We got to see Amy right.'

VINCE

I couldn't've been much higher than that sideboard. You wouldn't think that in a few years Amy'd be looking up at me.

She said they were taken when he was a soldier, in the war. There was the two of them sitting on the camel, laughing, Ray in front, Jack behind. And there was Jack all by himself, with his shirt undone, chest bare, holding a ciggy. But I didn't believe her, because I couldn't see what sitting on a camel, laughing, had to do with being a soldier. He was laughing in the other photo too.

I thought, That aint my dad, that aint my dad, laughing.

I said, 'He doesn't look like a soldier.' She said, 'That's why I like the picture.' She didn't explain.

She said it was in the desert, they were in the desert, like Uncle Lenny was too. It was before I was born.

The bananas in the fruit bowl came from Uncle Lenny's.

You had to be grown-up to be a soldier, that's what they said. It was like all the other things you had to be grown-up for, like you had to be grown-up before you could die. Which was a lie. The two things went together because in order to die you had to be brave, and soldiers were brave.

But I know now you don't have to be brave to be a soldier and you don't have to be a soldier to be brave.

'*Amy, can I have that photo? Just for a bit.*'

'*Course you can, Vince. You can keep it.*'

The sun's in his face and he's staring at you, grinning, still alive, like he knows you don't know who he really is. He's staring at you out of that brass frame like he knows he's in another world, peeping out at your one. He's wearing shorts and his shirt's untucked and unbuttoned and there's a tin helmet, tilted, on his head but it looks like it's something he's wearing for fun, and there's sand all around. He doesn't look like a soldier, he doesn't even look grown up. He looks like a kid on a beach.

LENNY

And if Amy was here I reckon she'd keep us all in check, she wouldn't have no misbehaving, we'd all have to clean up our acts. Which wouldn't be no bad thing. I can't see it passing off smooth. Four geezers and a box.

They're coming back now from behind the tower, not talking, like they've spoken and now they're thinking. Big Boy and little Raysy, like Jack and Lucky. Half shut your eyes, and you can see the one pair in the other. Maybe it's the attraction of opposites. It always seemed to me that when you saw Jack and Ray together, Ray was like this little midget Jack'd pulled out from under his coat, this little mascot. Meet my friend Lucky.

But you have to watch Raysy. Just when you think he aint got no advantage he pops up and surprises you, he pops out and does something canny. It's like he hides behind being small.

Vic's still looking at his lists. How much time do we give him? I bet Jack never guessed that to get to Margate he'd have to call in on the Royal Navy. You could say Vic's got a nerve, dragging us up here to look at all these names when it's Jack's day, like saying Jack aint special. But I don't hold it against him, my grouch aint with Vic. It's a question of duty.

CHATHAM

The sun comes out again and the obelisk casts a long, thin shadow across the lawn towards the curved wall, as if we're standing on a sun-dial. At the right time of the year, when the sun's low, the shadow must shift slowly, every day, over first one row of names then another.

We're moving off now, heading for the blue gates. Lenny's still loitering by them, like he was the one who let us in and he's waiting to lock up. Give him a quid for his trouble. Vic's finished, he's put his cap back on, but it's as though Vince has given an order anyway: time's up, back on the coach. We pass through the gates, not in a bunch, talking, but one by one, silent. It's like we've come out from seeing a show and none of us has got a neat comment worked out ready. Vincey's first, I'm last.

We walk back across the open hilltop. The sun and the view and the breeze are in our faces. There's no one else around and all you can hear is our feet scuffling and Lenny wheezing. Where the path starts to slope down towards the trees Vince suddenly comes to a halt and we all shuffle up behind him, like he's held up a hand. Our faces are all bright in the sunshine. He steps off the path on to the grass. He says, 'I'll catch you up, you all go on. I'll catch you up down there.'

We don't have to do as he says, we don't have to take orders, but it's true he won't have a job catching us. Judging by coming up. So we carry on, slowly, single file, gaps between us, me last looking over my shoulder at Vincey. He walks off across the grass, he don't seem to mind about his smart suit and shoes, and I see him stop on the edge of the hill and look at the view like Vic looking at the names.

I dawdle a bit behind the others. Maybe he wants me to do just that. Maybe he's giving me a second chance. But he just stands there, with the bag by his side, staring, like one of them stone sailors.

The sun goes in again behind the edge of a cloud but only for a moment. I look at the view too, I don't want to lose it either, but I turn and walk on down, following the others, so the trees come up and the view slips away. It's shivery among the trees.

We get back to the car but we can't get in because Vince has got the key, so we hang around in the car park, not talking, giving each other quick glances. Lenny looks at his watch. Vic's looking like it's all his fault, but you can't blame him, once he'd decided. It would've been a sort of affront to say, Not if it's going to mean trouble, not if it's up a hill, let's skip it.

And it's not him who's holding us up now.

We wait about a minute. Then we see him coming down the path, carrying the bag. It seems he's as keen as we are now to be pressing on, because he's walking fast, slipping now and then on the mud. His face is all fixed and distant as he comes towards us, like he wishes we weren't around.

I'd say he's done some blubbing too. We all need our moment.

He puts the bag with the box inside it gently on the bonnet, then he unlocks the car and moves round to stow his coat. We take off our own coats but none of us gets in, as if we've got to wait to be told. He shuts the boot then comes back round to the driver's door, twisting out of his jacket. He opens the rear door and slips his jacket, folding it, back on to the rear seat.

'Right,' he says, impatient, 'who's going where?'

Vic says, 'I'll go in the back,' quick as a flash. Lenny and me look at each other.

'So who's going in front?'

It's like he's Daddy and we're kids, and Daddy's getting in a temper.

Lenny looks at Vince.

'Okay Ray,' Vince says, 'in the front.'

It's not where I want to be, not now, but I get in and the big seat swallows me up.

Lenny gets in the back beside Vic.

Vince pauses for a moment by the driver's door, smoothing his hair, straightening his tie, scraping mud from his shoes with a stick he's picked up, then he takes the bag from the bonnet. I think he's going to say, 'So who wants—?' but he passes the bag straight to me. It's like he's passing it to me just so I can mind it for him, close and handy, it goes with being in the front. But I don't know how to take it, I don't know how to take charge of it.

''Ere Raysy, cop hold.'

He starts the engine, grabbing his shades from the dash, and moves off so quick the wheels slip and growl. He swings back through Chatham like everything's in his way. When you've been thinking of the dead you notice how the living hurry. We drive out and join up with the M2, Junction 3, Dover 48, then he really puts his foot down. He's driving like he's making up for lost time, like he's late for an appointment. But there aint no deadline. His neck's gone all tight and rigid. I look across the dash and see the needle flick past ninety-five. In a big plush car you don't notice the speed. Junction 4, Junction 5. So much for driving as fits the occasion. We're all sitting there like we ought to say something but we daren't open our mouths and I can feel Vic feeling that it's all his fault, but you shouldn't blame Vic.

VIC

But Jack's not special, he's not special at all. I'd just like to say that, please. I'd just like to point that out, as a professional and a friend. He's just one of the many now. In life there are differences, you make distinctions, it's the back seat for me from now on. But the dead are the dead, I've watched them, they're equal. Either you think of them all or you forget them. It doesn't do in remembering one not to remember the others. Dempsey, Richards. And it doesn't do when you remember the others not to spare a thought for the ones you never knew. It's what makes all men equal for ever and always. There's only one sea.

WICK'S FARM

He slows down suddenly, moving across to the inside lane, and we all breathe easier. He takes the slip road for the exit coming up, not saying a word. Junction 6, Ashford, Faversham. He takes the Ashford road, like he knows exactly what he's doing, though it aint the way to Margate, and after a mile or so he turns off that too. We're all looking at him, not speaking. He says, 'Detour,' eyes on the road, not budging his head, 'detour.'

The road gets narrower and twistier, trees arching across, hedges, fields. I suppose you could say we're in the country now, we're a long way from Bermondsey. The trees are all flecked with green. The sky's blue and grey and white, the sun coming in bursts. He takes another turn, and another, like there's a map in his head. We go along a ridge with a view off to our right, a big, wide view, wherever there's a gap in the hedge. It's as though he's got keen on views. Then the road climbs a bit, still on the ridge, and near the top of the climb he slows, looking this way and that, and pulls over where there's a wide bit of verge and a gate in the hedge. There's just a bare track leading off and down across a field, two chalky ruts, and there's one of those green signs sticking up and pointing by the gate: 'Public Footpath'.

He turns off the engine. We can hear sheep bleating in the distance. He looks at me and says, 'Raysy,' holding out his hand, palm up, fingers twitching, and I know he means the bag, the box, he means Jack. He says it in a way you don't argue with or ask why, so I hand it over. He takes the box out of the bag and tosses the bag back into my lap,

Rochester Food Fayre. Then he flips open the box and pulls out the jar and chucks the box back into my lap too. His face is set hard. He opens his door and gets out, holding the jar tight against his chest.

He doesn't reach over for his jacket or go round to the boot for his coat. He slams the door and walks over to the gate. The breeze whips his tie over his shoulder and balloons out his shirt. The gate's metal and clanky. He fiddles with a bolt, pushing up on one of the crossbars, then opens the gate just enough for him to slip through. There's a rusty streak on the sleeve of his white shirt. He looks out across the field, then he swings shut the gate, which clangs and judders behind him, and sets off along the track.

Lenny says, 'Jesus, what now?'

Vic don't say a thing, like it's all down to him, it's him who's given Vince the idea in the first place. Find yourself a hill.

I say, 'Search me.'

It's Lenny who gets out first, then me, then Vic. The breeze hits us sharpish. It's muddy underfoot. We ought to get our coats from the boot but Lenny's already moved to the gate, struggling with the bolt, like he's twigged quicker than us what's going on.

'Toe-rag,' he says, 'toe-rag. He aint got no prior claim.'

Vince is walking across the field to where it starts to slope steeply, his red tie flicking like a tongue over his shoulder. It's not so much a field as an open hillside. We can see the full sweep of the view, like we're standing on the rim of a big, crooked bowl. Down in the valley it's all green and brown and patchy, woods marked off with neat edges and corners, hedges like stitching. There's a splodge of red brick in the middle with a spire sticking up. It looks like England, that's what it looks like.

The field slopes up to the left, to a crest, where there's a clump of trees and, peeping up from the other side, a tar-brown stump of a building, a windmill, with its sails missing. In front of us the field slopes down gently, maybe for eighty yards, then drops away. There must be a whole chunk of the view you can't see till you get to the brow.

Near the gate the grass is trodden bare and sprinkled with sheep shit. There's a water trough tucked in by the hedge, galvanized metal. We can hear sheep and smell sheep and we can see them, off to the left, dotted across the slope. They're all staring at Vince as he walks across the field, except for the little 'uns, the lambs. They seem keener on running this way and that or tucking in under their mothers. Now and then one of them starts jumping about like it's stepped on something electric.

Lenny wrestles with the bolt.

'He aint got no special rights,' he says, 'he aint kin.' He frees the bolt. 'Never was, was he?'

He pushes open the gate and before Vic and me have slipped through behind him he darts off along the track after Vince. It's like the climb up to that memorial has got him in shape, it was just a warm-up.

Vince is getting near the brow, he hasn't looked back once. One elbow's stuck out where he's holding the jar and his shirt's billowing and flapping. If it wasn't that everything seems to have gone crazy, you'd say he looked a complete berk, out there in the middle of a field, holding a plastic pot, with his white shirt and his flash tie and a flock of sheep baa-ing at him.

Lenny's moving so fast me and Vic are struggling to keep up with him. He's about twenty yards away from Vince when Vince stops on the brow and stands there, steady, pausing but like he's already made up his mind about something. For a moment he looks like a man perched on the edge of a cliff but as we get closer, we can see the hillside dipping sharply away and we can see the hidden part of the valley below: a wood, a road, a farmhouse. Orchards, oasthouses.

Then we see Vince start to unscrew the cap from the jar.

Lenny says 'Toe-rag,' as if he'd known in advance what Vince was going to do.

The cap looks hard to shift, like the lid on a new jar of jam. We're just a few yards from Vince now and he can see us coming at him. It's like he's prepared for that, like he even wants us as witnesses. But he aint prepared for what Lenny does next.

Lenny snatches at his arm, the arm that's working on the cap, and Vince pulls away and lifts the jar up high so Lenny can't reach it. The cap's still on but it looks like it's hanging on loose, just by the thread. Vince dodges to one side but Lenny goes at him again. This time he grabs him by the tie and with his other hand takes hold of his shirt front. I see a wodge of Vince's stomach and a button flying. Then Vince goes down, sudden, caught off balance, arm held up high. He tries to hang on to the jar but as he tumbles, it pops out of his grasp and Vince and me watch it falling. We watch it falling keener than we watch Vince falling because when it hits the ground one of two things could happen, or both. The loose cap could fly off and what's inside spill out, or the jar could bounce bad and start rolling all the way down the steep slope of the hill.

But it comes to rest against a clump of thistles and the cap stays on.

Lenny scoots over and picks it up, twisting the cap on tighter. Then Vince lurches to his feet and goes for him. Vince's shirt's come untucked. There's a muddy green streak down his left sleeve to match the rusty brown one on his right. He tries wrenching the jar from Lenny's hands and slips again and puts a hand out to break his fall and Lenny pulls the jar clear.

Vince gets up, all fired up now, all hunched and snorting and puffing, and Lenny holds out the jar in front of him in both hands, teasing and sort of skipping on the spot. I've never seen Lenny so neat on his pins. Vince moves forward and Lenny moves back, dodging, like he could chuck the jar to Vic or me if that was the idea and we were ready to catch it, but he does a sort of rugby flip with it, low and quick to one side, so it lands on the grass away from any of us, then he steps round so he's between it and Vince, and puts out his fists and starts ducking and weaving.

'Come on, Big Boy. Come on, tosser.'

Vince holds off for a moment, thinking, like he's not so choked up as to take on a man Lenny's age. But he can see the jar on the grass behind Lenny, and Lenny don't look so past it, all of a sudden, he looks like a man with a purpose. He looks like it might be all over for him in just a while but right now he's planning on having his moment. Vic makes a little sighing, clucking sound beside me. Either of us could sneak round and grab the jar but we don't. I reckon Vic's not going to step in and be the referee, not this time.

Lenny says, 'Wasn't no love lost, was there? Was there?'

Vince goes forward, not putting his fists up, elbows out, hands splayed, like he's just daring Lenny, and Lenny goes forward and puts in a punch straight away, no messing, a good quick jab to the middle of the chest. It makes Vince stop and stagger, like he hadn't really bargained on it.

'That's for Sally,' Lenny says, gasping, then he puts in another punch.

'And that's for Jack.'

This time Vince don't stand and take it. He recovers, then comes in, grabbing Lenny's leading arm before Lenny can get his puff back. He holds Lenny's wrist and he shoves him twice under the throat with the flat of his other hand, like he could use more force if he wanted but he aint being so soft either. He moves his hand up on to Lenny's face, clawing and squeezing, and jerks Lenny's head back, once, twice, with Lenny's eyes sort of popping out between his fingers, then he takes the hand away so Lenny can breathe and Lenny says, 'Fists, pillock,' and wops Vince on the mouth. It looks like it hurts Lenny more. Then Vince takes hold of Lenny's arm with both hands and pulls him and swings him round, snarling, so they're twirling like a pair of ice skaters. He lets go and Lenny goes flying and tumbling. Then Vince goes and stands over him like you can't tell if it's to kick him or to see if he's all right. He puts out a hand and Lenny takes it, pulling himself up, then he socks Vince hard in the ribs and Vince shoves him back down again.

Me and Vic don't move an inch.

Lenny's sort of sprawled, half sitting, half lying, leaning on his hands, breathing and dribbling. Vince is standing over him, bent, breathing too. All you can hear is their breathing and the sheep bleating and baa-ing like spectators. Vince could get the jar now but it's like he's not sure of Lenny. He moves round slowly, so he's between the jar and Lenny, as Lenny pushes himself up.

Lenny's face looks like it's roasting and he's hee-hawing like a donkey, swaying on his feet. Vince steps back, gasping too, and picks up the jar. Then he comes forward with it slowly like it's him who's teasing Lenny now. You can see the look in Lenny's eyes, for all he's trying to hide it. It says, 'I'm beat, I'm done for. It's all I can do to breathe,' and all your feeling would be for Lenny standing there, breathing, except that Vince is swaying and staggering and gasping too and looking unsure at Lenny. And there's another thing about Vince. His face is all wet, his eyes are wet. He's clutching the jar like a kid holding a toy.

He says, 'I wasn't going to chuck the lot, I wasn't going to chuck the lot.' He's started to unscrew the cap again.

Lenny looks at him, not speaking, swaying, breathing.

'Just a bit,' Vince says, 'only a bit.'

Lenny looks at him then he speaks, all hoarse and croaky. 'So what's the idea? You going to stop off every ten minutes and chuck some more? A handful here, a handful there?'

Vince carries on unscrewing the cap. He wipes his face. It's like a temptation. It's like when you take a box of chocolates to someone who's ill, to someone in hospital, and you start tucking into them yourself, first one, then another. It's like when you're looking after what belongs to someone else and you go and take it for yourself.

Vince says, 'What's the meaning of "scatter"?' He wipes his hand across his face. 'What's the meaning of the word "scatter"?'

Lenny says, 'You ought to be ashamed of yourself, pillock.'

But it's like Lenny's ashamed of himself too, standing there, ready to drop. It looks like he's thinking he's hashed up the day.

Vince has got the cap off now. He looks quickly into the jar. The sheep are still staring at us. I reckon we must look as daft to them as they do to us, and I reckon anyone looking up from down below at the four of us on the top of this hill must think we're stranger-looking than the sheep.

Vince puts the cap into his pocket, then he hugs the jar closer to him and dips his free hand into it. His eyes are all gooey. He moves away from Lenny, turning his back towards him. It seems Lenny hasn't got the heart or strength to stop him. Vic and me don't stop him either. He moves to the edge of the slope, to face the view, his back to us all. In the distance there's a sort of trough of sunshine, a parting in the sky, but nearer to us a big, soft, sooty cloud is moving in. The breeze gets up. It's cold but I don't suppose Vince or Lenny can feel it. The ground smells of spring, the air smells of winter. Then there's a dash of rain.

Vince stands, facing the view, with his back straight and his feet planted. I'd say that shirt of his is pretty well wrecked and those trousers are going to need a good clean. Mandy'll need an explanation. He splutters like he's trying to announce something but he can't get it out or he don't know what it is. He delves in the jar and he throws quickly, spluttering, once, twice. It looks like white dust, like pepper, but the wind blows it into nothing. Then he screws the cap back on and turns, coming towards us.

'This is where,' he says, wiping his face. 'This is where.'

RAY

He said, 'So now I know, Raysy.'

It was a full day and a half after the operation that wasn't no operation, so he wasn't groggy and slow and confused any more. Sharp and clear as I've ever seen him, sitting up there in that little white smock thing, with the extra tubes going in, some round the back now. It seemed like every day they rigged up another tube. But there were others in there that were all tubes, tubes and wires and bottles and apparatus, complete chemistry sets. So you had to look close to see if there was really a human life, a human component still there somewhere.

But he was sitting up, straight and steady. I thought, It's like he's having his portrait done, his last portrait, no flattering, no prettying, and no one knows how long it will take. Two weeks, three. Nothing to do but sit still and be who you are.

I don't know what you say to someone when they say that they know. I reckon the imagination's a million miles from the fact. So I looked down at the bedclothes and up at him again and he was still looking at me, straight and steady, straight into my eyes, like if he could get a grip then I should, like he aint stopped being himself, just because. On the contrary.

He says, 'No telling, is there?' Then he says, 'Lambs to the slaughter, eh Lucky.'

MANDY

The road went on, black and curving and cat's-eyed, like the one sure thing in the wet and the dark and the spray, the one sure thing in the world. Not the place from or the place to but the road.

I said, 'So what've you got in the back?' For something to say. He said, looking at me, 'Carcasses,' and I thought, Trust my luck. After only six hours.

He said, 'Long way from home then?'

I nodded, feeling my head heavy, my neck sagging with tiredness.

He said, 'So where would that be?'

He leant forward, arms hugging the steering wheel.

I said, 'Blackburn.'

27, Ollerton Road, Blackburn.

He said, 'But not any more, eh?' pulling a packet of ciggies from his shirt pocket. 'Blackburn rover, eh?' grinning at his own joke. 'London, eh?'

I nodded.

He shook the packet of cigarettes, nudged one up with his thumb and drew it out with his mouth. He passed the packet to me but I shook my head.

He said, 'Day trip or for ever?' feeling for a lighter. I didn't answer. He flicked the lighter and I saw his face, red and bunched and knotty, in the flame. He said, 'How old are you, love?' breathing out smoke.

I didn't answer.

He said, 'Seventeen?' He took another drag on the cigarette, looking at the road like it was his road, the wipers dancing across the windscreen. '*Just seventeen, you know what I mean,*' sort of singing. He said, 'I can take you to London, love. I can take you where I'm taking my meat.'

He turned and I was looking straight at him. He said, 'What are you looking at?'

I said, 'You remind me of my dad.'

It's a good line, a handy line, stops 'em in their tracks. I'd used it before.

Besides, he did, just a bit. Remind me.

And it was him I'd blame, my dad, my dad Bill. It was him I'd give as my excuse, if I was ever called to account, if I ever found myself slinking back, or being carted in a cop car, to Ollerton Road. I wasn't the first to leave, was I? It was him who set me my example.

Maybe he was thinking of me right now, with his floozy in the Isle of Man, if that was where and how it was. Waking up in the small hours, lighting a ciggy. Rain on the window. I wonder what that Mandy's up to, I wonder what that lass is doing right now.

He used to say, 'You're a wicked girl, Mandy, you're a wicked girl.' But always with a sideways smile or a wink or a click of the tongue, whether I'd done wrong or not, as if it was only ever ten per cent a ticking-off and ninety per cent a show of approval. 'You're a wicked girl, I don't know what's going to become of you,' looking at me like one day he was going to have to come and pull me out of trouble. And I used to like saying, because it had just a touch of wickedness itself and because it was different from what the other girls said about their fathers, 'My dad's a sailor.' Sailor Bill. Barnacle Bill.

Not that working on car ferries made you a real sailor.

Fleetwood to Douglas, there and back inside a day. And in winter, Heysham to Douglas, an hour longer. But when I heard him leaving in the early mornings, trying to coax that clapped-out Hillman into life, I'd think, He'll be at sea soon, my dad Bill, the voyage out, the voyage home.

Except one day he never came back.

I never said 'seaman', it didn't sound right, though it was a wicked word too, a giggle word, if you said it the wrong way. Why is a ship like a rubber johnny? Because it's full of seamen. And he'd been a real sailor once, or so he said. He'd seen the world. Shanghai, Yokohama. But then he'd met Mum and the world-seeing days had come to an end, or so she said. One wild night in Liverpool. Brown arms, tattoos and a large pinch of salt. *Sailor, stop your roaming.* Though it's hard to imagine that ever having happened, it's hard to imagine Mum having been that woman, when you saw what she got for herself by way of replacement, that creep Neville from the Town Hall. 'Mandy, I want you to meet Mr Lonsdale.' Neville Lonsdale, Town Planning. And from then on we were going to lead a different sort of life.

He used to put that pasty face in front of mine, dimpling like a vicar, and say, 'So what do you want to be, Mandy, what do you want to do when you grow up?' As if it earned him points in her eyes. Someone at last with a bit of concern, with a bit of respect. Neville the devil. What I wanted to say was that I wanted to be wicked, I wanted to be wicked like Dad said I was anyway. I wanted to be Mandy Black, and I wanted to be wicked.

And so I was. I hung around in pubs and dance-halls, I twisted and shouted, I let hands scurry up my skirt, and worse. I let myself be pushed up against walls. I gave Mum and Neville hell, which was only what they gave me. But more than that, I said to my best friend and partner-in-sin,

Judy Battersby, 'How about it? London. Bright lights. You and me.' But she never showed up, she chickened out, the cow.

And I suppose what I always hoped, right up until the last moment, was that he'd come back anyway, with five years' worth of excuses. That he'd throw down his kit-bag then he'd throw Neville out the front door. Then I wouldn't have to run away myself.

But they found the Hillman in Liverpool, not Fleetwood. So he might have gone anywhere. Not a floozy in the Isle of Man but floozies all over, in Shanghai and Yokohama. I had this picture of him, which I still have, it's a daft picture but I still have it. That he'd sailed away to the South Seas. Grass skirts and coconut trees. He's still there now, thirty years younger, with a flower stuck behind his ear. Not the Isle of Man. Isle of Woman, more like.

He said, 'What's your name, love?'

I said, 'Judy.'

He said, 'Mick. Anywhere London or somewhere London?'

I said, 'Anywhere London.'

He said, 'I'll take you to Smithfield. Heard of Smithfield? There in two hours. It's all right, love, it's okay, you can nod off.'

So Mandy Black, or Judy Battersby as she was travelling as, arrived in London in a meat lorry and got carted away again in a butcher's van, without so much as a peep at Leicester Square. It's a famous story, it's done the rounds, it might even have reached Ollerton Road. Blackburn to Bermondsey, going up in the world. But now when I think of it, now when I see them huddled up in shop entrances and archways, in smelly blankets, I think, I was lucky. And when I think of that girl with a rucksack heading down the A5, I think, That was my adventure, my big adventure, though it hardly lasted twelve hours.

To run away from home and find another home in less than a day, though the new home wasn't a real home, any more than the one I left. The new home was all the opposite of what it seemed: a son whose home it wasn't but it was, a daughter whose home it was but it wasn't because she had to be kept in a Home, a mum and dad who weren't really a mum and dad, except to me.

Why should I have fitted into that? Why shouldn't I have taken off again like a shot? When the world was saying anyway everything is changing now, everything goes. It couldn't have just been him, Vince. That we were somehow, underneath it all, like *brother* and *sister*, worse, father and daughter. Just back from the Middle East, 'from the bleeding garden of Aden, sweetheart,' with his kit-bag slung in a corner of that bedroom he'd hardly moved back into before he moved out again for me. 'V. I. Dodds.' The smell of him in there, sweat and engine oil and Senior Service. Tattoos up his arm. 'You can lick 'em but they won't come off.' So it was like *committing incest*, like throwing the whole thing open, like being dangerous where you ought to be most safe. Safe as houses. And in a camper-van too, Uncle Ray's camper, like a pair of gypsies.

Blackburn to Bermondsey, aiming high. But that's where I stayed and that's what I became. Vince's floozy, Vince's wife, Vince's sister, daughter, mother, his whole family. And Jack and Amy's little grown-up girl. So it's as though I don't know any more who that lassie on the A5 was. As though in those twelve hours on the road I might have been about to become anyone. What do you want to be, Mandy? November '67. The year of Sergeant Pepper. Four thousand holes in Blackburn, Lancashire. It wasn't Wednesday morning at five o'clock, it was Thursday evening at eight o'clock. But I couldn't help carrying that song in my head, like my theme tune: *She's leaving home, bye, bye.*

He said, 'A doodlebug.'

I said, 'What?'

He said, 'A buzz-bomb. V-1. Flattened the house, killed 'em all, except me. I aint who you think I am, I aint Vince Dodds.'

I thought, I could have guessed that. Not just from the way you look but from the way you keep to your own separate space, from the way you were so ready to move out and kip down in this camper-van. But that was a sly move, wasn't it, Vince, a crafty move?

She can sleep in my room.

And what about you, Vincey?

I'll think of something.

I thought of saying to him, 'I'm not who you think I am either.' Because I don't know who Mandy Black is, not yet, I'm discovering.

But I'd already told Jack, sitting there in that meat van while we did a sort of dawn tour of London: 'I'm not who I said I was, my name's not Judy. It's Mandy, Mandy Black, from Blackburn.' And he said, 'So who's Judy?' And I said, 'No one.'

Old Bailey, St Paul's, London Bridge, the light breaking over the grey river.

Vince said, 'My real name's not Dodds, it's Pritchett.'

I felt him shrinking, slipping inside me. I sank down so my face was on his chest.

He said, 'It aint no secret. It's a known fact. Except he tries to pretend it never was a fact.'

'Who?'

He said, 'Old man. I mean, Jack. Why d'you think I took off in the first place? Why d'you think I joined up? Because I wasn't going to be no Vince Dodds. I wasn't going to be no butcher's boy.'

I said, 'But you came back.'

He said, 'I came back to show 'im.'

I said, 'It's easier for men. They can go and be soldiers, they can run away to sea.'

He said, 'You ever done a stretch in Aden?'

I started to lick his tattoos. One of them said 'V.I.P.', with a fist and a thunderbolt. I said, 'It says "Dodds" on your kit-bag. So what are you going to be, Vince? What do you want to be?' And he said, 'Motors.'

I said, 'Motors?'

He said, 'You saw that old Jag in the yard, didn't you? '59, Mark 9. It's a start, aint it? Aint any old jam-jar, it's a Jag. I'll make it like new again.'

Then he told me about motors, he told me all about motors.

I thought, It's never how you picture it, never how you picture it at all. Me and Judy Battersby knocking around the West End, getting picked up by a couple of fellers in a rock band.

A butcher's van, an ex-soldier with oil under his fingernails. Meeting a man from the motor trade.

He said one day Jack would come crawling to him, I'd see.

I licked the hairs on his chest.

I said, 'How do you know I'm who you think I am, either? How do you know my name's really Mandy Black? I could be anyone too, couldn't I?'

I put my hand on his sticky cock.

He said, 'I aint teasing you, I aint having you on. I'm telling you so you know what's what. I'm telling you so you don't get no wrong ideas. That's fair, aint it?'

I said, 'Yes.'

'That's only honest.'

I said, 'Yes, Vince.'

He said, 'I was only three months, I didn't know nothing, did I?'

I felt his cock stiffening under my hand.

'I'm telling you so you'll be prepared.'

'Prepared?'

'He'll try and do the same with you. They'll try and do the same with you.'

I said, 'What?'

'I bet it even suits them that you and me are doing this.'

'What are you talking about?'

'So I won't want to move on again, you neither. So we'll have to show 'em, together. We'll have to stay put and scarper at the same time.'

I said, 'How do you do that?'

He said, 'Motors.'

It felt safe in that camper, like a hiding-place.

I said, 'What are you talking about?'

He rolled me over and shoved into me and I lifted my knees and gripped him.

He said, 'They haven't told you, have they? Course they haven't. You don't know the half yet, do you?'

*

It's never how you picture it. Mrs Vincent Dodds, Mrs Dodds Autos. A husband in the motor trade, a daughter on the hustle.

The bright lights of London. There were bright lights all right. There were these rows of long, tall buildings, each of them lit up like a fairground, each of them full of meat and men and din, as if the men were shouting at the meat and the meat was shouting back. And outside it was still dark, extra dark because of the brightness inside, the air full of wet murk. There were lorries throbbing and reversing, the drizzle like sparks in their lights, and doors being swung open and puddles shining red and white, and more meat, on barrows, on shoulders, being lugged into the brightness, the men doing the lugging all streaked and smeared with blood, their faces red and glistening as the loads they were carrying. I thought, Jesus Christ, Mandy Black, where have you come to? And the noise like some mad language, as if it might as well have been the meat still yelling and protesting, still kicking, except that coming out of it I heard that voice, sounding unreal because I'd heard it before on the telly, on the radio, like a voice no one ever really used, but here they were all using it, natural as breathing, as if this was the very spot it came out of, the very spot. Cockney. Cockneys. Cock. Knees. Why do men from London get stiff in the legs?

He said, 'Smithfield Market, love. All meat and mouth, all beef and grief. I've got work to do but see up there,' and he pointed, leaning across the cab, leaning across me, putting an arm behind me. 'Kenny's caff. Good cuppa, good bacon sandwich. Stick around, I'll see you there,' and he winked.

The noise changed as I clambered down. It drew back then closed in on me like waves. Slop, slap, slurp, look what

Mick brought in. Like wading out at Morecambe, trying to keep your fanny dry till the last moment. I walked towards the caff, pushing my way through meat and men and noise, and if I'm honest, what I was thinking then, in the middle of my great adventure, was: I'll wait for him, my driver Mick. I'll cadge a breakfast off him, I'll go along with whatever nudgings, noddings and pretendings he wants to fit me into. Then I'll say, quietly, with a flash or two of the eyelashes, 'Can you take me back? Can you take me as far north as you're going?'

I never thought that an hour from then I'd be carried off to my future, to the rest of my life, in a butcher's van. By a big, round-armed, round-edged, big-voiced man who was like some uncle I never knew I had, who was like some man on the spot who'd been waiting specially for me to arrive. 'You come to the right place, sweetheart. 'Eart of London, Smithfield, life and death, Smithfield. See that over there? That's the Old Bailey. I'll take you by the scenic route, since you aint never seen none of it before. 'Op in.'

St Paul's, London Bridge, the Tower, like things that weren't ever real. The grey, wet light it all seemed made for. He slowed down, crossing the bridge. He said, 'You live in it all your life, then one day you notice it.' Then he said, 'Want a job in a butcher's shop? Quid a day, plus board and lodging.'

I said, 'My name's not Judy.'

He looked at me long and hard. 'And mine aint mud.'

And my breakfast date never showed up anyhow, or if he did, I never saw him, he never tried to come between Jack Dodds and me.

The smell, that had you trapped, of frying bacon. Steam and smoke and gab and cackle. Heads turning, smirking.

All pork and talk. I thought, This is worse than outside. All
with that look on their faces like you were a sight for sore
eyes but at the same time you'd invaded their precious territory. All chomping and guzzling and big and blood-smeared
and butchery. Except one. Except for this odd little feller in
a grey raincoat, a collar and tie showing underneath, who
looked as out of his way as I did, who sat stirring and
stirring his tea and peered up at me as if his thoughts were
far away but I might have just stepped out of them. I
thought, Buy me a breakfast, little man, buy me a breakfast.
You look as though I could handle you. You look sad and
safe enough to buy me breakfast, as if you don't use food
yourself.

So I sat down opposite him, at the table he seemed to
be saving for someone else, and he was just about to say
something, still stirring his tea like it would set solid if he
didn't, when in came these other three he seemed to know.
And one of them was bigger than the others, even bigger,
and put himself to the front like a sergeant, and I thought,
I don't know why but you know these things when you see
them, I could be taken in hand by this man. He looked at
me, then at the little man, then he looked at me again, like
I can remember men of a certain age looking at me once,
but not any more, Mandy Dodds, like they wished they were
ten years younger but they're facing the fact that they're old
enough to be your father. Then he looked again, smiling,
slyly, at the little man, who said, clearing his throat, flus-
tered, 'This is—' So I said, 'I'm Judy. From Blackburn.'

I saw the little pause in the big one's face. Then he spoke,
in that too loud, too bold voice, that didn't know, that had
never learned and never would and wouldn't care if it did,
that it was too loud and too bold, that wouldn't ever be

afraid of being heard: 'This is Ted. This is Joe. I'm Jack Dodds. And you've met Ray. You're all right with Ray. Ray's in insurance, Ray's lucky, small but lucky. He needs a good feeding up an' all.'

VINCE

I'll duff Hussein over too, same as Lenny, if he don't come good. I'll get him by his brown bollocks. One for the Merc and one for going cold on Kath.

The price of the motor and a thousand over, then we're all clean.

I've got to pay for this suit, this poxed-up suit.

Otherwise it's fist-in-the-face time, I hope he understands that. And I won't just go soft and easy on him, I won't just go through the motions, like with old left-hook Lenny here, old jam-face Tate. We aren't talking fruit and vegetables.

I don't even have to do it myself. There's people.

And anyhow I think he knows I hate his guts. That's half the pleasure of it for him. It aint just cars and pussy. It's that he knows I've got to smile and lay it on thick and act like I'm his humble servant when what I'm thinking is, You towel-head toe-rag, we used to shoot your lot when we was in Aden. And your lot used to take off squaddies' heads.

The sergeant said, 'We do engines, we don't do bodywork.'

It's that he knows he's got me where he wants me. It's that he knows somehow just by looking – because I aint ever told him, but I suppose Kath has, I suppose she would have gone and done – that there I was once, showing the flag, oiling the rag, in that stinking, flyblown heat-trap he'd be at home in, and now here he is at the bottom end of Bermondsey Street, slipping across from his City glasshouse, getting me to find him fancy cars, getting me to say,

'Right you are, Mr Hussein, yes sir, Mr Hussein,' at a wave of his wallet.

Oil for oil, that's what I call it, oil for bleeding oil. And all it is is his kind of fun.

There goes Vince Dodds who sold his daughter to an Ayrab.

He comes in, that first time, with his coat draped over his shoulders and his shades tucked in his top pocket and I can see he don't have to slum it. They're feeling the squeeze in the City, so I'm going up-market while they're going down, but that aint this one's caper. He don't have to deal with Dodds Autos, he could buy motors in Berkeley Square. Except he's got what they've all got, if you ask me. Haggle fever, call of the old bazaar.

All I've got to interest him is an '85 Granada Scorpio and he sniffs round it for a bit, more than he needs if he aint going to cut cake, but I see him looking at Kath, I see him clocking her as much as he clocks the car. She's sitting there in the office, behind the partition, with the door wide open, and it aint my fault she's wearing a skirt like an armband and a tight white T-shirt, and where he comes from they dress 'em up like nuns. It aint my fault she's grown up from being my little girl Kath, that she's eighteen and out of school and can't get no job. I said, You can work in the showroom, if you like, if it'll get you off your arse.

So I let him hover another thirty seconds till I can tell what makes him tick, good and proper. Women, motors and haggling. That's fair, them's fair hobbies. Then I go over, slow, unpushy, and say, 'Can I help you, sir?' And he looks at me, and one eye's saying he don't want to bother with the likes of me, he aint interested in a three-year-old Ford, and the other's still trying to peek round my shoulder at Kath.

He says, 'I was looking at the Granada.'

I say, 'Sweet car, sweet engine, all tuned and tickled. You won't get better value. Want to run it round the block?'

I can see him backing off, so I say, watching his eyes, 'Keys are in the office. Shall I get 'em?' Then I say, looking at my watch, 'I'd come with you myself, but I've got another client coming, three o'clock appointment. But I'll see if Kathy here can't do the honours. You in a hurry?'

And he says, looking at his own watch, it's a bleeding Rolex, 'Maybe not.'

So I poke my head round the office door and I say, 'Kath, will you go with this gentleman while he takes the Granada for a spin? I'm tied up myself. Mr—?' I turn round and he's right at my shoulder. He says, 'Mr Hussein.' I say, 'Mr Hussein.' Then I pick the keys off the rack and toss 'em to her and they land in her lap.

I'd never asked her to do that before and she looks at me, uncertain. But one thing you can say about Kath is that she aint no dummy when it comes to cars. I taught that girl how to use a motor soon as she could get a licence. Took to it like a natural, like her dad's daughter.

So she even backs it out for him, neat and nifty.

It aint my fault she was built like she was, it aint my fault she was her mother's daughter an' all.

I said, 'This is Kath, my daughter Kath. You're in good hands with Kath.'

Other client coming, my arse.

So I say when they get back, 'Well? Goes a treat, don't it? Vince Dodds don't deal in duds.' And he looks at me as though to say, Throw in the girl and I'll buy, and I look at him as though to say, Throw in an extra half-grand and she's yours. He says, 'Okay.'

Then he says, getting all chummy, 'My little weakness,

Mr Dodds, my little indulgence. I buy a car, then I grow tired of it, then I get another one, like toys.' The coat's a camel-hair. 'You should look out for anything I might like. I could make it worth your while.'

And I knew he never meant to buy the Granada. I knew he'd be back before long to buy another and there'd be extras in it if I so much as hinted that I was missing Kath around the place, that a girl of her age ought to be earning a decent living.

There goes Vince Dodds who pimps for his own daughter.

But it aint as if she didn't know what she was doing, it aint as if she can't take care of herself. Her mother's daughter. And she aint on no regular rummage. Not like Sally.

But now if he wants to ditch her, if he thinks he can chuck her out on the street, another motor, another muff, then he's got another think coming. I'll pop over to that posh pad of his and bust in the door. Then I'll bust in his head. And it don't matter, I don't care, if he don't buy the Merc and he never forks out that extra grand. Because maybe a grand aint nothing, it aint nothing at all, now Jack aint nothing neither. But Kath's my own living daughter, she is. She's a Dodds. And she turns up at Jack's funeral wearing the best little black outfit you ever saw, which must have cost half a grand for a start, half a grand if it was a penny. And maybe I aint done right by her, maybe I aint.

RAY

She would go and see June twice a week. Mondays and Thursdays, regular as clockwork, like she still does. And this was when I swung it so I only worked three days at the office, Mondays to Wednesdays, two days less for only a quarter less pay, taking into account my increment. Hennessy said, 'You're up for promotion, take it from me,' putting a finger to his lips. 'All you have to do is be a good boy till your annual review.' He was taking pity on me, I think, on account of Carol, and had put in a word, reminded them I was still working at the place. He said, 'About time too, Ray, if you ask me. How old are you these days?' I said, 'Forty-five.' But I wasn't interested in promotion, I wasn't interested in getting on in insurance. I was interested in the opposite. I said, 'They could do me a better turn than that. Less time for less pay, that's what I'm interested in, I don't want no leg-up.'

It stood to reason, with only me to consider. And a camper-van.

Besides, I was getting lucky, I was getting canny, I was starting to live up to my name. The gee-gees were doing me favours, if no one else was.

And why shouldn't a man who's all on his own, with no one to fend for but himself, arrange his life to suit his own hankering? Mondays to Wednesdays at the office, Thursdays to Saturdays at the races or on the open road.

It's just the gypsy in my . . .

And any shortfall in my pay-cheque the horses made up,

more or less, sometimes with extra on top. It's the same business, after all, the chance business. Insurance, gambling.

Hennessy said, 'And by the way, what do you fancy for Goodwood?'

So Amy would go and see June on Thursdays and I would be chasing off all over the country, following the nags. And for a long time I thought about it before I said it, for a long time I chewed it over, then one day I plucked up and I said it. I said, 'Amy, I aint going nowhere this Thursday. I suppose the horses can run without me. That's a long old bus ride you have to do. Let me drive you over to see June. Let me take you in the camper.' So she said, 'All right, Ray,' and I took her.

And it was either the second or the third time I took her, either the second or the third Thursday, that I said, 'I met you same time as I met Jack, did you know that?' She looked at me, puzzled, and she said, 'What, in the desert?' I said, 'Yep, in the desert. Egypt.' She sort of frowned and laughed at me at the same time. So I said, 'I saw your photo,' and when I said it my voice wasn't like I meant it to be, like I was just playing a game, answering a riddle, it came out different, it came out sort of like the truth. I aint ever been a dab hand with women.

She looked at me, long and hard, soft and sharp at the same time, and that was when I knew that she knew, or that she'd wondered all along. That I'd just had this thing about her, always. In spite of Carol, in spite of Sue, in spite of her being Jack's anyway, in spite of her having lost her looks by now. But there's a beauty in that itself, I reckon, that's a lovable thing, fading beauty, it depends on your attitude. And they aint all been lost. In spite of her and Jack getting stuck in their ways as if they'd been put in a mould long ago and come out and gone solid. But I suppose we all do that. We all need something to stir us up.

I'd had this thing about her always.

And I'd say it worked in my favour that Sue and then Carol did a flit, one after the other, because I reckon she took pity on me. Not Hennessy's kind of pity. Maybe she'd always taken pity on me, and if all it ever was was pity, I suppose I wasn't going to complain.

It was a long way over to that place. She'd get a 188 to the Elephant, then a 44, and sometimes she'd have to change again in Tooting. It wasn't so far from Epsom. So even by the route I took, the route I already knew, there was plenty of time to talk. But we used to hang around afterwards anyway and just sit in the camper or on one of the benches in the grounds if the weather let us. She said Jack had never seen June, or only the once, only that first time. He'd never gone to see her in the Home. I'd never known that for certain, though I had my guesses. I thought maybe there'd been a time once or he had his own arrangement still, his own private arrangement, he just didn't like to talk about it. But he never went. That was Jack's failing plain and simple, she said, that he didn't want to know his own daughter. And her failing, she could see it, she could tell me, was just the opposite, that she'd kept on coming, two times a week all these years, and it made no difference, but she couldn't stop now, a mother was a mother. And if he'd only come himself just now and then, just once in a while, it might have balanced things out, she might have spared some of her visits for some of his, and they wouldn't have become the people they'd become, pulling opposite ways on the same rope. But it was too late now.

She said she chose between him and her. It was a simple fact. She couldn't help it. She knew it and he knew it.

I said that was a hard choice, or I tried to say it, because choosing my words wasn't so easy either: to pick the one who didn't know who she was and maybe never would, not the one who was sound and whole and she'd been married to anyway for nearly thirty years. And she looked at me, slow and careful, as if it wasn't my turn to speak, and I thought I'd torn it.

She said, 'You think Jack knows who he is?'

I said, 'Never met anyone more sure about it.'

Then she smiled, she laughed under her breath. 'He's not such a big man, you know, when it comes to certain things. He aint such a big man at all.'

I said, 'He got me through, in the desert.' But I didn't say, like I half wanted, like I was half going to, 'And so did you.'

When she went in to visit I used to stay put in the car park, or I'd mooch around the grounds. There were lawns and paths and some of the inmates would be shuffling about. They didn't look so different. Like you could get mistook.

When I watched her walking across the car park and in through the entrance I used to think, She looks about as on her own as I am, and I'd start to ache. But it never occurred to me, not at first, that maybe it would clinch it if I went in to see June too, if I did what Jack hadn't ever. And maybe that's what she was wishing me to do all along. I thought I was holding back because it was only right, because it wasn't my place, I was only there to drive her. Or else I was just plain scared. But on the third or fourth Thursday I said to her, 'Can I come too?' And she said, 'Course you can, Ray.'

I don't know what you say about some things, some sights. I don't know what you say about a woman still in her twenties with a body that was just like any other woman's, soft and curved, and if it was dressed up better and you could blot out the rest, you might even say it was lovely, but with a swollen, slobbery head that only a mother could ever love. I don't know what you say about a woman who's twenty-seven years old and whose name is June but she don't know it because she hasn't even got the brains of a child of two. I suppose you should say that life's not ever so unfair that there's not a worse unfairness than yours, and that you can't ever get so stuck in your ways that there aren't worse ways of being stuck, like from the word go and for always.

But one thing I learnt sitting there that Thursday afternoon, not saying nothing, just sitting there, just like June herself, with that nurse eyeing us, wondering where I'd sprung from, was that Amy hadn't been going there twice a week for twenty-two years because it was some duty she just had to go through, a habit she'd just settled into, like she said. She'd kept going there because she'd kept hoping that one day June might recognize her, one day June might speak. You could tell that just by looking, by looking at Amy. And you could tell just by looking at June that it wasn't ever going to happen and that it was all wrong. It was as wrong that Amy had been coming here all them years as it was wrong that June had been born like she was in the first place, as wrong as there should be a mother of forty-six who still had her faded looks while her daughter aint never had any. But two wrongs don't make a right.

So I thought, I've made the first move, there's another move I should make now.

We sat on the bench, watching the pigeons. We didn't have to go straight back. It took half the time in the camper it would take her on the bus. I didn't know what to say about June, I didn't know what you should say, but I felt like saying some crazy things that didn't have nothing to do with June. I reckon Amy was all sort of fragile on account of having seen June for the first time with a stranger. Friend. I reckon one way or the other she needed a hug. I felt she was leaning on the little slice of air I left between us, like she should've been leaning direct against me, and I felt my pecker starting to grow like it hadn't ever much since Carol left. I wonder if women can tell.

But what I said was, 'Have you heard from Vincey at all? I hear they're going to ship 'em all back home.'

But next time when I picked her up I had the words all ready and the opportunity all crying out to be taken. It was a bright, breezy day in April. It was like this day, with Jack's ashes. I felt, Life can change, it can, even when you think it can't any more. All the same it took me all the way to Clapham before I said it. The sun was flickering through the trees on Clapham Common. I said, 'We aint going to the Home today, Amy, we aint going to see June.' Somehow I knew she wouldn't argue. I said, 'I've got a picnic all ready in the back there. Sandwiches, thermos.' It was the spring meeting at Epsom. I said, 'You fancy a day at the races?'

But we didn't see so much of the races. It must've been the first time I'd been to a racecourse without taking a proper punt. I parked up on the Downs and we wandered down to the track in time for the two o'clock. We did a bet with each other, like a couple of amateurs. Her horse against mine, a quid says, and I made sure she won. Conquistador, seven to two. I could have put fifty on it and come home flush. But the weather was changing and before the next race it came on to rain, like you might have said it was timed special. Sometimes luck just runs. So I said, 'Picnic time,' and we hurried back to the camper. I suppose two people know when something's going to happen, even when they're not so sure it ought to and they don't know how they're going to bring it about and they're as afraid of it as wanting it. But they know if it's ever going to happen, now's the time. There were curtains you draw across the windows in that camper, blue and white check, so no one would know. Except by the rocking of the suspension. But I don't suppose there was much of that. I said, pulling the curtains, 'Just like home, eh? Home from home.' The rain was drumming on the roof. I thought, It can't be helped, even if it aint right. I thought, Amy chose June, she didn't choose Jack, now I've chosen Amy. They weren't so faded. When the rain stopped we heard the crowd cheering for the three ten, the big race, the strange noise of people getting het-up over a bunch of horses. And afterwards that became our regular spot, Epsom Downs, every Thursday, for fourteen weeks, racing or no racing. Till Vince showed up, then Mandy.

LENNY

Well, I should've known better than to pick a fight I hadn't got a hope of winning. But that's one thing I aint ever known, better. They say it was the boxing bashed out my brains all them years back, but if you ask me there never was much brains there in the first place. I should've known better when I came out the Army than to get back into the fight game. You'd think that five years of shooting and being shot at and picking up the pieces of your dead mates would teach you a better way to make a living than trying to knock another man off his feet, but it was that or pushing a fruit-and-veg cart and that aint got no glory to it, nor quick readies neither.

I reckon I showed that pillock a thing or two, all the same. My chest feels like a bag of nails.

It's the way you're made. It's hard fighting against your own nature when it's in your nature to fight. We aint here to do the honours and pay respects to Jack because he worked so hard on his own nature he turned into some-thing else. We're here because he was Jack.

It's like when I got back from fighting for my country and there were more bomb-holes in Bermondsey than there was at Benghazi and they couldn't find nothing better for us than a pre-fab and a ration book, I'd say to Joan, It's better I get up there in that ring and knock some feller who's chosen to do the same smack against the canvas, than I let fly at all and sundry. That's for nothing, mush, now start something. I said it's the world that makes you want to kick and punch. And she said, 'Hooey. There's another way of going about things. You can hold your head up and put your mind to it and make the best of what's available, like most people.' She's that kind of woman. I said, 'Not on hand-outs and half a crown a day, you can't.' I said, 'Suppose I won the Worthington Tournament, that's fifty smackers. I'll put my mind to that.' I said, 'You used to like it when I won a bout, girl.' And she said, 'You're seven years older and you're going to lose.'

And I suppose it wasn't till Sally came along that I stopped proper, that I hung up my gloves and my hopes and started putting a button on my loose lip an' all. So you could say it wasn't Lenny Tate getting a hold on his own nature, it was someone else coming along and doing the trick for him, same stuff, same flesh, but different. Little Sally Tate.

It made me see too, when I got to know him and heard the story – and I never would've done if it wasn't for Sally and Vince taking a shine to each other in the playground – how hard it was for Jack, not having a little helper, only having June. How it was a darn sight harder for Amy. And how you couldn't blame Vince for being the mixed-up tyke he was. So I suppose you couldn't blame me neither for being a soft-brained berk and wanting Sally to be part of their family too.

And I think I could've forgiven Vincey in the end, if it wasn't for Sally hitching up with Tommy Tyson, and Tommy going along to Vincey's with a good-as-new BMW, only one previous owner, which he knew Vincey could see was stolen but he reckoned Vincey'd play along, being an old pal, so to speak, of Sally's. But Vincey don't take the car off him and what's more he puts the word out, and Tommy, what with his previous record and other offences taken into, does a spell inside, first of several. And I say to Vincey, 'You prick. You didn't have to take the car but you didn't have to finger Tommy. Tommy might be right where he belongs now, but you might have thought of Sally.'

He said he was doing his duty, wasn't he? His duty as a citizen. And I was the one who should've thought of Sally, seeing as it was looking like I'd disowned her.

He says, 'A hot car's a hot car. Two wrongs don't make a right.'

I might have forgiven Vincey. Sally might have forgiven me. I might never have gone spoiling for another fight again.

I reckon I showed that toe-rag, all the same, I did.

Gunner Tate. That's what they called me, because of having been in the artillery and because of the temper I used to have on me. It sounded good, like my fists were my guns. And in the semi-final of the Worthington they put me up against this scraggy kid who aint even had his call-up yet, same age as I was when I started fighting before the war. I said, 'No contest, no contest. What's the half-pint got that I aint got double?' And Dougie says, tying my gloves, 'Control on himself, and a big right.' I was thinking of the final before I even stepped in the ring for the semi. I thought, That's twenty quid for certain, that'll keep Joan quiet, and if it's me and Dan Ferguson in the big one, then it aint impossible. The bell went and I came out quick and eager and I thought, This one's going to be a cinch, two rounds, if that. Gunner Tate. Later on it became just a name that stuck: Gunner Tate, middleweight. Always pissed, always late. I came forward and he hung back, skipping round me, and I thought, You aint been nowhere, sunshine, and you aint going nowhere. You aint dragged five-fives through Libya, Sicily, all over sunnygunny Italy. You don't deserve nothing but I do. A man's got to grab a bit of glitter, a bit of pride, before he clocks off at the end of his stint. It aint worth nothing if you go down in the record books as having done distinguished service in the cause of fruit and veg. I came forward again for the quick kill and I saw his face, cool and sharp and steady as a machine. I thought, Six years between us, sonny boy, that cuts both ways. Then I saw his glove where his face had been. And then I didn't see nothing, nothing at all. Or rather I did. Because you know what they say about seeing stars. Well I saw 'em.

WICK'S FARM

We troop back across the field, not saying nothing. You can hear Lenny and Vincey breathing like a little duet. Vince is carrying the jar. He's holding it extra tight and careful. It's like the reason we're out here in this field is because the jar's gone and made a bolt for it and we've had to run after it and catch it. It's all the jar's fault. Except we know it aint, it's the other way round. It's all our fault. Fighting over a man's ashes. And the jar's sitting there in Vince's hands like it's shaking its head at us all, like Jack's inside there peeping out and sighing over us, with a bit of him left behind in the field for the sheep to trample on. He didn't expect this, he didn't expect this at all.

The wind's whipping up on our backs and as we reach the gate the shower hits us good and proper. We just get back inside the car in time to avoid a soaking. We get in the same seats as before. Vincey hands me the jar, wincing as he moves in behind the wheel, and then he looks around for something to wipe away the stains on his sleeve and trousers but he can't find nothing and he gives up and we all sit there for a moment, the engine not switched on and the rain beating against the windows like we might as well be in a boat. I look at Vincey's face and it looks far away and I can hear Lenny wheezing in the back seat. It's as though it's not a car, it's an ambulance. Meat wagon after all. It's as though we're all wondering whether we should press on with this exercise or quit now on the grounds of not being up to it. Two detours, one fight, a piss-up and a near-wetting.

Then Vincey sort of snaps to, and switches on the ignition and the wipers. We can see the rain sloshing down on the narrow road and the sky all grey and heavy, but up on the crest of the hill, by the disused windmill, there's a faint gleam on one side of the clump of trees, as though the clouds are going to pass over before long.

Vincey says, 'Right. We want the Canterbury road. Look out for signs to Canterbury. A28 and Canterbury.' He starts the engine.

Lenny says, 'Canterbury?' He stops wheezing. 'We might as well call in there an' all. We might as well pop into the bleeding cathedral.'

He says it like he's joking, but Vince sits there for a bit staring at the rain on the windscreen, not making the car move. He says, 'If you say so, Lenny,' all fierce. 'If you say so. Why shouldn't we take him round Canterbury Cathedral?'

I can feel Vic and Lenny looking at each other in the back seat.

Another fool's errand, another detour. Lenny's turn.

Vince puts the car in drive and we move off. He doesn't speak but I can tell from his face he's serious, he means it, he might even be wishing he'd had the idea himself.

It's even better than a royal blue Merc.

Vic don't say nothing, like he's already paid his forfeit.

So it's me who says, but like it's Vic who's speaking, while I hang on to the wet jar, 'Good idea, Lenny. Good gesture. He'd be honoured.'

RAY

He looks at me straight and steady, so straight and steady that my own face must be all a-quiver in comparison. I think, You have to sit straight and still for your final portrait, no shifting, no pretending, no ducking out. Then he says, like he can see what's in my head, like he sees the question I want to ask, 'People panic, Raysy. You don't ever want to panic.'

It's like what they said in the war. Number one rule for soldiers: Don't panic. Though I never understood how you could lay that down as a command, you can't command a man not to believe that fire'll burn him. Except Jack used to put it into working practice. Like when we ran into that trouble outside Sollum and that lieutenant, Crawford, is lying there suddenly like a bloody rag, with his next-in-line yelling, 'What do I do? What do I do?' and Jack says, 'What you have to do, sir, is assume command. If you don't, I will.' And I'm thinking, I'm bleeding glad I don't have to assume command, I'll settle for being commanded.

I suppose that's what he's doing now, assuming command, taking charge of himself.

I say, 'It's a tough one, Jack, it's a tough one.' Like I'm not talking about the thing it is, like it's just an extra tricky test you come out of afterwards.

He says, 'It'll be tougher for Amy.' Looking at me straight and steady. 'If you ever get the choice, Raysy, if you ever get the option, you go first. It's carrying on that's hard. Ending aint nothing.'

I say, 'Well, it aint an option I've got, is it? I mean, if anyone has. Seeing as there's just me.'

He looks at me. 'You never know. Still I reckon I'm lucky, being the first.'

'No, I'm Lucky.'

He doesn't smile, it's not like the old joke. I'm not lucky, you're Lucky. He looks at me. His eyes are like they don't miss nothing, his face is like you can't not look at it. I think, I've seen him most of my life, but now I'm seeing *him*. I'm not seeing Jack Dodds, quality butcher, Smithfield and Bermondsey, or Jack Dodds care of the Coach and Horses. I'm not even seeing Big Jack, Desert Rat, Private Jack of the Cairo Camel Corps. I'm seeing the man himself, his own man, private Jack, who's assumed command.

He says, 'It'll be harder for Amy. She'll need looking after.'

I say, 'She'll be here any minute. With Vincey.'

'I aint got much for her to be getting on with.'

I look at what he has got. A bed, a bedside cabinet. I reckon he hasn't got much more now than June's had all her life.

I say, 'If there's anything I can do, Jack.'

His hand's lying spare, empty, on the blanket and I see the fingers curl just a bit. Then his eyes close. The lids just roll down of their own accord like a shutter, like the eyes on that doll I bought Sue years ago one Christmas. Just for a moment it's like— Don't panic, don't panic. But his chest heaves. The swelling round his operation scar dips and rises.

I look at his face, at his hand lying on the blanket. I think, Everyone has their own space and no one else can step in it, then one day it's unoccupied. It's a question of territory.

He opens his eyes. It's as if he's been tricking me and he's been watching all along, through the slits, to see if I'm a different person when I think I'm not being looked at. But the lids open slowly. You see the whites before you see the whole eye.

He says, 'Still here, Lucky? Yes, there is something you can do for me. How lucky do you feel?'

VINCE

He's still lying there, with the mask over his face and the extra tubes, in the little unit where they put them after they wheel them out, the High Dependency Unit, and he don't know nothing yet because he aint woken up proper, he don't know sweet nothing. He don't know he's inoperable. And that geezer Strickland tells me it only took ten minutes, a quick opening up and sewing back together again, and he uses some word for it, a long fancy word, like something-sodomy. It's like he's pleased with what a quick piece of work it was. He don't spell it out for me plain and simple, he leaves me to work it out. Like it wasn't the two-hour job he said it could be if there was anything they could do. Inoperable, that's the word he uses, inoperable.

And I look across the corridor through the glass partition, where Jack's lying, number one on the right, and I think, He's inoperable, he can't be operated. He's still there but he's stopped running, he's pulled up at the side of the road. But that's how everything feels suddenly. Like we're all in some place where things have come to a standstill, and the rest of the world is whizzing on past, like traffic on a motorway.

He says, 'Is Mrs Dodds here?' And I say, 'Yes, she's gone back to get a cup of tea. She's with my wife.' Then he looks quick at his watch and he says, 'If you could fetch her, I could speak to her now, while I'm here. We could find somewhere private. Maybe the sister's office.' And I'm thinking, You turd. Because he aint thinking of the effect on me, or maybe he's thinking it aint important to me, I don't count, I'll just do as his messenger-boy, and I want to hit him, I want to smash his poxy four-eyed face. But I say, 'I'll go and get her.' He's already turning, as I say it, to a pile of notes some little junior doc's shoved under his nose. He says, 'I'll be here.' He prods his glasses with his finger and gives me a tight little half-measure of a smile.

So I go and find Amy and Mandy. But it's like I aint going nowhere, it's the corridors and swing-doors that move past me, like one of those old machines in arcades, with a steering-wheel and a picture of a road spinning round, so you got the feeling you were travelling though you weren't.

They're sitting there with their cups of tea, and they don't know nothing yet, only that Jack's alive, he aint sparked out on the table, possibility number three. But I can tell that she knows, straight away, just by looking at me, that she can see in my face what I don't even need to tell her. I say, 'He aint come round yet. Strickland's in the ward. He said he'd like to speak to you.' Then I shake my head just a fraction, like it's hard to budge it, and she looks at me like she don't want anyone to say it. As if it's all her fault and she knows it and she's sorry, and she don't see why she has to go before the headmaster and get punished extra for it, when it's punishment already, just knowing. But maybe the head-master's going to give her a second chance. Don't ever let this happen again. So she gets up, and as she gets up Mandy squeezes her arm. Then Mandy gets up too, giving me a little nod like a question. She looks good, Mandy looks good. And I nod back.

Then we go back along the corridors, which slide past and under us while we just pretend we're walking, and Amy don't say a word till we get near the ward, when she says, 'Uncle Ray ought to know.' I say, 'What?' She aint called

186

him that for years: Uncle Ray. Like Uncle Lenny. Like I'm a nipper again.

Strickland sees us coming and he says something quick to one of the nurses, then he ushers us into an office, it aint the sister's office, it's more like a store cupboard, and shuts the door behind us. There's only two chairs and he pulls one round for Amy to sit on and Mandy takes the other one, by the door. I stand close beside Amy, and Strickland stands in front of the desk with his arse half parked on it, and as he starts talking I put my arm behind Amy's head and clasp her shoulder and I feel her hand come across and grab my other hand.

He says he don't believe in not giving the facts straight, it don't serve any purpose otherwise. When he starts to talk he's looking at Amy but he switches his eyes pretty smart to me, as though in order to talk to Amy he has to talk to me, or he's seen something in Amy's face he don't want to look at. I can't see Amy's face. I have to look straight ahead, like when you're up on a charge, before they march you into the cooler. I have to look this bugger straight in the eye.

And when he's done, it's like Amy's pretending she hasn't heard him, she's pretending she aint even in the room. So it's up to me to keep things going, to ask the questions, though there's only one question, How long? Strickland looks pleased when I do, like we've shifted into a different area which aint his department, he's a repair-man, he aint a scrap dealer, and he'll be quit of all this just as soon as he walks out of this room. He starts talking about 'symptom control', which sounds to me about the same as 'inoperable', and it's while he's talking about this that I feel Amy's hands start to clutch and grab at me and I hear her start to catch her breath. Strickland carries on about symptom control, looking straight at me, but Amy keeps clutching and

187

grabbing, like her symptoms need controlling an' all. It's like her hands are climbing, scrambling up me and I'm a ladder, an escape route, up to some hatchway out of this room. But it seems to me Amy aint ever going to get out of this room, she's going to be locked up in it for ever, her own cooler. She's like June now. And I go rigid and fixed, like a mast, like a tower, while she clings and grabs at me. Thinking, She aint my mum, she aint my mum.

Then suddenly we're out of that room, as if we didn't do nothing, again, to make it happen, the world just shifted, twisted for us, and Strickland's disappeared, he's disappeared down his own escape route. Mandy's taken charge of Amy now, she's holding her and steering her towards the exit and looking at me sort of sharp, like this is a thing between women. But Amy aint Mandy's mum either.

Like my job's the thing between men. So I go back into the unit, before I follow them out, and just stand there by his bed, looking at him. He still aint so much as flicked an eyelid, he's just lying there under the mask, and Strickland said he'd speak to him, he'd speak to him himself, but he'd leave it a good twenty-four hours, even when he's come round, because what with the anaesthetic and everything, he won't take in proper what you say to him. But it seems to me that it aint Strickland's job to tell him, it aint really his job.

I stand by the bed, like I'm a tower, a mast still, but Jack aint trying to climb up me, he's just lying flat beneath me, and I think, It might be better if he died now, without waking up, so he'd never know and no one need ever tell him. Just him never knowing and the world travelling on and on without him. What you never know don't hurt. It's like I don't remember that bomb falling, I can't ever remember that bomb falling. They said so long as you could hear them, you were all right, it was when the sound cut. But I don't even remember not hearing it. So if that bomb had killed me too, I'd never've known I'd been born, I'd never've known I'd died. So I might've been anyone. I look at him like I'm looking down at a view. *Golden days before they end.* And I think, Someone's got to tell him, someone's got to.

RAY

I peered over the rim of my glass at Slattery's clock.

He said, 'It aint much good to you now though, is it?'

I said, 'How come?'

He said, 'I mean, now there's just you. Now it don't look like she's coming back.'

I said, 'Other way round, aint it? I can go as I please now, I'm my own man now. Free as a bird. If I want to take off for a couple of days, then off I go, and I don't have to worry about nowhere to kip.'

I took a swill of beer and smacked my lips like a man who knows what he's about.

He said, 'That aint no life for a man. All by yourself. Dossing down in car parks, at the side of the road.'

I said, 'Maybe it's the only life, maybe it's the only life for me right now.' Then I didn't say nothing for a bit. Then I said, 'Why you asking anyway, Jack?'

He said, 'I was just thinking. If you didn't need it, if you didn't want it, I could take it off you.'

I said, 'You? What the hell would you want with a camper?'

He said, 'Well, when Carol went and hopped it – excuse me, Raysy – it set me thinking. About me and Amy. Only natural.'

I looked at him and fished out a snout.

'I mean, not that Amy— Only that we got ourselves sort of in a rut. Only that we don't get about much, do we? And I reckoned what with Sundays and some help at the shop and some time off.'

He pushed his glass around on the bar.

'I mean, now Vincey's buggered off, good and proper. Overseas. And Sue— It's like the whole world's buggering off. 'Cept Amy and me.'

I looked at him, sharp, lighting up my ciggy. I said, 'You know that's what I thought an' all, don't you? I thought, Me and Carol are just getting all cooped up, we aint seeing much of the world, are we? I'll get us a means of travel. That's what I thought. Look what happened.'

'She buggered off.' He glugged some beer. 'But Amy aint—'

We stopped talking for a bit. There was just the sound of the Coach on a Friday night. Rattling on, going nowhere.

I said, 'Amy in the know about this?'

He said, 'No, I want it to be a surprise.'

I said, 'A surprise? That's what I thought with Carol too.'

He said, 'You must've paid a bit for it an' all. I'll give you a thousand. Straight cash, no messing. You don't need no camper, Raysy, all you need is some little pop-pop motor.'

I looked at him. Good price.

He said, 'Unless you think – she's going to come back.'

I took my eyes off him. I said, 'I'll think about it.'

And I did think about it, all that winter of being on my tod. I even said to him, 'You still in the market?' like I was ready to sell, and he says, 'Still a grand. Amy'll be chuffed.' But I was thinking about something else too, another use for that camper. And after we skipped seeing June, that first time, and drove over to Epsom, I said to him, 'I've made up my mind, Jack. It aint for sale.'

CANTERBURY

The road twists along between the hills, with orchards climbing up the slopes on one side, all bare and brown and trimmed and lined up like the bristles on a brush. The sign says, Canterbury, 3 miles. There's a little river on the other side, then a railway line, and the road and the river and the railway line wiggle along the valley as if they're competing. Then we come out by some houses and some playing fields, and Vince says suddenly, 'There's the cathedral.' But I don't see no cathedral. I see the gas-holder in front of it, and I see the cars zipping along the A2, just ahead, Dover one way, London the other. If we'd approached by a different route, down them hills where the A2 comes, we'd've seen it like you're supposed to, all spread out before you with the cathedral sticking up in the middle. We cross the A2 and a sign says 'City of Canterbury – Twinned with Rheims'. Then as we get closer in I still can't see no cathedral but there are big old stone walls in front of us, city walls, and it starts to look like a town you're meant to arrive at, at your journey's end. Except it's not our journey's end, we're going on to Margate, by the sea. Jack never specified Canterbury Cathedral.

Vince follows the signs to 'City Centre'. We haven't hardly said a word since we last got back in the car, since Lenny came up with his idea, like we've all been thinking it was a stupid idea in the first place and maybe we don't have to go through with it. But now we're here, with the cathedral just a few streets away hiding somewhere, like it's seen us if we aint seen it, it's too late to back out.

Besides, Vic suddenly says, all eager and cheery, as if he's remembering how it was him who got us hiking up to that memorial, that he's never seen Canterbury Cathedral, he's never stepped inside it. Vince says, 'Me neither, Vic.' His voice sounds all sweet and mild, like you wouldn't think that half an hour ago he nearly punched Lenny's face in. Lenny says he's never been anywhere near the place. I say, 'Nor me.' Vince says, 'Aint no racetrack in Canterbury, is there?' But no one laughs, and it's like we're all thinking we might have lived all our lives and never seen Canterbury Cathedral, it's something Jack's put right.

We get a glimpse of it suddenly, the cathedral tower, popping up over the tops of buildings, and Vince aims as best he can for it, as if he thinks we can drive right up to the front door, in a car like this. But it ducks out of sight, like it's playing tricks with us, and the streets take you this way and that, so Vince says, 'I reckon we could walk it,' and pulls into a car park.

We get out of the car. I'm still holding the jar and I look at Vincey like it's for him to take, it's his by right now, his trophy won in a fight, but he says, 'You hang on to it, Raysy.' So I bend down and find the plastic bag that's still lying by my feet under the dash, and put the jar in it, and I think, I'm the one who's going to carry Jack into Canterbury Cathedral.

We must look a strange bunch. Me and Vic aren't much the worse for wear but Vince is all scuffed and mud-stained. He puts on his coat, which hides most of it except the bottoms of his trousers, where it's worst. Lenny looks like he's been pulled through a hedge. He's hobbling slightly but he's trying not to show it. It's like we aren't the same people who left Bermondsey this morning, four blokes on a special delivery. It's like somewhere along the line we just became travellers.

Vince straightens his tie and gets out his comb.

We follow the signs, 'To the Cathedral'. The streets are narrow and the buildings crooked, like that street in Rochester, as if they've come out of the same picture-book. There's whole bits where cars can't go and people are walking in that same haphazard way. Tourists. The pavements are all wet though it's not raining. But now and then the wind suddenly gusts up and, judging from the sky, it looks as though there's more rain coming, more than just a shower.

We turn another corner and there's an old arch and we go through it and suddenly there's nothing in front of us except the cathedral itself, and a few bits of chained-off lawn and cobbles and people walking. It's a big building, long and tall, but it's like it hasn't stretched up yet to its full height, it's still growing. It makes the cathedral at Rochester look like any old church and it makes you feel sort of cheap and titchy. Like it's looking down at you, saying, I'm Canterbury Cathedral, who the hell are you?

I reckon I wouldn't mind if it was just me, passing through in the camper, taking a look, seeing the sights. But I feel all keyed up, with the others, and holding Jack. There's an entrance through a big arch, where people are milling around and lining up to go through some smaller door inside. We head towards it and it's as if, because I'm carrying Jack, I have to go first and they make way for me, and I look up at the arch and the walls and the carvings and the funny knobs and pinnacles and I feel like I felt at the Home when Amy said yes I could go in with her.

LENNY

Canterbury Cathedral. I ask you. I should've kept my big trap shut.

Still, dose of holiness'll do us good, I suppose, the way things were going.

So glory be. Lift up your hearts for Lenny.

VIC

Well it makes you feel humble. It makes a man in my line of business feel humble to think of what they've got in here. Tombs, effigies, crypts, whole chapels. When all I do in the normal course of work is box 'em up and book 'em in for their twenty minutes at the crem.

He's got himself a guidebook, biggest, flashiest one he could find. *Wonders of Canterbury Cathedral.* Chose it like he chose that tie, I suppose. He stands, flicking through, as if he doesn't want to look at the cathedral, just the guidebook, giving us snippets, as if we can't make a move till we've had the lecture.

He says, 'Fourteen centuries. Fourteen centuries, think of that.' He says, 'They got kings and queens in here, they got saints.'

His coat's hiding most of the damage, but there's a smear of drying mud up his left trouser leg.

'They got cardinals.'

I look at Lenny and half wink and jerk my head just a little, as though I'm saying, 'Come on, let's go. Let Raysy suffer.'

And it's not a bad idea, considering, to get the two of them separated for a bit.

He says, 'They got nineteen archbishops. You know, if we'd thought, we could've taken him to Westminster Abbey an' all.'

Lenny and me shuffle off slyly, along the side-aisle, over the worn stones, as if we could be treading on tiptoe.

It makes you feel humbled. But it makes a man in my

line feel relieved we don't all get to choose or we don't ask for much when we do. Canterbury Cathedral, please. I suppose we're doing our bit for fair dos for the deceased by bringing Jack in here, all thanks to Lenny. Levelling things off, like death's supposed to.

But then he didn't have his sights set so low, as I recall. 'Any lodgers?' he'd say. So I said, as if I was touting for custom, 'You ever thought what you'd want, Jack?' Half a wink. And he looks at me, face wrinkling, and says, 'Ooh, I don't know if you'd be up to it, Vic. I'm thinking big. I reckon nothing short of a pyramid.'

VINCE

Amy said, 'Will you go in and see him?' and I said, 'Yeh, I'll go and see him.' She wasn't crying and her voice was clear and steady. She wasn't insisting or demanding. It was like she was asking a polite, considerate question, like a host to a guest. I even reckon she was holding her head a bit higher and her back a bit straighter, as if this was an important day, a very important day, and she had to see it got managed proper, like something special had happened to her and she wanted to share it.

She'd just come out. She'd just been to see him herself.

I said, 'Yeh, I want to see him.' Like I couldn't have said no, even if I'd wanted to. You don't refuse to see someone's prize possession.

She said, 'You go through the door and ask the man,' and I thought, She don't know it's happened yet.

So I went through the door and asked the man. He had a rumpled white jacket and a pale podgy face to go with it, and he looked at me like I shouldn't expect him to understand what a big deal it was for me, any more than he should expect me to understand how it wasn't for him.

It said 'Chapel of Rest'. He said, 'Mr Dodds?' and I wondered which one he meant. I said, 'That's me,' when maybe I should've said, 'That's him.' He said, 'Through there.'

There was this little room with a glass partition down the length of it and an opening at one end you could step through, otherwise you could just look. On the other side of the glass there was Jack, raised up on something and lying on his back, and I thought, That aint Jack, he aint real. I suppose I was right.

You could only see his head because they'd wrapped him up in something like a pale-pink curtain or a tablecloth, right up to his chin. It was covering what he was lying on an' all. Like Jack was just his head, it wasn't a body, there wasn't no dead body.

I went through the opening and stood beside him. It smelt cold. I thought, He don't know I'm here, he can't ever know I'm here. Unless. I thought, He aint Jack Dodds, no more than I'm Vince Dodds. Because nobody aint nobody. Because nobody aint more than just a body, than just their own body, which aint nobody.

Except you can't see his body under that tablecloth.

Then I just stood there looking at him and I felt myself going straight and tall, like I wasn't just standing there, I was holding myself proud and stiff, like Amy. I was standing to attention. Like the only proper thing to do was to go stiff and straight and still and stony just like Jack was, out of sympathy. Except upright.

And I thought, I should see him naked. Because we all are, aren't we? He's naked underneath, under the tablecloth. I should see his body. I should see his hands and his feet and his knees and his bleeding bollocks an' all. I should see Jack Dodds' body. Because this is Jack, Jack Dodds, but he don't look like Jack, he looks like the bleeding Pope. Because naked we come and naked we. But they've kitted him out so he looks like the Pope.

RAY

I say, 'It's all right, Vince. You go ahead.'

Because I've sat down suddenly in one of the wooden seats in the side-aisle, clutching the bag, like some old geezer on a shopping trip who's run out of puff.

He looks down at me, holding the guidebook, and I can see Lenny and Vic at the far end of the aisle. I reckon they moved off pretty smart, like they knew me and Vincey might have business to discuss.

He says, 'You okay, Lucky?'

I say, 'Yeh, give me a mo.'

He flips shut the guidebook. 'Gabbing on a bit, was I?'

I say, 'No, it wasn't that.'

He looks at me.

There aint no hiding, if it's true what they say, least of all in a church. Because *He*'s supposed to see everything, innermost thoughts. But I reckon if Vince can't tell, if he can't see my innermost, and if it was his thousand in the first place and he gave it to Jack in his dying days, on his death-bed, he's not going to ask for it back, not now. Like asking for the money back you've put in the collection box. He aint going to tell no one.

And Jack aint going to tell no one.

He looks at me. 'You sure?'

'Yeh, give us a mo. You go on.'

He looks at me. Then he looks round quickly at the pillars and the arches and the windows, then back at me as if he's twigged the situation. Except he aint twigged it all. And I'm saying to myself, Miserable sinner. That's what you're supposed to tell yourself, miserable sinner. You're supposed to sink down on your knees. But all I'd been thinking, suddenly, was that it's a far cry, all this around me, from what I'm carrying in my hand, all this glory-hallelujah, from Jack and his drips. What's a plastic jar up against this lot? What's the lick and spit of a human life against fourteen centuries? And it was the same as I thought at that crematorium, though I never told no one, that none of it had to do with him, none of it. The velvet curtains, the flowers, the amens, the music. I stood there, looking at the curtains, trying to make it have to do with him, and Vic says, touching my arm, 'You can go now, Ray.' Because nothing aint got to do with Jack, not even his own ashes. Because Jack's nothing.

So I had to sit down, sink down, like I'd been hit. Like Vincey'd taken a swing at me an' all.

He says, 'Okay, Raysy, fair enough. Take it easy.'

I say, 'Here,' handing him the bag, looking at him, 'I'll catch you up,' and he takes the bag, looking at me. He half moves to slip the guidebook into it but thinks again. Then he walks off, slowly, along the side-aisle, along the row of pillars, in his camel-hair coat, mud on his trousers. Lenny and Vic have reached a spot where some stone steps go up and they stop there for a bit like they're wondering which way to go. Then Vince catches up with them. He taps Lenny on the shoulder and Lenny turns and Vince holds out the plastic bag and Lenny takes it.

RAY'S RULES

1. It's not the wins, it's the value.
2. It's not the betting, it's the knowing when not to.
3. It's not the nags, it's the other punters.
4. Old horses don't do new tricks.
5. Always look at the ears, and keep your own twitched.
6. Never bet shorter than three to one.
7. Never bet more than five per cent of your kitty, except about five times in your life.
8. You can blow all the rules if you're Lucky.

LENNY

He gives me the bag. He don't look at me, he looks at the guidebook. It's like the only reason he's given me the bag is so he can flick through the guidebook. But I can see it aint. He's studying that guidebook like it's got all the answers.

He says, 'They got the Black Prince in here somewhere.'

I say, 'Who's he when he's in?' Maybe they got Snow White an' all.

He says, 'I reckon we should find the Black Prince.'

I say, 'Whatever you say, Big Boy.'

So we shuffle on, down some steps and up some steps, past all these geezers made of stone, lying face up, flat out, out for the count.

I reckon he's sorry, that's what he is. I reckon he's trying to make amends. We've all got a bit of that to do if you look back over the years. Excluding Vic maybe. Clean hands, as always.

Seeing as there's three of us here involved, counting Raysy. And Sally's paid her price, if you can say she ever deserved to in the first place, being the innocent party, or at least the least guilty. Since I don't suppose it happened while she was looking the other way. It was Vincey's doing in the first place, but it was me who said, when she came right out with it and said she wanted to have the baby, 'No you don't, my girl.' My first fully weighed-up response as a father, words just shot from my gob. She said he'd come back and do right by her. I said, 'Don't talk bollocks, girl. What book've you been reading?' And she aint ever forgiven me since.

I reckon that's when it really happened, that's when we really parted company, though it wasn't till later, till she teamed up with that Tyson toe-rag, then started taking on all-comers, that I washed my hands altogether, did a Vic. Daughters, eh Raysy?

It was me who found the doc to do the job. O'Brien. And it was me who found the money to pay him. I need a winner, Raysy, I need some readies double quick. So Raysy was a party.

You just leave it all to me, girl, you just make yourself ready. Well, you should've thought of that. You just make yourself nice and ready.

And the fact is I never even spared a thought at the time for that poor little unborn perisher. Except it went through my head, like some sort of excuse, like some sort of cock-eyed warning, that it might turn out like June, it might turn out to have been better not born. Settling up for your sins. So, either way, you end up short.

And the fact is that when you can remember, just a few years before, loading and firing, loading and firing, whacking it home and knowing that that's a few more of 'em blown to bits, and not thinking twice about it, even being glad, because it's them not you, less of them to do it to you and it's only what's asked of you, any case, what you're trained for, then what's one little unborn sod who aint ever going to see the light of day?

Gunner Tate.

And what they call a sin and a crime and against the law at one time aint at another, is it? Like if it'd been five years later, we could've solved that little problem, no fuss, all above board and legal. Different time, different rules. Like one moment we're fighting over a whole heap of desert, next we're pulling out of Aden snappy.

It's only now that I think what it might've been. It. He. She. A whole life. All these stony geezers. It might've been the next Archbishop of Canterbury. It might've been Kath, Kathy Dodds. Different mother, same result: Vinccy's brat. Same old game now, it seems, for Kathy as for Sally anyhow. Just better luck at it. Turns up at the funeral dressed to kill.

I'm carrying the bag, but like it aint got nothing to do with me. *Rochester Food Fayre.* Vic's walking ahead. I tap him on the shoulder. I say, 'Here, Vic.' Like it's a relay, a relay round Canterbury Cathedral, and it's his lap.

VIC

He says, reading, ' "Edward Plant— Edward Plant— Edward Plantagenet. The Black Prince. Son of Edward the Third. English commander in the Hundred Years War. Fought at Cressy and Pottiers . . ." '

Sounds like a proper soldier-boy. Looks like one too, with his helmet and his chain-mail and his coat of arms. All level in death.

' " . . . Married Joan, the 'Fair Maid of Kent'." There you are, Lenny, he got spliced to a Joan an' all.'

Lenny touches my arm while Vince reads. He holds out the bag for me to take. Vince lifts his eyes, noticing, as if he's the teacher and we ought to listen. Pay attention at the back.

I take the bag.

' " . . . Died in 1376." '

Well Jack, if it's any consolation, if it means anything to you, we had you rubbing shoulders, so to speak, with the Black Prince.

RAY

It smells of stone and space and oldness. The pillars go up and up, then they fan out like they're not pillars any more, they've let go of their own weight and it's not stone any more, it's not material. It's like wings up there, arching and reaching, and I know you're supposed to gaze up and think it's amazing and feel yourself being raised up too, and I'm gazing, I'm staring, I'm peering hard, but I can't see it, I can't make it out. The next world.

But I reckon I could fly to Australia. Cross this world. Money I've got. Save Sue the trouble of doing it, other way. When. If.

Though I reckon she would, I'd lay odds she would. Though you'd think it'd serve no purpose, you'd think it'd be immaterial, and there's a hundred things you could better put the fare towards. New car, swimming pool.

It's a far sight further, Sydney to London, than London to Margate, a far cry further. And when she got here she'd only wonder why she ever came, it wouldn't be like the place she left years ago, roots, there wouldn't be no country churchyard with birds tweeting, God knows where I'll get shoved. But someone's got to do it, you've got to have someone, and I bet she would.

But I could save her the trouble.

LENNY

I found that doc to do the job. O'Brien. I'd like to know what register he was on or had been struck off of, I'd like to know how he washed his hands.

Doctor. Butcher more like. Family butcher.

Which strikes me as funny now. You shouldn't joke in church. Because when Jack in that bag there was still up and breathing, or not up but still breathing, flat on his back like one of these holy Joes but not yet turned to stone, he went and said to me that he always wanted to be a doctor.

I stared at him, a bit lost for a comment. He said, 'You know, a doctor, a quack, a sawbones. Cure the sick, chase after nurses, that sort of thing. I'd say live meat's better than dead meat any day, wouldn't you?'

I looked around at the other bed-cases and I looked back at him, because I thought he must be having me on, and he said, 'What are you sniggering at, Gunner?'

I said, 'Well it's a turn-up, Jack.'

This Black Prince feller don't look like he ever smiled.

Vince says, studying that guidebook, 'I say we should take a gander at the cloisters, then make tracks.'

I say, 'Okay, Big Boy, you lead on.' Vic and I have a quick smirk at each other and we traipse on, following Vince, like we can't leave till we've done the lot, it's obligatory.

You shouldn't joke in church, or in hospital, it seems. But it's either a crying shame or it's the biggest joke out to end up wishing we was something we aint. And I'd rather laugh than cry. And, thinking it all over and sizing it all up, I'd say Big Boy there's got the last laugh, since he knows he aint Vince Dodds, he knows he never was, though it's looking like he'd like to change his tune over that. But there aint none of the rest of us know who we really are. Boxer. Doctor. Jockey.

Except Vic.

We're slipping through the doorway that leads to the cloisters. It looks like we've lost Raysy.

Live meat's better than dead meat, that's what he said, though we'll never know June Dodds' honest and considered opinion on that. And Sally'll always have wanted to have had that baby, that pillock's dead baby, though she could've done without some of the live meat she's lived off since. It's a thin line sometimes between the one and the other. But flesh is flesh. It can't be denied.

Maybe the first thing I ought to do after we've done our duty by Jack here is go and pay Sally a visit. It's me, girl. It's your old dad, remember? It aint just another passing prick.

It can't be denied. It shouldn't be encouraged either, sometimes, but it shouldn't be denied. It's like I shouldn't be thinking right now, when I'm taking a turn in the cloisters, of Amy, forty years ago, when Sally was a nipper, fresh back from the seaside. But I am all of a sudden, I am. It don't do when you're escorting her dead husband's remains for their final disposing to think of the way her tits used to point and the way her frock used to hang on her. But I am.

You shouldn't ever have wicked thoughts in church, but you do, you want to have 'em, like it's an encouragement. You shouldn't think such things when you're an old man of sixty-nine with no breath in your lungs and nothing but a penny whistle between your legs, but I do, I am, like I'm free to, seeing as Jack's in the bag. I'm thinking of how she'd kiss and pet Sally and I'd be jealous of my own daughter, and how I used to think Jack was the luckiest bastard alive.

And this was my idea, to come here. Dose of holiness. It wasn't for *him*. Who's he going to tell, who's he going to brag about it to over a slow beer at the end of the day? My mates did me proud, they carried me round Canterbury Cathedral.

It was for us, to put us back on our best behaviour, to clean up our acts. Seeing as how Amy aint here.

I'm undressing her in my heart.

It's just as well your thoughts don't show in your face, though that aint such a let-out with my mush. Face like a fire alarm. But you can't help your face, even less than your thoughts. You can't help flesh being flesh.

It's like Jack used to say, I can see him holding forth now in the Coach, that there was more than one meat market at Smithfield once, bad old good old days. That night he was extra merry and Raysy wasn't, bad run with the nags I suppose. It was Vincey's birthday, Vincey's so-called birthday. And that new barmaid. You shouldn't think of a barmaid's bum. Raysy trying to make some joke about the Coach never going nowhere. Everyone tanked. And Jack saying, 'Cock Lane, Smithfield, famous for it once. You wonder how they think up the names. Cock Lane off Giltspur Street. We've all been there, aint we, Raysy? Cock lane, cock alley, cock passage, we've all driven the coach up there.'

VIC

So I said, 'I'll just have to go myself.'

Trev looked up.

I said, 'That was Tony. Won't be in. Looks like he's down with the same bug as Dick. They're dropping like flies.'

Trev said, 'There's Roy. There's me.'

I said, 'It's out beyond Sutton. You've both got to be at the crem at three thirty. It's pushing it. I'll have to go. Can you deal with the Harrises?'

Trev nodded. 'And if you're not back before I go to the crem?'

'You better put the Closed sign up. Late lunch. We can't ask Maggie here to hold the fort.' I was standing by the window, and I smiled. 'Unless you want to ask Jack Dodds to swap trades for half an hour. He's often said.'

And it was only then that I realized: the Fairfax Park Hospital and Home, Cheam. That was where June was. Where Amy went, where Jack didn't.

'It's all right, I'll go. Make a change for me.'

So a little after half past one I took the forms and the keys and went round to the lock-up and drove off in the black van with the blacked-out rear windows, what we called the Black Maria. The hearses were more friendly: Doris and Mavis. A ship is always she.

It wasn't as though I expected to see her. It wasn't as though it would look any different, because June was there, from all the other homes and hospitals that are an undertaker's regular port of call. Homes, Hospitals and Hospices, where people hexpire. And the worst are the Homes, since

211

you know they aren't homes at all, it's just a sweet-sounding name for a clearing-station for the handicapped or the old, or a stand-in for that word you mustn't use any more: asylum. And you know that for lots of them it wasn't such a short stay, that this was where the deceased *lived* maybe most, maybe all of their life, and that life, in this case, meant a kind of death, a kind of not having a home to go to.

Like Bernie Skinner always says – like any landlord – after the third time of calling time, 'Aint none of you got homes to go to?' With that sudden fierceness, as if he's insulting his own customers, as if he really hates all boozers and loiterers and it's the worst disgrace you can throw at a person, to have no home to go to.

And they're always sad anyway, these pick-ups from long-term institutions. Taking them out of one box just to put them in another. As if there was never any choice in the first place, and if you'd listened carefully you could've heard the sound of a coffin being nailed, long before I showed up. I picked up a prisoner once. Wormwood Scrubs. Heart attack, fifty-one years. I said to the warder, 'What was he in for?' and he said, 'Murder. Murdered his missis three years ago. Turned out to be a life sentence after all.' Or a merciful release.

But the outcast and the outlawed have to die too, the shunned and forgotten, and somewhere there's a reluctant relative who has to step uneasily forward. And you never ask, it's not your place, what exactly this death means to them. Though you can see sometimes it's not the simple, neat thing they'd hoped for, a merciful release. Your job is to provide a decent funeral, decency and respect with regard to the final disposal, everyone deserves that. It's not your job to pry.

What you learn in this business is how to keep your mouth shut.

There were brick walls and a gateway and a drive and gardens and trees, so that though it was the edge of London you might have been arriving at someone's country mansion. Except the mansion had got mixed up with what looked like an old-style barracks block, with grilles on the windows, and, once through the main entrance, there was the usual sour-milk smell of Institution, the usual squeaky corridors leading off, the usual rattle of things being shifted by trolley.

The receptionist looked at my ID and the forms, and I thought, Some day someone will do this for June, someone will come with the papers. Release of the body. It'll be the next main event. The receptionist picked up her phone and tapped out a number, then looked at me, the way people do when they're on a phone as if they're not looking at you at all but at the same time they're staring. She had hair permed stiff as wire and glasses hanging from her neck on a chain, and I thought, She's been here long enough to view everyone as inferior, everyone as suspicious. Long enough to know that if you put her in charge she'd run it a whole lot better. Beaky face, twisty mouth. She held the receiver clamped to her ear, starting to look cross at being kept waiting and starting to look cross at me for seeing her being kept waiting, and I thought, as I do sometimes, it helps to calm things down, And you too, sweetheart, one day, you too. Release of the body.

Then she said crisply into the phone, 'I see. I'll tell him,' then to me, with a sort of relish, 'You'll have to wait. The superintendent's on a late lunch, he won't be back till three.'

I said, 'I can wait,' thinking, I'm damn glad I didn't send Trev.

She scanned the forms again, as if they might have changed, then handed them back, looking at the next thing on her desk, like I was being dismissed. Then just at the point when she knew I was going to ask, she said with a little huff, as if I should know, 'Round the back of the main building and across the service yard.'

But I would've known anyway. There's always an incinerator chimney. There's always a blank double door like the back exit of a cinema. If there's no one about and there's no other sign, you bang with your fist on the double door. Someone comes to a window and sees the Maria reversed up.

She said, 'Three o'clock.'

It's a sort of distaste. Stigma, that's the word. Like you don't want to know the man who takes away your rubbish. I'm used to it, it's natural. The old man used to say an undertaker's half lord, half leper. You shouldn't hold it against.

I thought of asking: Is there somewhere I could get a bite? Then reckoned better of it. Then I thought, for a mad moment: Twenty minutes – I could see June. Just see her. Out of plain curiosity, out of I don't know what. See what Jack never sees. I could find out and just go, a black jacket will take you most places. But then I thought, No, seeing June might not be so hard, might not be so bad, but first you had to get past this charmer.

I said, 'Three o'clock,' folding the forms back into my pocket.

But I looked towards where the corridors led off, thinking, So this is where. And this is where Amy comes twice a week, year in year out. I wonder if she says hello to this cow, I wonder if she gets a smile.

And it wasn't till then that I realized that today was

Thursday. Thursday afternoons: it was one of Amy's after-noons. And I felt myself sort of bracing up, lifting my shoulders and tugging my lapel, the way you do when you might meet someone unplanned, the way an undertaker has to do most of the time. You never know who you might bump into, you never know whose toes you might tread on. It's not just a job, it's a place in the community. That's what the old man said. There's some who say I'm the next best thing to a vicar, and I say, 'That's all right. Call me Vic.'

So I stopped being the humble pick-up man. I became the full-scale, knock-'em-dead funeral director, and she must've seen, because I made her eyes flick away from me.

I said, 'Nice out, I'll take a stroll.'

It was an airy, breezy day, the sunshine coming in quick splashes. I walked out on to the forecourt, checked the Maria was parked okay, then took one of the paths that fanned out across the lawns, feeling like a truant, feeling that I was enjoying this, the boss doing the hired man's job, this slipping in and out of a part like the sun dodging the clouds. Feeling that for twenty minutes I had a special angle on the world.

There were rose beds and trees. Patients were out exercis-ing, taking the air too. What do you call them? Patients? Inmates? Residents? Some of them moving oddly or stand-ing oddly still. A thin man came towards me, his lips and his fingers clenched round the stub of a cigarette as if he was trying to pull a long piece of string from his mouth, but it was pulling back. Others looked quite normal, only the old clothes gave them away. But even then. So if you weren't careful. And how would you *explain*? So you think you're an undertaker, do you? You better come along with us.

I sat on one of the benches while the sun came out and

went in, came out and went in again. The man with the cigarette turned and came back, as if I'd taken *his* bench, and as he passed me he snarled like a dog, dribbling, his teeth showing. I wasn't afraid. Have no fear. I wondered if Amy was afraid, whether she'd been afraid when she first came. But women aren't afraid, or not of the same things. I thought, You see all the dead, all the bent and broken or plain stretched-out dead, and you think, These people are strangers now, total strangers. But it's the living who are strangers, it's the living whose shapes you can't ever guess.

And that's when I saw them. There must be something that makes you look. Sitting on a bench, on a bench on another path, in front and to the left. I saw Amy's head of brown hair, the breeze stirring it, the sun putting colour into it, and that way she had of sitting, plain and straight and simple, as if she was waiting her turn. But not before I saw Ray, looking small beside her, almost like her kid. His little coconut-shy head, and that way of scratching his neck, I'd recognize that gesture anywhere, the fingers reaching right into his collar as if a whole mouse had dived in there. I thought, I wonder if he knows, he's definitely thinning on top, bit of pink showing through.

If I'd taken another path I might have walked straight past them. But now I slunk back, behind them, to the van, half thinking I should tread on tiptoe, and then I saw it, it must've been there all the time but you don't see what you don't expect to see: Ray's camper, on the far side of the car park, sludge-green and cream, that funny bit on top that opens up like an accordion for extra head-space.

I climbed back into the Maria. From the front of the van I could see them clearly, fifty yards, ten o'clock, Ray on the side of the bench nearest me. It seemed to me that though they made the shapes of two separate people sitting on the same bench, so you might have thought it was just a chance encounter, they also made a single shape that was the two of them together.

Ray leant forward and lit a cigarette, cupping his hands against the breeze. Then he took a puff, took the cigarette from his mouth and with the same hand, elbow on knee, stroked his bottom lip with his thumb. There was a paper bag wedged between them with the remains of something, because Amy dipped her hand into it and threw crumbs for the birds pecking near their feet, sparrows, pigeons. She did this quickly, with a jerk of her arm, as if she half wanted to shoo the birds away, not feed them, but the crumbs kept them coming back. Ray didn't feed the birds. He smoked and rubbed his lip and scratched his neck. Then he sat back and at that exact moment Amy leant forward as if they were a machine that worked like that. She stroked her leg just below the knee as if she had an ache there.

I looked at my watch: nigh on three. But the superintendent could wait. I'd waited for him. Though it's a serious transaction, release of the body. You need the signature and the verification and the date and time, and you shouldn't be late for the dead, just because they're dead. One of my rules. Don't dilly-dally with the deceased. I'd've given Tony a bollocking.

Five past three and they were still there on the bench, and nothing in the van to pass the time, save an old thumbed *A to Z* and the forms in my pocket. But I had them by heart. Jane Esther Patterson. Date of birth, date of death. She was eighty-seven. Cause of death: cerebral haemorrhage. Next of kin: John Reginald Patterson. Son. I must ask the superintendent, if he's not shirty with me, how long she'd been in for.

(I did. He said twenty-eight years.)

I watched Amy lean back, without Ray leaning forward this time, and dip her hand again, briskly, into the bag and throw. You felt they both wished they hadn't stuck that bag between them. Then Amy picked up the bag and started crumpling it into a ball and brushing down her skirt as if she was about to stand up, and just before she did, Ray reached out and clasped her far shoulder, then shifted his hand to the back of her neck, the fingers reaching under her hair, just like they'd done into his own collar. As if he'd been meaning to do that all along, or something like it, but it was only her moving to get up and him not having another chance that pushed him to it. Then Amy hesitated for a bit, her head sort of wriggling against Ray's hand. Then she got up like she'd meant to, and Ray jumped up too like he was on a spring and they started walking back towards the car park.

I hunched down in my seat but I don't suppose they could see me, with the reflections on the windscreen, if they were looking anyway. It was like just for a moment they'd been two younger people and now they were two older people trying to act their age. It made them look funny. But I suppose if you were going to look funny, this was the place to do it. Amy dropped the balled-up paper bag into a litter bin and Ray flicked his fag-end a few feet in front of him and stepped on it. They walked separately, like people being careful to walk separately, as if they just happened to be on parallel courses.

I suppose it can happen a lot here. Visitors crossing paths. Time to spare, burdens to share. Regular lonely-hearts' club.

They passed maybe four or five car-widths to the left of me and this time I ducked right down, nose to the passenger seat, acting funny too. Then I lost them as they passed out of sight behind the back of the van. But I watched in the wing mirror, and I had a clear view of the main gate out of the side window. It's one thing about a van, you can see over the roof of a car next to you. I heard an engine start and a bit of reverse gear, then I saw the camper creeping out towards the gate, past the little 'Out/In' bollard with its arrows pointing. The turn to go back was left. The other way took you out of London: Ewell, Epsom, Leatherhead. I watched Ray brake, flash his indicator and turn right.

You shouldn't judge. What you learn in this business is to keep a secret.

RAY

I said I felt about as Lucky as I'd ever felt. Being Lucky.

So he said, smiling, he felt about as Jack as he'd ever been, or was ever going to be. About as sweet jack all.

Then he looked at me and I thought, just for a second, He aint saying it's down to *me*? Like when they first brought him in here, before the op, before he *knew*, and I felt everyone looking at me sort of special, like I was the man of the hour. Ray'll swing it, Ray'll fix it. All Jack needs is a dose of his old mate Raysy. And while we're at it, we'll take a bet on the surgeon doing a top-notch job.

I thought, It's a terrible burden having all this luck.

But he looks at me as if he can see how he's putting me on the spot, when it's not me who ought to feel on the spot, it's him. And he says, like he's shaking his head at what I'm thinking, 'I've come to terms, Raysy,' slow and firm. He says it again as if I haven't heard. 'I've come to terms. It's Amy I'm thinking of.'

Which makes me hold my eyes, wide open, on his as if I'm lost if I so much as blink.

He says, 'I've come to terms, but I aint squared up with Amy.' I look at him. I don't move an eyelid. 'I don't want to leave her in the lurch.'

I say, 'It's not your fault that you—'

He says, 'It's not that. I aint played straight with her.'

I look at him. He looks at me.

He says, 'It's money I'm talking about. We was all set up to buy that place in Margate, weren't we? Westgate. And the whole world thought this was cos Jack Dodds had finally

220

seen the light and decided to start a new life. And everyone thought it was a crying shame that just when he did, he finds out there aint going to be no more life.'

I say, 'Including me, Jack.'

He says, 'Including you. Including Amy. Except what everyone don't know is I had to sell up or fold up. That's why I did it. What the whole world don't know is I took out a loan to save the shop five years ago, and it comes up in a month. Wouldn't have been no problem. I sell the shop, sell the house, buy a little bungalow in Margate, a little tinpot bungalow, and I scrape through on the difference, just about. Except now it's all off, aint it? All bets off, eh?'

He looks at me like I should know best.

I say, 'Why not've sold up five years ago and paid yourself what you went and borrowed?'

He says, 'Cos then I had to make a living, didn't I?'

I look at him.

He says, 'I'm a butcher, Raysy. That's what I am.'

I keep looking at him. It's him and it's not him. It's like he's been hiding. He says, 'It's something I aint got to do now, make a living.'

I say, 'So you never – saw no light?'

He says, 'No, Raysy.' I don't believe him. 'And no new life, eh? Not for me.'

He looks at me.

I say, 'How much?'

He says, 'Seven large ones when I took it on. Now they'll want nearer twenty.'

He sees me whistle silently.

He says, 'We're not talking bank managers. It was a special sort of a loan. A private loan.'

I say, 'Not Vince?'

And he laughs. He tips back his head and cackles so it

hurts him and I find myself reaching for a paper bowl, I find myself looking at his call-nurse button. 'Vince?' he says, half choking. 'Vincey wouldn't've lent me money if I was dying, would he?'

I say, 'So who?'

He says, 'Vincey wouldn't've forked out for the shop, would he? He wanted me to sign on at the supermarket.'

'So who?'

'One of his mates, from the early days. One of his – business pals. Rough stuff, you understand.'

He looks at me like he's in for a scolding.

I say, 'You'd've been better off taking a long shot on a two-year-old. You'd've been better off coming to Uncle Lucky.'

Even as I say it I see which way the wind's blowing.

He says, 'Would've been a big 'un, Raysy. Where would I have got the ante? But it's funny you mention that.'

He looks at me, starting to smile, so I nip in quick. I say, 'You told Amy about all this?'

He shakes his head.

I say, 'You going to?'

He says, 'That's a tricky one, aint it? What I'm hoping is I won't ever have to, there won't be no need. It's funny you mention her.'

He pokes with his finger at the empty paper bowl I've been holding all the while. He says, 'You look like you're begging, holding that.'

I put the bowl back where I got it.

He says, 'I don't know what she's going to do. I mean, when I'm— She might want to stay put. She might want to go ahead with that bungalow anyway. It aint kiboshed yet, it could still go through. Either way, I don't want no debt-collector knocking on her door. I don't want her finding out she's got twenty grand less than she thought she had.'

It's like he wants me to tell him the solution.

He says, 'That's a nest-egg, aint it? Twenty grand. That's what they call a nest-egg.'

I say, 'So, for all she knows, it was just you seeing the light too. It was just you going for a new life. Glory hallelujah.'

He looks at me as if I'd know the answer to that too.

He says, 'Some things are best not known.'

I say, 'Why Margate?'

He says, 'I don't want to leave her in the lurch. I want to see her right.' And his eyes shut suddenly, the lids drop in that heavy way, as if it's more than he can do to keep them open, like he's nipped out for a moment without saying and left me guessing.

Then he opens his eyes, as if he never knew he'd shut 'em.

I say, 'So what do you think she's going to do?'

He says, 'Depends. Maybe you'd know what she's going to do.'

I look at him.

He says, 'I need a winner, Raysy. I need a winner like I've never needed.' He lifts his right arm slowly off the bed-cover. What with the tubes going in it, it looks like he's not lifting it but it's being lifted, like the arm of a puppet. 'And I've got the ante this time.'

He moves his hand towards the bedside cabinet and opens the little drawer, the drawer with his few odds and ends in it. His hand shakes. He struggles with the drawer and I half go to help him but I know it wouldn't do to help him because there aren't many things he can still do for himself.

He takes out his wallet. I've never seen Jack Dodds' wallet look so fat.

He says, 'Here, have a look inside. Back compartment.'

He hands it to me. I take it and flip it open while he watches me. I don't see no photograph. There's a great wodge of notes.

He says, 'There's a thousand smackers. Eight hundred in fifties and a bunch of twenties.'

I look. I rub the top note with my thumb. I say, 'You've got a *thousand*, cash, in this place?'

He says, 'Who's going to take it, Raysy?' He looks around at the other beds. 'These poor bastards?'

I say, 'So where did you—?'

He says, 'Be telling, wouldn't it? Take it out. Count it.'

I shake my head. 'I believe you.'

He says, 'Never my strong point, was it?'

'What?'

He says, 'Sums. Rithmetic. Never had it up here like you.' He gives his head a little lift like he's trying to nod at his own skull. He says, 'Take it out anyway. I need a winner.' He looks at my hand on the wallet. He says, 'It's Doncaster coming up, aint it? First of the flat.'

I think, And all things being normal, I'd be there.

I say, 'It's a thick 'un, Jack, a thousand quid to make twenty. A thick 'un.'

He says, 'It's a thick 'un.'

I say, 'And if I put it on the wrong nag?'

He says, 'But you won't, will you? You can't. Amy needs it.'

I think, Your money or your life.

He says, smiling, 'Anyway, just think of it as the price of a camper. A thousand quid, remember? But you didn't want to sell it, did you?'

CANTERBURY

I can't see them anywhere. It's like they might have gone and left me in Canterbury Cathedral. So I wander back down the aisle to where I was when Vince took himself off, in case they come looking for me, and I sit down again on the wooden seat, elbows on knees, thinking, I'm the odd one out now.

Thinking, It's like he's looking at me now, knowing. Better make your mind up, Raysy, better make it up quick. It's like it wasn't just the dosh, it was me an' all, the two together. There's the money, Ame, and there's Raysy. You'll be all right now, you'll be all right with Lucky. Nudge, wink. I reckon you'll see each other right.

It's like I should've been him.

I sit there, keeping an eye out, but I don't see them anywhere, so I get up and find the way out, and then I spot them, standing on the paved area, looking out for me. I think, Friends. The sky's dark and threatening and the wind's cold but they don't look like they're getting peeved. They look like they're glad to be here together, like all's forgiven.

I think, Maybe.

Vince says, 'We was beginning to wonder, Raysy, we was beginning to think you might've got lost.'

Vince is holding a guidebook. Vic's got the bag. I'm not holding anything but it's like everyone can see that Raysy's got a lot of something that aint his.

I can feel the cathedral behind me, looking at me.

Vince says, 'We was in the cloisters. Did you clock the cloisters?' Like I ought to have done.

I say, 'Yes, I saw the cloisters,' thinking, Small lies are easy.

Then we head back the way we came, out through the gateway and along the narrow streets, except we take a different narrow street from the one we came up. It's called Butchery Lane, which is why we take it. Vince says we ought to. Then as we turn into it the rain comes pelting down. But there's a little pub half-way along, the City Arms, and it's open, and Lenny says a quick one wouldn't hurt, would it?

VIC

Then he says, straight-faced, serious, sitting there in my office, hands pink and scrubbed from a day's butchering, like he's a special sort of client who's come washed and ready for his own laying out, 'As a matter of fact, Vic – I can say this to an old matlow – I wouldn't mind being buried at sea.'

AMY

Well they must be there by now, they must have done it. Tipped him in, chucked him. For all I know, they're halfway back again or they're making a day of it, they're out on a spree, donkey-rides all round, now the job's done, down there in Margate.

But I still think this is where I should be. My own journey to make. Their journey and mine. The living come first, even the living who were as good as dead to him, so it'd be all one now, all the same, in his book. And I've already said goodbye to him for the last time, if not the first. Goodbye Jack, Jack old love. They can say that June won't ever be the wiser if I missed this day with her for the sake of one last day with him, there have been missed days before, about a dozen of them once, long ago, and you don't ever get a second chance to scatter your husband's ashes. But how do they know she wouldn't know? And someone has to tell her.

If she won't be the wiser, he won't either.

And I don't think I could've done it. Stood there on the Pier, when it should've been the Jetty anyway, waves below me, salt in my eyes, stood there with them all watching me. You first, Amy, whenever you're ready, take your time. Wind up my skirt. The way the day's turned out, I'd say it's blowing half a gale down there in Margate.

This is where I belong, upstairs on this bus. It seems to me that for years now I've been more at home on a number 44 than I have been anywhere else. Neither here nor there, just travelling in between. I don't know if I could ever have made my home in a bungalow in Margate. 'I'm packing it in, Ame,' he says. When I'd long since given up on him, when I'd long since thought it could never happen, when I thought, One day he'll just drop dead there, behind the counter, in his striped apron, cleaver in his hand, and that's how he'd want it, another carcass to deal with. 'I'm jacking it in. Geddit?' Ha. 'It's a new life for you and me, girl.' I don't know what caused it, what suddenly tipped him over, what blinding flash. But he looked at me as if I'd be overjoyed, as if he wasn't looking at the woman he'd been looking at for fifty years, he was looking at someone new. He said, 'Margate. How about Margate?' As if we could put the clock back and start off again where it all stopped. Second honeymoon. As if Margate was another word for magic.

That's when I knew that the tables had turned. It was me who'd thought all those years ago, when I first said goodbye to him, that you always get a new beginning, the world doesn't come to an end, just because. I still had the power to choose. I chose June not him. I watched him set solid into Jack Dodds the butcher, Jack Dodds, high-class butcher, have a bit of mince, missis, have a bit of chuck, because he couldn't choose June too, couldn't choose what was his, it was all he had to do, and I thought I'm the one who can still change. I did, once. But when he looked at me then, like he was looking at someone I wasn't, I knew I was stuck in a mould of my own. Of this woman who sits every Monday and Thursday afternoon on a number 44 bus. Even a week after her husband has died.

As if it was my fault, after all, for deserting him, for saying goodbye. Once, twice.

And she'll never know. Never.

Margate, Margate. And what about *June*?

There's something about a bus. A red double-decker, sloshing and chugging through the rain, with its number up front and its destination and its route, which doesn't change from one year to the next. As if as long as there's a number 44 going from London Bridge to Mitcham Cricketers the world won't fall apart, London Bridge won't fall down. As if, if it's true what he always used to yanter on about and only because his old man used to spout the same, that Smithfield is the heart of London, bleedin 'eart-a-Lunnun, then the red lines of the bus routes must be the arteries, bleedin arteries, and veins.

Never once in a cab. On Jack Dodds' takings? And never on the Tube, though it's quicker, Northern Line, all the way to Morden. Because I like to see, I like to think while I'm journeying, while I'm in between. I like to look around me. And only a dozen times in a camper. How many times was it? Not much more than a dozen, eh Ray?

But why have I come upstairs today? Upper deck like a ship, swishing through the rain. To prove I'm still an able-bodied woman, not one of the old crows downstairs? To prove I can still choose? To get a new view of the world slipping by? Lambeth, Vauxhall, Battersea, Wandsworth. How could I have done it, Ray, stood there with you, sharing his ashes? This is where I belong, number 44. Have a bit of ash, missis. And as long as the red buses keep on running, then the red blood will keep on flowing, the heart will keep on pumping, pumping. Oh Ray, you're a lucky man, you're such a *little* man. Oh my poor Jack.

RAY

So I spread the *Racing Post* in front of me with the whole Doncaster card. Then I lit a ciggy and I got out my form book and my notes. Ray Johnson's Register, '87, '88, '89. Always keep a log of your bets. Then I scanned the races and runners, doing the calculations in my head that come natural after a while, the eliminations, the percentages, the fields to go for and the fields to stay clear of. People think I'm Lucky Johnson and it's all done by sixth sense, and sometimes it is, sometimes a flutter's a flutter. But the reason why I'm quids-in, just about, with the nags, and Jack Dodds and Lenny Tate won't ever be, is because everyone wants to believe in hunch bets, and it may look like luck but it's ninety-per-cent careful clerking, it's ninety-per-cent doing your sums. I aint worked in that insurance office for nothing. People think it's horses from heaven, answering your prayers, but it's learning how to beat the bookie, and if you want to beat the book-keeper, keep a book.

So I studied the runners, stroking my jaw, thinking, Long odds, long odds. Off-course bet, so there's the tax. On a thousand quid. Thinking, Early-season handicaps are a pig in a poke. Thinking, If I was there it'd be easier, it's always easier if you're there. You see the nags, you get the scent, it aint no blind date. And you get the compensations. The hooves on the turf, sun on the silks, Irish gab. The whole great ballyhoo of beer and hope. Thinking of all the things Jack won't ever look on or listen to again.

The smoke from my ciggy curled towards the window.

Fluffy clouds after showers, a breeze, the going good to soft. The going.

I looked at my watch: eleven thirty. Only a fool bets early, the scent changes, every minute, there's the sums and the scent. Only a fool bets early. But what if? Suppose, if Jack.

I kept not looking at the name looking up at me from the middle of the list for the three five. Twenty-two runners. What's in a name? They call me Lucky. Only a fool bets on a name. And Jack can't be saved, he can't be.

I thumbed my notebooks, jotted some figures. Rule number one: value for money. But Jack don't want value for money, he wants a one-off winner to end all winners, to save his bacon, his fried eggs and bacon. He's not in the business of averaging out.

So this aint your regular sort of bet.

But I kept not looking at the name staring up at me. Rank outsider, twenty-to-one the field. Though it kept staring back at me. There's luck and there's luck. There's safe luck that keeps you from harm, that keeps bullets from hitting you or makes you live to a hundred and five, and there's wild luck that makes you grab at gold. There's the sums and there's the scent, getting stronger, and sometimes the scent is all there is, and you can tell all you need to know about a nag from the tilt of its head. It's like it's the bet that's the thing but sometimes it's just the run and the rush and the roar of the race. Sometimes it's just the glory of horses.

So I stubbed out my ciggy and lit up another and took a pace or two across the room like I couldn't sit still. I stood at the window. Back end of Bermondsey. And the track at Donnie a wide, flat gallop. You'd have to be a fool. I felt the flutter in my ribs and the luck in my veins. What you do it for in the first place, why you're in it in the first place. I opened the window like I was short of breath. I felt the air and the smoke in my nostrils and the life in my limbs and Jack's money burning a hole against my heart.

Miracle Worker.

AMY

But it was easy to make a man smile in those days. Even that tallyman, Alf Green with his puffed-out chest, the sticks dangling from it, and his black tash and his stare like a sergeant-major's, watch out if your stick didn't tally, used to crack his face just a little bit for me, just a bit. Unless I imagined it. You'd think he might've stretched a point now and then, called six bushels seven. Me there by the bin in my thin frock, hot and sticky, and him with his notcher. Seven bushels the shilling-tally and you were pushing it to make two-and-six a day. Hard work, up at the crack. But don't tell me there weren't short cuts, and more than one way of collecting hop tokens. Shirley Thompson should've been a champion picker, tokens she had. Two hundred bushels the week, except it wasn't all bushels. She'd end up with nearly ten pounds' worth, not counting extras for cash. And her ma and pa in Deptford would be chuffed with her for the fiver she'd hand over. Our little Shirl, champion hopper.

And don't tell me that there weren't general compensations. Doing it for free, getting it for free, down there in the garden of England, with the sunshine and the fresh air and the haystacks and the hop-bines, and that feeling, though it was stay-put and keep-at-it work, bins all in a row, three or four to a bin like a factory outdoors, of being set loose. On the loose. Living in huts and tents like natives, living on the land, no fixed abode. No hawkers, no gypsies, no dogs, no hoppers. The smell of fry-ups at night. Wood fires, billycans, oil lamps, natter.

The gypsies came with their caravans and horses, needing the hopping just like us, but made their camp separately, over by the wood, eyeing us like we were the ones who'd pitched up where we shouldn't, and I used to envy them because they were a stage further at being outlaws than us and because they were professionals at it and we were just amateurs and when we were back again in Bermondsey, all bricked up and boxed in, they'd still be wandering the woods and lanes. I used to envy them their nut-brown skins, against our London dough, white turning red, like a barber's pole. I used to watch one of them lead his horse every evening to the pond for watering, just as us hoppers finished. Though no hopping for him, it seemed, city chits' work. Big feller. Bare-backed both of them, him and his horse.

I suppose you could say it was more than envy.

My mother said I never should

And I didn't, though I might've. I played with Jack Dodds instead, Jack Dodds from the other end of Bermondsey. It's a big wide world. And I don't know what Shirley Thompson did, what Shirley Thompson used, but she never got herself knocked up, but I did, first time of asking.

He was a muscle man too, a big man, even bigger, if not so trim. I don't mind admitting, that's how I liked 'em, or thought I did, big hunks of men. What more could a girl want than a big hunk of man? And I knew he had his eyes on me, down there on the next row of bins, I knew he had his feelers out. Whereas Romany Jim wouldn't grant you a glance, a flick of his head, not while you might be looking back. And Jack never thought it was man's work either, with those big hefty hands. Oh, all shrunk to the bone. Like picking flowers, he said. She loves me, she loves me not. Like counting buttons. I said, 'So what d'you come for?'

He said, 'Reasons.' And I said, 'So what d'you do when you're not picking hops?' and he said, 'Be telling, wouldn't it?' But someone whispered in my ear, when they saw how the wind was blowing, 'Butcher's boy,' and he gave the game away anyway when we took that walk, Sunday evening, round by the farmyard and stopped to look at the pigs, and he eyed 'em over like he was looking at something familiar from a new point of view, like he was weighing out sausages.

Like picking flowers, threading beads. But it was hops that brought us together, it was hop-picking that started it. The way your life gets fixed for you. *Drink up, Vincey, have some more baby-juice.* And it was pickings of another kind that clinched it. It's all pickings.

He brings round a bundle of newspaper with about two pound of runner beans wrapped up inside that he said he got from one of Wick's hands, though for all I knew he'd rifled 'em direct, and says did I want 'em? And I say, Yes, if he'll help me top and tail and string 'em, like I was doing him a favour. Uncle Bert and Benny were down the Leather Bottle, drinking hop-juice, spending tokens, leaving me to do supper, and he'd have been down there too if he hadn't also been spying out his moment. Runner beans. He said, 'All right.' So I went inside the hut and got a saucepan, two knives, a colander. You used to have to take everything like that, pots, pans, washtubs, the lot, like refugees. Then I went to the standpipe for water and came back and gave him one of the knives and only then did I flash him a smile, a real you-never-know smile, like a traffic light on amber. You never know how one thing leads to another.

Then I sat down on the hut step and spread the beans out on the paper on the grass in front of me and I put the saucepan down on the step beside me, deliberate, because there was room there for two. I said, 'There's a chair inside if you want it,' and he said he was all right sitting on the grass. Copping more leg. I tossed him a runner and I could tell he'd never strung beans before. He might've known how to chop brisket but he didn't know how to string beans. I said, 'This way.' Then I jammed the colander between my thighs so my skirt all rucked and tightened up. I said, 'Chuck 'em in here. See if we can't fill it.' Because I wanted him to see, I wanted him to know, if it wasn't plain as pie, that there was a bowl there, a whole bowl of me waiting. Unless he thought it was like a piece of armour. So we started filling the bowl. He aimed and he threw, rather than reaching across and dropping, and of course some of those bean slices started missing, some of them missed by a long way, some of them went down the front of my frock. It was an old cream thing with blue flowers on and buttons down the front. I suppose he was looking at those buttons, counting them. So we filled the colander. And I said, 'What next?' twisting a strand of hair around my finger. I said, 'Uncle Bert and Benny won't be back for a while yet,' the colander still between my legs. 'Unless you was thinking of joining them?' He said he wasn't thinking of doing that, looking at the beans. So I said, 'Wait there. You can take me for a walk.' Then I picked up the colander and stood up, shaking bits of bean out of myself, tutting, and I picked up the saucepan and took them inside and came out again, smiling, and he was smiling too.

I thought, What are you doing, Amy Mitchell, what are you doing? You don't even know this boy. You don't even fancy him, not that much, not so much. But the air was soft and ripe and still. And there was that feeling inside me, between me, like a bowl. And who should we see as we crossed the road by the pond but Romany Jim, with his horse. Clip-clop. Things come together in this world to make things happen, that's all you can say. They come together.

But you'll never know, June, that that was how you came together. Or not quite together, not quite. Like Jack won't ever know it was the sight of that gypsy. The things that do and don't get told. You'll never know, you never had the chance, about warm August nights and colanders. You'll never know, you'll never need to and maybe you're better off as you are, how one thing leads to another. If you lead a man to water, he'll drink. And there you are with your bellyful, trying to tell yourself that you're no more to blame than he is, but feeling anyhow, you can't help it, that you've got him on a rope, saying, I do, I will, in a borrowed suit, with the rest of them looking on like butter wouldn't melt. Hitched, they call it.

But it was only after you arrived that I felt him tug away, tug and twist and turn against me at the same time, as if it really was all my fault now, my problem, not his. There you are, you see, look what happens. And it would've been better all along, wouldn't it, if we'd done what other couples do when a hot night in a hop-field catches up with them?

But I thought, It's not a punishment, because one thing leads to another, it's not a punishment. The important thing is not to take it as a punishment.

I don't know how I scraped up the money. No hop-picking that summer. How could we? No extra shillings. And this extra mouth to feed. Except it was being fed for us, it was being taken out of our hands. I nearly got down on my knees with Dad and with Uncle Bert. I said, Jack and me never had no honeymoon, did we? And now, and now. Have a heart.

I think I was ready to ditch you then, I think I came as near as I ever did to chucking you.

I said to Jack, We're going to Margate for the weekend. No, don't ask, all fixed. Just get your old man to give you the time off. Say it's your honeymoon. Steamer from Tower Bridge. Wanting him to say, to show, that if he didn't want her, then he'd better still want me, he'd better. Wanting me to say or show that it was all right if he didn't want her, so long as he still wanted me. You won't ever have to know, June, what hard-nosed little tricksies we can be.

I bought a new summer frock. Undies, shoes, stockings, swimsuit, the lot. Uncle Bert went and hocked his grand-father clock.

And the sun came out, like it was on our side, and the waves sparkled and I wore my new frock, etcetera. Except the mother inside you sneaks up on you when you least want it. You won't ever have to know that either. Even when you're only eighteen and you're at the seaside, ice-cream and Punch and Judy, in a new swimsuit, and men are eyeing you. Yes they were, left, right and centre. I must've looked like I was anyone's.

I thought, Well you had your chance, well I gave you your chance.

The Pier, the Jetty, the Sands. Dreamland.

I thought the war might change things, put everything in its place. So you think you've got troubles. Bombs whistling down on Bermondsey, whole streets going. I thought, He might be killed. Or I might. Or you might. A stray bomb on a home for the hopeless, no one need grieve, a mercy really. What hard-nosed. But what the war did was to push things further the way they'd gone. It was me and you together, no one else near and dear, and it was Jack far away being a soldier, not being killed, being one of the lads again.

With Ray Johnson. So when Vince Pritchett, but forget the Pritchett, dropped into my lap, into our lap, I ought to have known it wouldn't help a bit, it wouldn't win him back. You can't make a real thing out of pretending hard. You can lead a horse. That Amy Dodds' a kind soul, taking in that Pritchett kid, what with her own little problem. Ah, but that's the reason, aint it, don't you see?

From then on it was me and you, and him and Vince. Meaning him and Vince against each other, him and Vince at daggers drawn, cleavers drawn. But it keeps men together, it keeps them occupied, fighting.

Yes it was here, Vince, here. This was where. Here, in the garden of.

And what *you'll* never know is that it was even truer than you once believed, before you learnt better. All done with hops, all done on the hop. Because it was in a hop-bin. A twenty-bushel hessian hop-bin, slung between its trestles. All-round privacy, could've been made for the purpose. Like two rabbits in a sack.

And what you'll never know either is that three nights later up on that hill, near that old windmill, which had its sails then, he looked at me, firm and steady, straight and steady, and said, 'You're beautiful, d'you know that? You're beautiful.' It's not what you expect from a butcher's boy. It turns you over to hear a man say that, fills you up. To be alive, to have lived to hear a man say that, any man, and to know, by his smile, that he means it.

Like you never did, June, or could or ever will.

The things that do and don't get told. The tallyman would come with his sticks and his notcher, to count your bushels, to take a look at your bushels. With his stony face that said, I'm the tallyman and don't think you can get round me. Your stick better tally, your notch better marry,

serious business, tallying. 'Now then. Mitchell, Amy . . .'
Never smiling. So maybe I imagined it, but maybe he
would've smiled, just a hint, just a glint, if he'd known, that
it was in that very bin.

VIC

Just as well, I thought, I was still in my uniform. All the nice girls. Only a month or so from demob. Four-year stripe now as well.

But she said, 'So what do you do then, Vic, when you're not mucking about in boats?'

I thought, Well, here it comes, it had to come, and I know just what follows. First she'll look at my hands, just a dart of a look like she thinks I won't notice, but I will. Then she won't look at me at all but she'll start taking a keen interest in the features of this thrown-together dance hall, except she won't be looking at them either so much as doing some quick rethinking in her head. Then when I ask her about the next time, she'll come up with all the usual excuses.

And she was the best of the bunch so far, Pam Summerfield, the best of a not-so-long and not very long-lived list, best as a straight eyeful but more than that. A bounce, a balance, a nerve. Like she wasn't going to miss out on any fun going, she wasn't going to not take her chances then regret it later, but there was something there that was for the long course too, that wasn't born yesterday either.

And she was kitted out as good as you could expect for Gosport, Christmas 1945. Pink and black number, like she meant serious business.

The band was playing *Chattanooga Choo Choo*.

I said, 'Ships, not boats.' But I thought, You've got to be straight with this one, and I'm not going to come the old son-of-the-sea, and she was going to have to ask sooner or later, and maybe her asking now was a sign.

So I said, 'I'm in the undertaking trade. Family business.'

She looked at me. She didn't look even for one moment at my hands. She looked at me and said, 'Well I never, Vic, well I'd never have guessed. Well at least you won't be out of a job, will you?' Then she looked down then up again quickly as if she wasn't going to change her course, and there was a smile just in one corner of her mouth. 'So you'll be used to handling bodies then.'

RAY

He says, 'Wanna do a deal with the yard?'

Springing it on me quick and sudden, looking at me with that cocksure, you-aint-going-to-refuse-me look, like he can see me thinking, He must be joking, since what's he got to do a deal with? But he's not joking, he's serious, and he knows I'm going to come round, just wait and see, to whatever it is he's fishing for.

I say, 'What deal? We already got a deal.'

He says, 'We aint got a deal, we got an arrangement.'

I say, 'A pretty good arrangement I'd say, from where I'm looking. So what's the problem?' Thinking as how he's got two cars in there now that he's stripping down to fancy up. There's a Rover as well as an Alvis, not to mention recent use of the camper. Recent use. Like the place has become his home.

He says, 'A very good arrangement, for which I aint ungrateful. But that was like your kindness. Your kindness to an ex-soldier-boy who wanted to mess around with motors, who wanted to keep his hand in as a mechanic. I can't expect that to go on indef, can I? I can't expect to rely on your kindness.'

He picks up his pack of ciggies and shakes a couple up out of the foil, all neat and practised, and offers me one and lights it. He says, 'I aint ungrateful, Uncle Ray.'

Uncle Ray.

And I think, I wonder if he knows how I got it all wrong, read the picture all wrong. How I thought he could do with a bit of taking under my wing, seeing as how Jack once took me under his. Seeing as how I might not be here otherwise, twenty-five years on, having a beer and a smoke with Vincey in the Coach, I might be lying under a cross in Libya. Least I could do was return the favour, give the lad a help-out on his return to Civvy Street, and take him off Jack's hands. Except Jack didn't see it that way, I should've known. He hadn't given up, even after five years of having to. Dodds and Son.

My foot in it, my big little foot.

And things had shifted now anyway, they'd shifted into a whole new picture, what with that girl sleeping under Jack and Amy's roof, at least part of the time, what with all the comings and goings, what with it seeming suddenly like everyone was looking for a new place to pitch their tent. What with them afternoons at Epsom.

I hear that you and Auntie Carol. I'm sorry to hear that, Raysy.

And maybe I'd never've let Vincey use the yard, maybe I'd never've picked him a horse to buy his first used car with, Shady Lady, Sandown, six to one, if Amy hadn't said, 'Vincey's coming home, he'll be home in a month or two. I think we better stop this.'

He says, 'Besides,' and he pauses to light his own ciggy and to blow out a big cloud of smoke, he looks at the smoke like he's looking at his life. His knuckles are all cracked and blackened. 'Besides, now I'm going into business, I'll need premises, I'll need to do it all proper. If you're going to have a business you got to have premises, aint you?'

I say, 'You're going into *what*?'

He says, 'You heard, Raysy.' Raysy. Getting cockier, lifting his beer and taking a swallow. 'It's like I always said all along, I aint just doing it for fun, except maybe you thought I wasn't serious. But I want to do it proper, see, I want to do it right. Otherwise you could always say, "You know that arrangement we've got, Vincey? Well, I don't want to keep it going any more, sorry, I've got other ideas for the site." And that would be that, wouldn't it? I wouldn't have no choice.'

I say, 'But I haven't got other ideas for the site.'

He says, 'Well maybe you should have, Raysy. It's good commercial space, aint it?'

I look at him. I say, 'It's not a site, it's a scrapyard. It's still got Dixon written on the gate.'

He says, 'Exactly. And Charlie Dixon popped off over a year ago, didn't he? Since when you aint been collecting rent or nothing. You just been being a bleeding office-boy. And chasing horses.'

I say, 'That's my look-out.'

I look at him. He blows out another swirl of smoke.

I say, 'So what are you suggesting? You pay me rent? What with?'

He shakes his head. 'I'm talking ownership, I'm talking buying.'

I look at him. There's something in his face that stops you laughing.

I say, 'Same question, twice over. What with?'

He says, 'I'm asking you to make an investment, Raysy. In Dodds Motors. A non-cash investment, you don't have to fork out a penny. An investment of time. There aint no Dodds Motors now, course there aint, but there will be in five years, I'm telling you. You sell me the yard as premises but you loan me out the asking for five years. Come five years, I pay you your price plus a percentage. If I can't stump up – but I will – the yard's yours again. Plain and simple, can't lose. Soon as I've got another car on the go

246

and I've got the margin, I'll give you a deposit. You'd get to keep that an' all.'

Maybe he can see me thinking that I ought to laugh but I can't. I say, trying to look like I know when my leg's being pulled, 'Why should I take on a cock-eyed offer like that? Why shouldn't I just put it up for the highest bidder?'

He takes a swig of beer, squeezing his lips on it slowly. 'Seems to me you aint been rushing to do that this last year or so. Seems to me that you aint minded me parking my motors in your yard anyway, for free. That's where your kindness comes in, and my being grateful. That's where I'd reckon on us having a special understanding.'

I look at him. I think, He bounced right out the way of a V-bomb.

He says, 'I aint forcing, I'm only asking. If I've put other ideas into your head then that's my problem. It's a gamble, course. But you'd understand that, wouldn't you, Uncle Ray? With me it's motors, with you it's horses.'

But he looks at me like it's a certainty, a racing certainty. The glint in his eye sharpens. And that's when I think that he *knows*. I don't know how, but he knows. By scent, by doing the same. Sleeping in that camper. And not just sleeping.

Chasing horses.

That's why he thinks I can't refuse him.

He says, 'Nother one?' holding out his hand, all smiles, to grab my glass, but I shake my head, like I don't want to interrupt a different sort of flow. All flowing his way.

I say, 'What about the price?' like I'm not interested, I'm just raising an objection, testing him. Thinking, he won't have a straight answer to that, because he knows anyway he aint got a hope.

But he says, quick as a shot, his hand still hovering by

my glass, 'Two grand. Plus twenty per cent over the five years. Twenty per cent. Call it five grand to come – after I've put down a deposit.'

Like he's done his sums.

He blows out another cloud of smoke then he stubs out his snout, taking his eyes off me, looking at the ashtray, while I look at the smoke now, floating up and disappearing, because I know and he must know, without any asking around, that that's still a cheap price, even in 1968, even for a disused junkyard round the back of Spa Road. And if I'd've known what would happen in five years' time, if I'd've known what those years would do, but Vincey had his finger on that pulse too, I'd've said, Forget it, Vincey, just forget it. I aint selling. Have it for nothing, meantime.

Value for money.

He says, looking up, 'I'm only offering, I aint insisting. I'm only putting it to you. You sure you won't have that other one?'

I say, 'Yes.' Then I say, 'Yes, I'll have another one,' in case he gets me wrong.

He says, 'Think about it. You could be in there at the beginning of Dodds Motors. Founding father. Bernie! You here?'

I think, Maybe he doesn't know, but I won't ever know that he doesn't know.

Then Bernie comes out of hiding and pours us two more pints and Vince pays for them and I say, before I take a sip, 'There's just one thing in all this, Vincey.' Realizing as I say it that it's taking me down the path he wants me to go.

He says, 'What's that?'

I say, 'It's called a butcher's shop.' Realizing it's like I've committed myself. 'It's called Dodds and Son.'

He stops his beer half-way to his mouth, looking all hurt

and taken-aback, like it seems I didn't understand him and he had reason to suppose I did. He says, 'Do me a favour, give me a break. I thought you was on my side.' Giving me the little-lost-orphan look.

Then he smiles quickly and lifts his glass. 'Cheers.' So I lift my glass and drink. He says, 'Just think about it.' Then I drink some more, not saying nothing, then I say, 'I'd want to keep the camper there. I'd still need my own space for the camper.' He looks at me and says, 'Course you can. No charge. I'd even give it a regular once-over for you. And if you ever wanted to trade it in, I'd see you got a good deal.' He holds his glass to his lips and it's almost as though I see him wink.

'That's not as though I'm agreeing,' I say.

He says, 'Course you aren't, Raysy.'

I think, Jack won't forgive me. Either way, he won't ever forgive me. Wound a man once, you can wound him twice. I think of him down there at the shop even now, chopping and weighing, not knowing, while we sit here drinking. He always had a rule: no boozing at lunchtime, not even a quick mouthwash, not when you're handling knives.

Then Vince downs the rest of his pint quickly and looks at his watch, hands all grubby, not like Jack's. There's the tattoo on his forearm, blue and red, made in Aden, a little scroll with his initials on with a fist holding a thunderbolt on top: 'V.I.P.'

But 'Dodds Motors'.

He says, wiping his mouth on his wrist, 'Better dash, gotta see a man about a car.' Grinning. He slips his packet of ciggies into the breast pocket of his shirt and gets off his stool, giving me a nudge on the shoulder with his knuckles. 'Think it over,' he says, sloping off, like it's nothing special, like it aint neither here nor there.

And I sit there for a while, finishing my own beer slowly, getting out my own packet and lighting up again, Slattery's clock edging round to quarter to three. Then I say, 'Ta-ta, Bernie,' and go down to Billy Hill's, like I'm not thinking, and I put a one-pound bet each-way on a steeplechaser at Sedgefield, thinking, It's not to make, it's to decide. If it's placed, I hang on, if it's not, I sell. You shouldn't bet on superstition. And it comes in fourth in a nine-horse race. O'Grady Says, five to one. So I walk out, thinking, That don't settle nothing, and I go over to the yard, thinking, Either he'll be there or he won't, and if he is.

And he isn't. There's the Rover and the Alvis, sitting there in the sunshine, like someone's ditched them, with a panel off here and a panel off there, and the Alvis with its back end hitched up on two stacks of bricks, and his tools and oil cans and greasy rags lying around. I think, He ought to have an inspection ramp. Lying all day on his back with his nose up an oil sump. The camper's parked outside the lock-up, the weather being mild for the middle of February, and it being in regular use at the moment. Regular and irregular. But it's not in use right now, either kind. I think, I haven't had a good trip out for a while, on account of making room for that girl, on account of being so accommodating.

I think, I sell Vince the yard. I never sold Jack the camper.

Then I just stand there in the middle of the yard, in the middle of my own yard, with the lock-up that used to be Duke's old stable, and the new blocks rising up against the fuzzy blue sky and the railway arches running across, every arch some joker's business premises, and the smell of dust and rust and the rumble of traffic and something banging away on a building site somewhere. I think, First Johnson, then Dixon, then Dodds. Or Pritchett. It's a question of territory. It's when you say, This is my patch, this is my pitch, that the trouble starts. TowcesterUttoxeter.

So let him have the yard.

And now I think that he never knew, he never knew then and he doesn't know now either. Because he'd've said, by now, he'd've come right out with it, today of all days. Surely he would.

I reckon he was only so cocksure and keen because that's how he's made, and because he was getting it at the time, from Mandy, in my camper. Not even guessing. But he still had me selling him that yard for a knock-down price and missing out on value for money, so I reckon that's another reason why I should keep that thousand.

AMY

And I suppose now he's given me my chance, that's what he's done. Tit for tat. Thrown it back at me. You were the one, girl, who wanted me to believe that life don't ever play so mean that you don't get a second chance, that it don't start up again just when you think it's finished.

Well, here's your chance. That feller you lived with for fifty years, the one with the striped apron and the jokes for the housewives, he was just a stand-in. And now he's gone, see, just when you thought the real Jack might be putting in a fresh appearance. Let's all go to the seaside. Funny that, pops up again just to pop off. Don't know what you've got till you miss it, do you missis? Have a bit of best end. So here's your chance, here's your life all over again. And it's never too late.

Though it's easier when you're eighteen.

He levelled up the gun, one eye looking along the barrel, the other squeezed tight, and of course I thought, One day he might be doing this for real, not tin ducks but people. Or someone might be doing it to him. There must have been a few of them that summer taking pot-shots in side-shows and thinking it wasn't such a game. But I suppose his call-up came at just about the right time, so far as he was concerned. Get me out of this, get me out of here, put me somewhere where I can start again. It's possible, after all. Facing bullets would be easier, he'd be good at it. *'Ere, Nursey, take a peek at this.* I suppose I knew already he'd be better at facing some things than others.

'Have a go, have a go for the lovely lady. Three shots for tuppence.'

But I thought, like the fool I was, If he hits then we'll find a way somehow, if he misses, never.

He said you'd think they'd be able to do something, these days, you'd think they'd come up with something. *They.* To make dud babies whole again. As if they could wave a wand. It was the only time we ever talked about her, in that guest-house bedroom with its fine view of the tram depot, the only time she ever came up in the conversation. Then he said did I know he'd had this idea once, it was just a stupid idea, of being a doctor.

But he said he wasn't no doctor, was he? No more, he said, than I was Florence Nightingale.

So I knew it wasn't the simple rescue operation I thought it was going to be, the simple kill or cure. Margate or bust. Because maybe you don't ever get your life over again, try telling it to June.

Which I have been these fifty years.

Best thing we can do, Ame, is forget all about her.

The ducks moved along in a never-ending row, on some hidden belt, each one painted red and white and green, but scratched and dented where shots had hit, each one with one big eye fixed open wide and its beak curled up in a smile, as if it was only too eager to be shot at again, to disappear with a ping and a clang then pop up again.

I stood behind him on the boards of the Jetty, with the lights and the noise and the crowds and the slither of the sea in the dark below, you could just feel it. The white cliffs looming towards Cliftonville. A steamer was moving out across the bay, chugging back to London, all lit up, like most of its passengers. I thought, Maybe he's thinking it too: hit or miss, kill or. Three ducks says that life aint finished yet. He seemed to take an age to fire each shot. Ping! One duck. Three more swam past, each one giving him the eye. Ping! Another duck. Ping! And after another two slipped goggling and smiling by, a third took a dive in the pond that wasn't there.

'Good shooting sir! Every one a winner! You see, folks, it can be done. They may be ducks but they don't know how to duck, do they? Any more now, any more? So what'll it be, sir? The chocs, the china or the teddy bear? Let the lady choose, shall we? The lucky lady.'

And like the fool I was I chose the teddy bear, the big yellow teddy bear. What would I want with that? Except to show the world it was my lucky day, our lucky day, and I was the lucky lady. He didn't smile, he didn't even look pleased. He just looked at me as I smiled and held the teddy bear, as if there was something he didn't understand. And now, when I remember it, I know I never hugged him, like you do, for winning a prize. I just hugged that teddy bear, laughing. I thought, Which way now? Back to the shore or on to the end of the Jetty? Maybe it should've been the shore. All the wrong choices, and him having just made three shots count. But you don't go on the Jetty just to walk half-way and then turn round again, teddy bear or no teddy bear, you don't go on without going to the end, it's what you do. And just for the time it took to walk to the end of that Jetty I felt, everything is still possible, everything is still floating, the water lapping and slapping beneath us, and I didn't notice, or care if I did, that the smile he'd put on his face now was like the smile on one of those ducks. It was only when we got to the end that I thought, This isn't true, it's only a picture, a seaside postcard, and maybe that's what he was thinking. How could I laugh and smile and act like life was a holiday? My whole stupid idea of going to Margate. The breeze was flipping my skirt. Men were eyeing me. Lucky teddy bear. I thought, Just to be free again, with just the breeze and the night and the sea and the men looking. Having your pick. As if this was your starting point once more. Lambeth Vauxhall.

There was a strap rubbing on one of my shoes, my new shoes, so I gave him the teddy bear while I stooped down to fiddle. Maybe I just wanted to hide my face. And I think even as I handed it to him I knew what he was going to do. There he was for a moment, a grown man, on the end of a pier, holding a teddy bear, a man on the end of a pier. He looked at it for an instant like he didn't know why he was holding it, like he didn't know what it had to do with him. Then he stepped nearer the railings. And then there wasn't any teddy bear, there was just Jack. Goodbye Jack.

RAY

But I didn't put my coat on and go down to Billy Hill's. 'George, I've got a thick 'un for you.' Where I'd look a fool slapping down a thousand cash, even if they took it. Where I'd lose all credit for being a canny punter. 'So what's the game, Raysy? Looks like you've gone and won already.' And where I might be tempted to say, any case, to declare to the assembled company, all the gluttons for punishment and two-quid no-hopers, 'This is for Jack, I'm doing this for Jack. You know, Jack Dodds, it's to save his skin.' You'd have to be a fool to back a horse called Miracle Worker, you'd have to be a fool to own and train one. You'd have to be a bookie's bosom pal. Still, if Lucky Johnson here has a fancy.

I picked up the phone there and then, third ciggy on the go, and dialled a number where I knew they'd take a four-figure punt, no questions asked, even from the likes of me. Where they'd say, 'What's the asking?' And I'd say, 'A thousand, to win, tax paid.' And they'd take down my credit-card number and read me back the details without so much as a wobble in the voice, Miracle Worker, thinking, There's one born every minute, there must be harder ways of making dough.

Thirty-three to one.

But it's different if you *know*. And if it don't come in, which it will, then Jack'll get his money back. I'll foot the bill for this bet, recoup it on another. Jack'll get his thousand back, and that's my conscience squared. Price of a camper.

'All placed, Mr Johnson. Thank you for calling.'

And it has to be in my name, it can't be in Jack's. Because supposing. Just supposing.

Then I put Jack's thousand in a spot I use, behind a cupboard. I aint carrying a grand in cash around with me more than I can help. And I put on my coat and shoved my cigs in my pocket and looked around the room before I left like I hadn't ever looked at it before. It looked about the loneliest room on earth.

And you're flogging the family home an' all.

I walked in the direction of the Coach, thinking, If I'm so sure, I could pop in the turfie's anyway and put on a bet of my own, or pick out a combination to cover my loss. Which wouldn't be logical, if I *know*, and it'd be tempting fate, either way. This isn't my day, it's Jack's day. You've got to keep it simple. Though it aint.

Or I should go and see him, now, tell him. Maybe that's why I'm legging it along this street like there's somewhere I ought to be going. 53 bus to St Thomas's, Westminster Bridge. Tell him what his money's riding on, tell him that the bet's on me, either way. Least I can do, Jack. Except I don't want to have to look him in the eye, or have him look me in the eye. And if he's got any sense, he'll tune in on his earphones, on his radio, that's one thing he can still do. Racing from Doncaster. And he'll know, because he will, he'll know too.

So I slipped into the Coach. Quiet for a Friday. Bernie says, in his just-between-you-and-me voice, bringing me my pint, 'What's the news on Jack?' I say, 'I went in last night, I'll go again this evening. It's just a matter of time, Bern.' Looking at Slattery's clock. Quarter past two. And Bernie shakes his head, like what's happening to Jack is something that ought not to be possible, like it's a miracle working the opposite way. I say, 'You having one too, Bern?

Have one on me. Fetch me a sandwich while you're at it. Ham, no mustard.' And up on its shelf, high up at the end of the bar, Bernie's telly's all set up and switched on, the screen angled and the sound pitched just right, so that any Joe sitting at the bar can keep his eye and ear on what's showing, without having to move an inch to order a drink. Racing from Doncaster. Lincoln Handicap meeting.

Bernie brings my sandwich and sees me looking at the screen and says, 'One or two on, I suppose?' And I say, 'No, as a matter of fact, I haven't. It don't seem right somehow, does it? What with.' Bernie nods, approving. 'But there must be one or two you'd fancy, any case?' he says. I say, 'Be telling, wouldn't it?' biting my sandwich. Bernie smiles, like he knew I'd say that. He pours his drink, nodding at the TV. 'And I suppose you'd be there, wouldn't you? If it wasn't for.' And I say, 'Yep.' Like Jack should've thought.

Cheltenham too, Gold Cup, then Doncaster, first of the flat.

He says, 'Cheers, Ray,' lifting his glass. 'Good health all round.' I say, 'Good health.' He says, 'Sound up high enough for you?' I nod and he waddles off, tea-towel over his shoulder, like he does when he knows conversation's not what's required. But he can see me sitting there, eyes glued to the screen, more than you'd think necessary for a man who hasn't got a bet on. He can see me lighting snout after snout and knocking it back, quicker than usual. Steady drinker is Ray, slow and steady. 'Make the next one a short, Bernie. That's a long short.'

'Caning it a bit, aren't we, Raysy?'

But when the three-five comes on I'm not thinking like a punter, a chancer, needing a slug of courage. I'm thinking like a jockey. I'm thinking like I'm the jockey and I don't have no choice. Some feller called Irons, never heard of him,

Gary Irons. Heavy name for a jockey. I'm thinking what does a jockey do saddled with a horse called Miracle Worker? And a name like Irons. I'm sitting on a bar-stool in the Coach but I'm being like a jockey, my toes up on the top rung, my knees braced and squeezing, arse wanting to lift. All I need is the whip. I watch him come out of the paddock, deep chest, sheepskin noseband, and head up to the start and I see in the way he rides out the way he'll ride back, I see the way he takes the turf and hits full gallop quickly, long, clean strides, a stayer, a finisher, and I think, It's this horse's day, it's this jockey's day. Any old irons. It's Jack's day. And then it's only seeing what you saw already, seeing what you knew in your head, it's only letting the horse make the race for you. I watch him run like he's never run before and never will again, or not at these odds, hold the midfield, find the gap, move up to make his challenge like he's dispensing with preliminaries, and with four in front and maybe three lengths in it, kick forward and take them all as if there's a spare gear in him and he could do with another furlong to really find his pace.

Sometimes it's just the glory of a horse.

I don't move a muscle when it passes the post. Or when they lead it round to the enclosure and the jockey dismounts and unsaddles and pats its head, and it dips its neck and snorts like it aint done nothing special. I don't move a muscle when they click up the result and the SPs to confirm. Shortened a shade, but I don't need no SPs.

Thirty-three to one.

Bernie says, 'Someone's lucky day.' And I say, 'Yep,' picking up my whisky glass, draining it, looking through the bleary bottom of it. Then I look at my watch and at Slattery's clock and put my empty glass on the bar and dismount my stool. 'Well, must be getting along, Bern. See yer.' Bernie says, 'See yer,' taking the glass. It's hard to imagine Bernie not being there, like Slattery's clock, behind the bar.

Then I go out and I think, I should go straight to see him. Twenty minutes if I'm lucky, lucky even with the bus. I should go straight and tell him. But if he's got any sense, he'll know, he'll've tuned in. Lucky came good, he came good.

And there's his thousand pounds, left for safe keeping. He should have that back, I should take him that. And there's the little matter of how to hand over the winnings, on account of it can't be cash, though that's how he'll've pictured it, if he's pictured it, that's how Jack Dodds will have pictured it. Big wad of readies, shopkeeper's preferred. Thirty-four thousand smackers to stash in that bedside cabinet, like he's ringing up the till. Nursey, you'll never guess what I've got.

But it'll have to be a cheque, Jack. I used my own name, for convenience. Shall I make it out to you? Or to Amy?

So I returned to quarters and got out Jack's thousand and counted it, to be sure, though it hadn't been touched. Eight hundred in fifties and two hundred in twenties. Then I phoned that special number again, to make sure about pay-out, sounding pretty cool, I reckon, for a man who'd just won thirty-odd thousand pounds. I thought, The tax is on me, Jack, I'll give you a cheque with three clear noughts. Then I felt like I could hardly stand. I thought, I must've had one too many at the Coach, I shouldn't've gone on the scotch. Wasn't no need, was there, if I knew? And I shouldn't go into that place now, the HDU, breathing beer and whisky and wobbly on my pins. Breathing booze over Nurse Kelly.

So I made myself a strong cup of coffee and sat for a bit

to steady up. Half an hour won't make no difference, and if he's got any sense — But instead of steadying up, I dropped off, I slipped away, in a twinkling, and next thing I knew the phone was ringing and it was an hour later though I didn't know it, and my coffee was standing where I'd put it, hardly touched and cold, and outside the sky was thick and grey and shaping up for rain. I picked up the phone and I knew the voice. It was Amy's voice. But it sounded strange and I couldn't make sense of what it was saying. She said, 'He's gone, Ray, he's gone.'

MARGATE

We come in on the Canterbury Road, past faded, peely bay-windowed terraces with that icing-on-an-old-cake look that buildings only have at the seaside. Hotels, B-and-Bs. *Vacancies.* The buildings look extra pale against the grey, piled-up sky, and against the clouds you can see little twirling specks of white, like broken-off flakes of the buildings, like scatterings of white being flung about by the wind. Seagulls. You can feel the wind, even in the Merc, bouncing up the side-streets and jolting into us, and we're all thinking, Any moment now we'll see it, we've got to see it, it can only be just over there. Then we see it, as we come over a brow and a gap opens up in the buildings: the sea, the sea. With the whole of Margate spread out below us, the front, the bay, the sands, with Cliftonville beyond, except you can't see the sands, or precious little of them, because the tide's right in, like Vic said it would be, and the sea's grey and thick and churny like the sky, with white spray flying up. And that long harbour wall out there on the far side of the bay, the only thing you can see that's like a pier, with the spray lashing up against it extra fierce: that looks like where we've got to go, that looks like where we've got to do it.

With a storm brewing.

Lenny says, 'Journey's end. 'Allelujah. I need a pee.'

Two extra pints in Canterbury.

He says, 'Looks like it's expecting us.'

Vic is sort of perking up, like he's coming into his rightful element. I'm thinking, You could get blown clean off that wall. I'm holding Jack again, in his bag, in his jar, and I hold on to him tighter, like I already need the extra ballast. Vince is looking all cool and careful and deliberate. He don't say nothing. He only had the one at the last port of call, but I reckon we're all glad we took a little extra on board to steady ourselves for what's to come. He drives on slowly down the hill, the sweep of the bay ahead of us, his eyes looking this way and that. It's not exactly thick with traffic or bulging with trippers. It's not season.

We join the front proper and he pulls up by the kerb, leaving the engine running. It seems he's heeded Lenny's little problem. Sudden sight of all this water. One thing it's not hard to find in a seaside resort is a public bog, and he's drawn up close to one, it looks like a blockhouse. But he don't stop at that. He opens his driver's door and gets out. There's a great gust of air. He walks round to the pavement, lifting his head and scanning the bay, his messed-up white shirt flapping like a flag, then he opens the passenger door for Lenny, courtesy itself, like a chauffeur. He cocks his head towards the blank-walled building on the other side of the pavement. 'Make yourself comfy, Lenny,' he says and it sounds as though he says it with a smile. It's like he wants things from now on to be proper and seemly, with no snags and upsets like a bursting bladder. 'Anyone else?' he says. But I'm not feeling the call. I switched to whisky, taking a tip from Vic.

Lenny edges out of his seat, all abashed and obedient. More raw air swirls round the car while his door's open but Vince, out on the pavement, doesn't seem to mind. It's as though he wanted the excuse to be the first of us to stand on the front at Margate and breathe in the briny. I twist my head round so I can see him hoisting back his shoulders and holding up his chin. You can hear the din of the waves. I hold on to Jack. Little pin-pricks of rain are peppering the windscreen and being dried off again almost immediately as if, despite the clouds, the sky's too het-up to start a real downpour. All wind and no piss. Lenny stands on the pavement and takes his own lungful of air, half like it does him a power of good and half like it hurts. He looks around, hunched and braced, and looks at Vince, straight and tall, looking around beside him. He says, 'Remember it, Big Boy? Remember it?'

VINCE

So I walk into the hospital with the money in my inside pocket. Eight hundred in fifties, rest in twenties, rubber band, brown paper envelope. I think, There can't be many people who turn up at this place like they're hitting a casino. And I hope he understands it wasn't easy. He ought to know a thing or two about cash-flow, him of all people. He might think that kind of dosh is just pocket money to me, because I wear a four-hundred-quid suit, because I flog jalopies for readies on the spot, but he ought to know about margins, now specially. Sometimes cash flows and sometimes it don't. Right now it's hardly trickling.

So Hussein better.

And when am I getting it back? You can't deny a dying man a favour, any crazy thing he asks, but that don't mean. You can't take it with you when you go, but he will, *he* will.

I think, I might as well be taking this money to chuck it off the edge of a cliff.

But then I come out the lift and walk down the corridor, with the usual traffic of trolleys and wheelchairs, and there's that smell again that's getting so familiar you can smell it when it aint there. I'm standing in the showroom and I can smell it. I'm breathing in cars but I can smell it. Like the smell of the swab they give you after a jab, only scaled up, and beneath it the smell of something stale and thin and used up, like the smell of old tired papery skin. I suppose it's the smell of— I think of all the patients in this hospital, heads in beds, I wonder what the tot-up is, I wonder what today's takings are. And I think, I've done what he asked,

I've only done what he asked, and if I don't ever touch this money again, still it's cleared my conscience, aint nothing on my conscience.

So I stride down that corridor with my head held high, like I'm back on the square at the depot and the sergeant's called me out. *Deetail!* And I look at all those poor crumpled-up bastards and old girls in their wheelchairs, thinking, I bet you aint got a thousand pounds to give away, have you? But it's only money, aint it? Only paper.

I walk in, and there he is with his tubes and his pumps and his meters and his belly all swolled up like he's pregnant. I can see he aint looking so good. I mean, given he's buggered in the first place. Today he's having a worse day than yesterday. Every day's a notch in only one direction. But I can tell what the first thing on his mind is, so I don't play no tricks, I don't tease. I pull out the envelope, giving a quick squint around, like the place is full of spies and thieves, and hand it to him, looking at him, thinking, I aint ever going to see this money never again.

I say, 'There you are, Jack, as per promise. You don't have to count it.'

Though I bet he does, soon as I'm gone. He just takes a quick peek inside the envelope, feeling the thickness, stroking it with his thumb, then he looks at me, up and down like he's taking in the whole of me, like he's that sergeant inspecting my turn-out, and says, 'You're a good boy, Vince.'

AMY

They'll be there now, where we might have gone. Ended up
or started again. New people, old people, the same people.

He looks at me while I sit by the bed, holding his hand,
his thumb moving gently, dryly, in little circles round the
base of mine, and I think, We aren't going to look at each
other so many times again, there aren't going to be so many
more times we'll speak. First you count the years, the dec-
ades, then suddenly it's hours and minutes. And even now,
when it's his last chance, he's not going to mention her, he's
not going to say a word about her. It's like we could be back
there now, fifty years ago, in that guesthouse, with me
seeing, with me knowing clear as day suddenly that he
didn't ever want to know. *You'd think they could come up
with something.*

He looks at me like he's sorry for having left it too late,
for having to be going just when he was going to put things
right. He would've been a changed man, course he would,
change of heart, the world would've turned upside down
just for us. Like he's sorry for having been the man he was.
Is. But he's not going to mention her, he doesn't say he's
sorry on account of her. He doesn't even look so apologetic
for the things he's making you think he's sorry for. He looks
at me so firm and straight and steady that I have to look
away myself, just a flicker, though you'd think there
shouldn't be time for that, not a second to spare from looking. But I think, I'll always see his face, I'll always see Jack's
face, like a little photo in my head. Like a person never dies
in the mind's eye.

But he doesn't mention June. He mentions Vince, who isn't, who wasn't ever ours. He says, 'Vince'll look after you. He's a good boy. He aint such a bad job.' He says that I'll be all right, I'll be looked after, but he doesn't say how he never looked after June, he doesn't say, 'And give June my love.'

So I think, Then I won't mention Ray, I won't say a thing about Ray. Though it's my last chance, and it's the time for it, at the bedside, now or never.

He won't mention June so I won't mention Ray. Fair dos. What you don't know can't hurt. But he looks at me with that unflinching, unblinking look, so I have to dart my eyes away again. I look at the next bed which, just for now, is empty, the sheets and covers stripped off, and when I look back, his own eyes haven't budged an inch, they're looking into me and beyond, like he'd like to step right through me and go on then turn round and come back and hug me. And he says, like it's his last word on everything, on why he's lying there and why I'm sitting there holding his hand, and why it had to be him, why I was saddled with him and not a thousand others, luck of a summer night, 'All a gamble, aint it? Ask Raysy. But you'll be all right.'

MARGATE

It doesn't look like journey's end, it doesn't look like a final resting-place, where you'd want to come to finish your days and find peace and contentment for ever and ever. It aint Blue Bayou. If you look one way, beyond the public bog where Lenny's disappeared, there's only grey thick sky and grey thick sea and a grey horizon having a hard job trying to mark the difference between the two, and the other way, across the road, it's like someone's put up a frontage in a hurry to outstare the greyness, it's like the buildings are a row of front-line troops drawn up to put a brave show on it, but it don't help exactly that they've been dressed up in joke uniforms.

Flamingo. Tivoli, Royal, Grab City.

Vince says, 'Marine Terrace.' He's got back in the car while we wait for Lenny. It's like he's decided to be our tour guide again, like in Canterbury Cathedral, except this time he's reeling it off out of memory. 'Marine Terrace, Margate. "Golden Mile".' But it's a short mile, it's about two furlongs and it don't look so golden, not in this weather, it don't look like it's made of gold. *BurgersHotdogsIcesShakesTeas PopcornCandyflossRock.* There are signs and coloured lights, some of them on, some of them flashing, everything rattling and shaking in the wind, and here and there a pavement placard on a chain lying where it's been blown flat. Most of the arcades look shut but one or two are lit up, all flickering and winking. By one of the entrances there's a geezer in a flat cap and a donkey jacket, perched inside a little booth, like he's only doing his duty. But they aint exactly flocking in.

Vince says, 'It's not season, of course.'

You can imagine Vince running an arcade. It's not so different after all. Dodds Showrooms.

Mirage. Gold Mine. Mr B's.

More little spots and spatterings are dotting the wind-screen and Vince turns on the wipers but only gets a smear, so he turns them off again. The rain doesn't want to rain yet, though the sky's getting darker every second.

Vic says, 'Timed it perfect, didn't we? Wouldn't have thought, by this morning.'

Vince says, 'Well we're here.'

The sea don't know that.

Vic says, 'It's not good scattering weather,' as if the thought hadn't occurred.

Vince says, 'Depends how you look at it.'

I'm holding the box.

Vic says, 'Fair old wind.'

I say, like I only want to be sure, 'Where's the Pier?'

Vince says, slow and patient, 'You're looking at it, Raysy. That thing right there that you're looking at, that's the Pier.'

I say, 'It don't look like a pier.'

Vince says, 'But it's called the Pier. It's a harbour wall but it's called the Pier.' Then he launches into his tour-guide patter. 'There used to be this other thing called the Jetty, which looked like a pier, which you went on like a pier, where the steamboats came in. But they called it the Jetty, and that thing over there which is really a harbour wall, they call that the Pier.'

I say, 'Sounds reasonable. So what happened to the other thing – the Jetty?'

Vince looks at me like I ought to have mugged up on

that too. 'Got swept away, didn't it, in a storm. Nineteen seventy-something. I remember Amy saying, "Did you hear about Margate Jetty?" I reckon that's why Jack specified the Pier. He didn't mean the Pier, he meant the Jetty. That's what we all remember, going on the Jetty. But he must've remembered there wasn't no Jetty any more, so he settled on the Pier.'

I'm getting confused so I don't say nothing.

Vince says, 'You can't see it from here, it must be behind the Pier, but there's supposed to be a bit of the Jetty still left, still standing, all by itself out to sea.'

I say, 'Well maybe that's been swept away today an' all.'

Vic says, 'This isn't a storm.' Voice of authority.

I think, Course not, looking at the spray.

The seagulls are whizzing around the sky like they're either having the time of their lives or they wish they'd never taken off.

Vince says, peering across the pavement, 'What's he doing? Gone for a paddle an' all?'

Then we see him, emerging from the lee of the walled-round entrance to the Gents. He can tell we're looking at him and he staggers a bit, deliberate, at the point where the wind catches him, pretending it's worse than it is. All the same, he glances grimly up at the sky, then he smiles, weakly, like a man always can when he's just emptied his bladder. He looks like the one who's always last and knows it, always keeping everyone waiting. He stands for a moment, with the railings and the grey sea behind him, as if because it's the seaside and he's the focus of attention he ought to do a quick comic turn but he can't think what, so he just stands there grinning, awkward, like he's having his photo taken. This is me at Margate. Shocking weather. He goes up on his toes all of a sudden, holding up his fists, rolling one shoulder, jabbing with his right. I reckon Lenny's face is its own comic turn. Then he moves towards the car, like it's hard work, he could be swimming for it, and opens the door. There's a blast of air.

'Aint weather for the beach,' he says.

'Mad March days,' Vince says.

Vic says, 'It's April.'

'April bleedin fools,' Lenny says.

'Mad Gunner Tate,' Vince says, like he didn't mean it to mean anything, it just came out.

'Mad Jack Dodds,' Lenny says, shutting the door. 'April first yesterday. You think he's whisked it all up special?'

You can't tell from holding the jar, no little trembles. Just the engine purring.

Vince looks at Lenny in the driving mirror then he looks straight ahead. We sit by the kerb.

Vic says, 'Well,' as if the moment's come.

Lenny says, 'Well.'

I don't say nothing. It's like we're all waiting for someone else to give the word and maybe it needs to be me since I'm the one holding Jack, I ought to sense him saying, 'Come on, lads, get shifting.' But I don't say nothing. I aint taking command.

Vince is staring ahead, his hands resting square on the wheel like he's driving though we're staying still, it's a pretend car. The windscreen's all silvery, the sky's like lead. Then just as I'm about to say, 'Come on, let's go,' we start to move anyway. As if Vince hasn't done nothing and the car's decided for us, as if we're all just payload and it's switched itself into motion, like that belt suddenly starting to move, you could hear a little clicking sound, that carried Jack's coffin out of sight behind the blue velvet curtains.

It doesn't look like the end of the road, it doesn't look

like what you'd aim for and work for. It looks like it's trying to keep going all year round something that only happened once one whoopsy weekend. So this is what you get, this is where you come. I reckon it's all about wanting to be a kid again, bucket and spade and a gob full of ice cream. Or it's all about being on the edge, which you are, other sense, and you know it. Not where the road's going, just where it don't go no further, on account of the ogwash. End of the road, end of the pier. Splash. And if the seaside was such a fine and wonderful thing in itself, then there wouldn't be no need, would there, for this whole china-shop of Amusements? All of them trying to tickle your fancy like a troop of tired old tarts. Like it aint the coast of Kent, it's Cunt Street, Cairo.

Flamingo. Tivoli. Royal.

Vince lets the car roll slowly forward, barely touching the gas, as though it knows what to do, a Merc has a mind of its own, like Duke always knew the way home anyway, and I can see what he's doing, I can see how he wants it to be. It's like the car has become a hearse, a royal blue hearse. Because this is Jack's last ride, along Marine Terrace, Margate, along the Golden Mile. Last ride of the day, eh Jack? Vince looks straight ahead, hands on the wheel, like he don't want no distractions. *Mirage, Gold Mine, Ocean.* They're all painted up and decked out like poor men's palaces, except one, at the end of the parade, looming over them all, a bare brick tower with just a few big words on it. It looks more like the way into a prison than a funfair. We've already passed it, but we all noticed, as we came down that hill, the big wheel rising up behind it and the big dipper, black and spindly against the grey sky. It's what Margate's famous for, it's what people come here for. *Dreamland.*

AMY

And the most I've wanted, the most I've hoped in fifty years, believe me I've never asked the earth, is that you should have looked at me, just once, and said, 'Mum.' It isn't much to have wished, all this time. Damn it, you're *fifty years old*. You should've fled the nest by now, you shouldn't want me around, you should be leading a life of your own. For God's sake, Mum, I'm a *big girl*. Well, all right then, go on then, big girl, have it your own way. It's your life, you go and ruin it.

I've tried to know what it's like to be you. To be in that Home always, which I only visit. To be in that body all the time, which I only look at twice a week. Which shouldn't be so difficult, should it, since it was once part of mine? Flesh of my. But I think when they snip that cord they snip off everything else too. They say, You're by yourself now, you're as different and as separate as all the others, it's hoo-ha thinking otherwise. And when I tot up all those twice-weekly visits, then it seems we haven't shared each other's company for much more than one whole year, which isn't much in fifty, which isn't much for mother and daughter. But if you look at it another way, it's one whole year of just visiting.

That's what I am, that's what I've been: a visitor. And when I went in to see Jack, in that little room, Vincey waiting outside, to visit Jack's body, like you could say I was a visitor to it when it was alive, but I haven't counted up the times in fifty years, I thought: What's the difference? He isn't ever going to turn into something else now, but don't kid yourself, Amy Dodds, that was just as true of Jack alive as dead.

So what was true of you, girl, was true of him. And maybe that's why he never came to see you, because he'd already visited himself, looked in on himself somehow in that little room where his own body lay, knowing he wouldn't alter. Maybe that was his sacrifice for your sake: no hope for you so none for him. His sacrifice of all those other Jacks he might have been. But pull the other one. Maybe Jack Dodds, my husband, was really a saint and I never knew it, I never cottoned on. And I was the weak and the selfish one. Hello Mum.

Best thing we can do, Ame, is

You bastard, you butcher.

I stood there with my hand on his cold forehead, cold as stone, thinking, This is the only Jack that ever was or will be, the one and only, my poor poor Jack. Thinking, They'll have fetched him out the fridge and they'll pop him back, like he used to do with his pork and beef. Say something, Jack, don't just go dead on me too.

Thinking, I've got to look strong and proud and steady for Vince. At least we gave that poor little hopeless bundle a home.

I said, 'Will you go in and see him too, Vincey?'

I've tried to know what it's like to be you, girl. To know what it's like to have missed what you've missed and not even know that you've missed it. I've tried to know if it would have been better or worse, if we'd known beforehand and if we'd had the choice, to have put you out of your misery before you even knew you were you. If you do know that you're you. So Jack and me would've been free to lead different lives, thanks to you having laid down yours. Your sacrifice.

Except it seems that course of action never did much good for Sally Tate, poor little missed-her-date Tate, not in the short term, nor in the long. It seems she just ended up visiting too. Jailbird of a husband. Then having visitors of her own, paying guests. It's a living, you can see what drives a woman to it. And Lenny Tate has turned his back, washed his hands. It's your life, you go and ruin it. Though his own life hasn't got so much left of it, by the look of him these days, he's a bit of a ruin himself. And whether Joan Tate has turned her back or not, or what she thinks, I don't know. Except I think she always knew Lenny had a soft spot for me.

And then there's the crime of it, as it was in those days, bad old days, a crime. Chop it up for you, missis? Though why crime, when a good half of the world, when you think about it, when you think of all the misery, must be wishing for a good half of the time it'd never been born? You and me should be so lucky, June. And anyhow the fact is, the sad fact is, that Sally really wanted Vince. And I hadn't stopped wanting Jack. Let's all go to Dreamland.

Runner beans. Colander. Holes in your head an' all.

This bus is crawling today. It must be the rain, turning the roads to rivers. Atrocious weather. But a bus always gets through. I'll be late today, girl, but it makes no difference, since when did you ever know about the time or the day? Even if sometimes on these Mondays and Thursdays I've thought that perhaps you're *waiting*. You're thinking, It's Monday, it's Thursday, so she'll be coming. I hope she's coming, I hope she never forgets.

And I don't want this journey to pass quickly anyway, not today. Time to think, while the bus chugs, time to prepare what I've got to say.

I've tried and I've hoped and waited for fifty years and

you can't blame me now. You can blame me that you were born in the first place but you can't blame me now. Fifty years is pushing it. And being born may be the big mistake in the opinion of a good part of this world, but once you have been, don't snivel, get on with it. That means you too, my girl, even you. There's only you now to show it, to prove it: that it's not the same as if you *never were*, that it's not as if you might as well have *never been*. Fifty years is beyond the call, for bringing up baby. And I'm sorry about the false hopes and promises, and the moments of weakness, I'm sorry about all the second-stringers, VinceySallyMandy. But that doesn't excuse you from being the one you really are. JuneJuneJune.

I've got to fend for myself now. Though you don't know that, how could you? Look at me, a poor defenceless widow-woman, sitting on a number 44 bus, upstairs, though God knows why, with the world outside, what you can see of it through the fogged-up windows, turned all atrocious. And Bermondsey these days like the back of beyond. Safer where you are, girl, believe me. And now, because we're running late and it's the time they let them out of school, we've gone and stopped at a stop where a whole pack of 'em are screaming to get on. Navy-blue brats. They're piling upstairs, pushing and shoving and yelling like they don't know how just to speak. And I know they're only kids, kids letting off steam, but they scare me half to death. They scare me half to death twice as much as they might if Jack was still here. It shouldn't make any odds, should it, since he wouldn't be here anyway? He'd be there, behind his counter, nice bit of topside missis, not here on this bus with me. Not coming to see you, ever. And never asking, never: How is she? How's June? But it scares me to death that though he's not here, he's not there either, where he always was, nice bit of leg. He's not even propped up on those hospital pillows, like it seemed he was for an age too, for a whole lifetime, being visited. Tell you what, Ame, you come to my place. Even then never saying your name. He's not anywhere. Or by now he'll be washed out to sea or mingling with Margate Sands, if it's all gone to plan, all done before this weather set in. And I know what they'll be saying, thinking: She should've come, she should've been here, she should. Blame me for that too, blame Ame. But someone's got to tell you.

What I'm trying to say is that it's your own damn fault. If no one ever kissed you, no one ever missed you, except me. It's your own damn look-out. And it's too much to hope, I suppose, too much to expect that after fifty years without a peep, without a whisper from you, you should be waiting now, knowing, waiting to say: I understand, I've always understood. It's all right. Forget me.

What I'm trying to say is Goodbye June. Goodbye Jack. They seem like one and the same thing. We've got to make our own lives now without each other, we've got to go our different ways. I've got to think of my own future. It was something Ray said, about how much was I short.

You remember Ray, Uncle Ray? He and I came to visit you once, that summer I missed those Thursdays.

I've got to be my own woman now. But I couldn't have just stopped coming without saying it to your face: Goodbye June. And I couldn't have said the one thing without saying the other. It won't mean anything to you but someone's got to tell you, no one else is going to. That your own daddy, who never came to see you, who you never knew because he never wanted to know you, that your own daddy

RAY

When he was stripped to the waist for digging in, lorry-loading, ammo-lugging or when he was at what the Army and no one else calls ablutions, and once when he was kipping in the shade of a busted wall at Matruh and I was supposed to be standing guard, half the time there's nothing a soldier wants more than sleep, I'd fish in his breast pocket and take out that wallet. I must've looked like a thief except I wasn't taking nothing, and I'd pull out that photo and wish I was him. There's crazier things that keep you sane, when you're lost in the desert. Though if I'd been him and had her, I wouldn't't've had him to be my shield and protector, to place himself between me and the bullets, so to speak. I wouldn't't've been little man hiding behind, I'd've been big man in front. Large target.

And I'd only've felt twice-over exposed and unprotected, any case, on account of having recently heard that the old man had died. Because news travels slow in wartime. But he was dead weeks before, when I'd never known it. He was dead when I was sitting on that camel with Jack, when we was eyeing up them tarts. When I'd scarcely set foot in Africa. Me, Africa. Well, Ray boy, you'll see a bit of the world, you'll see a bit more than the back end of Bermondsey, but keep your bleeding head down, that's what I'm telling you. Which were two bits of fatherly advice I couldn't see how you could ever fit together.

Not a bomb, his chest. And you wouldn't think it would make any difference to your immediate safety and security, him not being there any more, when he wasn't there anyway, as far away alive as dead. Except it takes away a sort of allowance, a sort of margin. It makes you feel you've moved to the front, you're next.

And it's strange to think it was that way round. When you'd expect. When I'd dropped him a postcard only just before I got the news of him, to say I was alive and well and enjoying the sunshine, if I didn't exactly wish he was here. Though he could've done a roaring trade, I reckon, what with all the scrap metal lying around, and the air would've been good for his lungs, dry and clean, except for the dust and the smoke and the petrol fumes and the bleeding flies. And he must've been shaping up, bracing himself to get some message about me, Pte. Johnson, R., that I was a goner. Jack said, 'Well he's spared that worry anyhow.' Him flaked out under that wall just like a dead 'un. And I thought of a time in the future when I might have to say to the girl in the photo, 'Mrs Dodds? Amy Dodds? You don't know me, but I knew Jack. In Africa.' Holding in my hand a little bundle of what the Army calls personal effects. 'My name's Ray Johnson. I only live just round the corner.'

And just remember, Ray boy, you weren't meant for scrap.

It was a photo taken at the seaside. Somehow you could tell that. Summer frock, summer smile, seaside photographer. And now I know where.

We're moving on round the curve of the sea front, still at this snail's pace, solemn and slow and proper. We ought to hurry up if we want to beat the rain. Except it looks like we're going to get a soaking anyway, judging by the spray hitting that harbour wall, I mean Pier. The wind must be coming smack across the bay, west to east. The frontages are getting less grand and there's not so much wide road between them and the sea. They look more flimsy and forlorn, on account of they're more exposed or on account of they never had so much in the first place to put up a show with. *Mario's Coffee Parlour.* Some of them look shuttered up for good. *Rowland's Rock Shoppe. The Ruby Lounge Free House.* I reckon Lenny's got his eye on that, old ruby face. I reckon we've all got our eye on that. *Casanova's Take-away. Femme Fatale – Lingerie, Health and Beauty.*

It aint much. It aint much to write home about, if it's what you get. If the sea's just the sea, wet desert, and the rest is knick-knacks. A pier, a postcard, a penny in a slot. Seems to me you could say that Jack and Amy were spared, after all, Amy was spared. It's a poor dream. Except all dreams are poor.

Thirty-four thousand.

I could see the world. It can't be all sea and desert. I could see the other side of the world, Sydney Harbour, Bondi Beach, it must knock Margate into a cocked hat. I could see Sue, before she gets a message, saying— Before she says to Andy, who I reckon aint wearing that Afghan jacket any more, 'It's the old man.'

A goner.

And I could say, I'm sorry. I'm sorry I stopped writing. Because it was me who stopped first, I'll admit that, but I had my reasons. I'm a small man but I've got my pride and I aint good at admitting things. It was because of Carol. It was because Carol went and left me, dumped me for some other joker, and I was ashamed and afraid to tell you because I reckoned you'd think, for all that you and she used to be daggers drawn, that it was my fault somehow, or I was only pitching for sympathy or it was something to do with you having taken off in the first place. I thought not writing at all was better than thinking up lies, that's what I thought. Except, now you know that and now you know

I haven't told you for nigh on twenty-five years, it probably puts me even more under suspicion. And for twenty-five years you must've been thinking that there was Carol and me on the other side of the world, but me mainly, and we'd just decided not to write. Out of sight, out of mind. Must've made you all the gladder you hopped it. But here I am anyway, now, telling you, saying it to your face. Carol left me about six months after you did, that's a fact. And the fact is I stopped missing her a long time ago, that's how it is, but I aint ever stopped missing you.

Now, where are them grandchildren of mine? And the swimming pool. And aren't you going to show me some koala bears?

I could see the world. It might be better than seeing racetracks. WincantonWolverhamptonYork. It might be better than chasing nags. Have you heard? Old Lucky Johnson's given up the horses, aint going to put on another bet. The world's full of lonely, out-of-luck men, hanging round racetracks, betting shops, checking football results, tearing up chitties, tooling about on Sunday afternoons like prats, plugged into metal-detectors.

And I could say to Susie, And another thing I haven't told you. I haven't come all this way all on my ownsome, no, girl. Wait there just a moment. There's someone I— This is Amy. Amy, remember, your Auntie Amy as you called her? Except she aint your Auntie Amy now, not any more. You know what this trip is, don't you? It's not just any old trip, it's not just a family reunion.

Except then I'd have to come right out with it, wouldn't I? Own up. Me and your Auntie Amy. Just like your mum and— More to the point, I'd have to put it to Amy first, ask her, take the gamble. You don't get nothing without asking, nothing ventured, nothing gained, first law of wagering. But you don't get nothing neither, sometimes, by stirring up old embers. You just get ash. She said, 'We ought to stop this, I ought to start seeing June again,' looking like a nun who'd done a bunk from a convent. She said, 'I can't not see June.'

You fancy a trip to Australia? Down under?

And suppose she said, 'Forget it, Ray, that was over twenty years ago, wasn't it? We're old people now.' Suppose she just said, 'Forget it.' So maybe I'm better off on my tod, like I always was anyway. Seeing the world on my tod, going down under all on my tod, with thirty thousand smackers in my wallet, for ballast. No one need know. Vincey don't even know where his thousand went. I'd bank on it.

It won't happen again like that, miracles don't work twice. And it would've been sort of Jack's gift anyway, one way or the other.

Or maybe I should just give her the money, straight, clean. Here you are, Ame, it's thirty thousand, it's to see you right. Don't thank me, thank Jack and a horse. Except then I can't see how I couldn't tell her. That it was sort of meant like a sign, like a permit, like a blessing on the two of us, to carry on where we left off. And then it would be do or die again, your whole life on a yes or no. What do you say, Ame? And the whole world would have to know, if I was lucky. Not me seeing the world but the world seeing me. Raysy's a dark horse, aint he? Snappy work, if you ask me.

But then *he* knew all along. That's the long and the short of it. Had it all taped and sewn up. Just like he was, lying in that bed, sewn up. As if he was saying, These are my shoes, Raysy, go on, step in 'em, wear 'em. You always should've worn them, if there was anything other than the rule of blind chance in this world, if we could all see and choose in the first place. You and Ame. If we could choose. And you'd be riding Derby winners and Lenny'd be middleweight champ. And I'd be Doctor Kildare. And Vic? I reckon Vic's where he wants to be, I reckon Vic's got it all sorted out.

Go on, take 'em. They're about four sizes too big but I'd say you can walk in 'em.

If we could all see. We're coming up to where the Pier starts now. *Barnacles Free House. Thanet Match Room – Snooker and Social.* If we could all see and choose. Bookies would go broke. But a few things happen anyway, a few things happen. Like we haven't seen or chosen them though we would've if we could've, but they happen anyway, like they saw and chose us first, they saw us coming, like we aint been missed or overlooked altogether, even though we aint the tallest, smartest, niftiest, sharpest punter in the neighbourhood. The sky's pressing down like it's got to burst and Vince is looking for a place to pull in, and what I'm thinking is I'm holding the jar and I don't deserve. The sea's the colour of desertion. It's the colour of wet ash. The rain's coming. Oh Ray, you're a lovely man. To have lived and heard a woman say that to you, even if it aint true. You're a lovely man. The rain on the roof, the noise of the crowd like waves. With tears in her eyes and a flame in her throat: Oh Ray, you're a lovely man, you're a lucky man, you're a little ray of sunshine, you're a little ray of hope.

JACK

He said, 'Jack boy, it's all down to wastage. What you've got to understand is that what comes into the shop aint what goes out. Whole art of butchery's in avoiding wastage. If a butcher could get cost on what he chucks in his waste-bin and his fat-drawer, he'd be a happy man, wouldn't he? He'd be laughing. If you take away the weight of the wastage from what you buy in and divide what's left into what you paid, that'll give you your real cost to set against your takings and don't you ever forget it. Bone'll cost you and fat'll cost you and shrinkage'll cost you and not having your cutlery ground'll cost you. And ending up, because of poor keeping or poor cutting, with lots of measly scraps of meat that aint fit to sell to no one'll cost you more than anything. You got to keep a constant eye on wastage, constant. What you've got to understand is the nature of the goods. Which is perishable.'

MARGATE

Vince parks the car and I'm holding the jar, thinking, I don't deserve, I don't deserve. There's a rough sweep of ground, between the road and the sea, with a little old squat building in the middle of it, with a clock tower, a customs house or something, and the Pier leading off behind. On one side there's the inlet of the harbour, like the Pier's armpit, with a concrete ramp going down, and on the other there's just sea-front, high and railed, curving out the opposite way, with cliffs in the distance, murky white in the grey light, and seagulls doing stunts or lining up on the railings with their wings braced and akimbo. It's like that way it's not beach and sands any more, it's just open sea, North Sea, next stop Norway, and the Pier was put here in the first place to form the bay and the beach and the harbour, sheltering arm against the elements. Only trouble is the elements are coming the opposite way today.

Vince says, 'Right,' opening his driver's door before he's hardly switched off the ignition. 'Let's do it, let's do it.' It's like that slow drive along the front was just tightening his spring and now he wants to move fast. But the sky's telling us we ought to get weaving anyhow, you wouldn't think a sky could get so heavy without bursting. Vince looks up, holding out a cupped hand, half to feel for drops but half to beckon to us, fingers wagging, to get out and shift. It's still only spitting at us, teasing, but the waves seem to know that something's coming. They're jostling and squirming like animals at feeding time, like they're getting ready to get more wet.

Lenny says, 'We could wait a bit. Jack could spare a quarter of an hour.'

Vic says, 'It's not a passing shower. It's dirty weather setting in.'

Aye aye skipper.

Vince moves round to the boot to get his coat, leaving his door open. Cold air swirls round the car again, so does the niff of the seaside: tarry and bilgy and mucky, same time as it's zingy and clean. It smells like something you remember, like the seaside you remember, except I never got taken to no seaside. *It's Tower Bridge Pier or nothing, Ray boy, for you and me.* It smells like memory itself, like the inside of a lobster pot.

Vince comes round to where we can see him again. He's carrying all our coats and jackets, like he's Daddy again, but we don't move. I reckon it's because we're all scared. We're all scared all of a sudden. Vince bangs with his fist on the roof above Vic and Lenny, and Lenny ducks, instinctive, his mouth going flat and wide, his eyes going up and rolling, all froggy. 'Come on,' Vince says, 'let's go.' Then Vic opens his door and Vince hands him his coat. Then I open my door but I stay sitting, holding the jar as if it's too heavy to lift. Then Vince comes round to his open door to take the car keys, and drops my coat for me on his seat. I look at him, holding Jack, as if to say, Do you want? Would you like? And he says, 'Hold on to him, Ray,' as if he remembers he's already done some carrying and chucking, a bit of Jack which got lost on the way. 'Hold on to him.' Which means it'll be up to me. He says, 'I don't think we need the bag any more, do we?' So I pull out the jar and drop the bag at my feet. *Jack Arthur Dodds.* The rain's started to spit harder. Then I grab my coat and get out and Lenny opens his door and gets out. Vince hands him his coat and shuts his door, locking up. Then we're all standing in the wind and the noise of the sea, struggling to put on our clobber. I juggle with Jack while I get my cap on, jamming it tight against the wind, but I don't like to put him down on the tarmac. I can see the jar's going to get wet and slippery. Supposing I drop him? Vince is going bare-headed anyway, that slicked-back hair of his is all over the place, but I've put on my cap now and I wonder if I should've done.

'Come on, come on,' he says, 'let's go.' And it don't seem such a contradiction all of a sudden that it's taken us all day to get here but now we've got to act quick. When you thought of it beforehand, pictured it in your mind's eye, you saw it all paced and slow and ceremonial, with Vic maybe offering a few tips, acting like a marshal, not all whirl and scramble and rush. It's true if we'd got here earlier, like we could've, there might've been calm, space, sunshine, time. But it's as though the weather was needed all along to push us to it, like the elements aren't so much against us as behind us. Like all the while we've been teetering and tottering towards some edge, and now there aint no more hanging back. On account of the heavens being about to open.

The Pier's wider than it looked from a distance, it's as wide as a road, which means maybe we won't get so soaked, not from the spray anyhow. On the seaward side, the side that ought to be taking the worst but isn't, there's a raised bit running all the way along, several feet higher, like a defence, except there's what looks like the remains of old railings and lamp-posts up there, rusty and stumpy, as if once long ago you might've taken a jaunty stroll along the top, if you didn't get blown away first. But now it's closed off, the steps up all crumbled, and down below, on the main level, where we're walking, there's signs saying THIS LAND IS PRIVATE – TRESPASS AT YOUR OWN RISK. So we'd have our excuse for turning round and backing out. No go, Jack, we'd've been trespassing. Except who's going to stop us, day like today? No one else around. And, any case, special circs, special request, special mission. It's like another whip to drive us on.

It's broad and it's solid. I'm glad it aint a jetty, sea thrashing around underneath. But it's potholed and patched and uneven, it wouldn't be an easy walk at the best of times. In the inner wall of the raised bit there are arched bays clogged with rubble and rusty cans and litter, and further on, where the raised bit gets higher, there are lock-ups and lean-tos butting up against it, for storing God knows what, the paint on some of them weathered right off, the woodwork underneath all grey and feathery.

It looks like a dump, that's what it looks like.

It's about two hundred yards long, two hundred and fifty, but Jack said the end, he specified the end. We walk on, spread out, but as if it's the weather that's forcing us apart, it's not our choosing, as if each of us is fighting his own little fight with the elements. We keep to the right, away from the drop to the sea and the beating of the spray, but now and then great showers of it carry to us, flecks stinging our faces, the main offering slapping down with a noise like gravel being flung. Up ahead, on the inside of the curve of the Pier, you can see the waves slicing in and forming peaks, each one like a mad animal trying to scurry up on to the flat surface, lashing out with its tail when it realizes it can't. We don't speak. We can't speak, strung out from each other, but I reckon I couldn't speak anyway. Because there's something swelling up inside me, in my chest, where I'm holding Jack under my car-coat, like there's waves beating at my own harbour wall.

I hadn't expected it, I hadn't reckoned on it. It's like a

part of me's taking charge of me, telling me what to do, telling me how to act.

Vince is walking ahead, maybe four yards, purposeful, one hand thrust in his coat pocket, the other holding his collar to his throat. There's the mud of Kent on his trousers. Vic has drawn level with him but off to the left, as if he's not bothered by a bit of extra spray. His head's up and there's a set to his face that could almost be a smile. And Lenny's somewhere behind me, or I hope he is. I ought to turn round, give him a helping hand, grab him by the arm and pull him along, which wouldn't be easy, holding Jack as well. But it's Vince who suddenly stops and turns, to check on us stragglers, and as I carry on walking it's him I grab by the arm, not worrying about Jack, my other arm and the feeling in my chest are taking care of Jack. I grab his arm, pulling it, squeezing it, and as I draw up close to him I say, 'I've got your thousand. I'll give you back your thousand. I'll explain.' And I'm glad that all the noise and commotion mean there can't be no lengthy conversation, and that all the spray flying about means that Vincey can't be sure of what's going on in my face. But the look in Vincey's face is like simple plain relief, like light's suddenly splashed across it. It's like he can wait for the full story but right now he's shot of some little nagging side-problem and he can give the matter at hand his full attention. We both turn and look at Lenny, hunched, hobbling, flame-faced, battling towards us. He draws level and he says, 'I reckon Amy made the right decision after all.'

We move on, slipping back into our own separate spaces, Vic several yards ahead now. It looks like Vic's going to win this race. Victor. And as we carry on it's like the rain decides it's time it fell proper at last. Nothing changes in the sky but the rain just starts to rain in earnest. It sweeps in on the wind as if it's tired of the spray making a poor job of wetting us, so in seconds we're soaked and it's running off our noses and chins, but I'm not sorry about that. And either the wind takes away some of the weight of the rain or the rain cuts through the force of the wind, because it's like with the rain everything gets softer, safer, like we're in the thick and there's nothing more that can be chucked at us now. The light's all dim and gauzy across the bay as if there's furls of giant lace curtains swirling about in it, and the waves don't look so angry any more, and maybe Vic was wrong about it not being a passing shower because low down in the sky in the distance, inland, there's a faint thin gleam. We choose our moments.

It's not far to go now. I don't know if I say it spoken or just in my head but I say it, 'Not far to go now, Jack,' holding him inside my wet coat, 'nearly there.' And, now we've come right round the arm of the Pier, you can look across through the murk at the centre of Margate like we're on opposite shores, different lands. You can see Marine Terrace and the parade of arcades we passed earlier, with their sprinkled lights, like little toy buildings trying to wave at us, trying to say, Here we are. And behind them, against the pale band in the sky, you can see the outline of the big wheel and the dipper and even imagine there's some mad buggers up there right now, in the swaying seats, in the rattling cars, screaming and shrieking in the wind and the rain like they're crazier than we are.

Vic has reached the end. He stands there for a moment looking out. Captain on the bridge. Up above him, on the raised section, there's a harbour light on a tower like a miniature lighthouse, but where he's standing it looks like there's just a stone platform and a drop. He starts to pace about, waiting for us. It seems right that Vic's there first, to inspect the pitch, check the facilities, it wouldn't do if something wasn't up to scratch. We come up to him and he turns and looks at us, standing square and straight, like the wind's decided to go round him, and gives us one of his all-present-and-correct smiles. He's looking specially at me.

He says, 'Here we are.' But there aint nothing here but huge great slabs of stone laid as flags, all pocked and pitted and puddly, and a low granite parapet, like kerbstones, half broken away, and the wind and the rain and the spray. On one side the waves are smacking and crashing, and on the other they're gurgling and clucking like they're trying to apologize. One way there's Margate and Dreamland, the other there's the open sea. Except it aint just the open sea, because now we can peer round the end of the raised bit, we can see it: a rusty mass of old iron-work sticking up out of the water about three hundred yards out, the waves surging around it, like what's left of a fallen-in bridge.

'It's the Jetty,' Vince says, shouting against the wind. 'It's the Jetty, the bit that never got swept away.'

I hear Lenny say, 'Today could be the day.'

We're at the end and I'm holding Jack. I reckon you know what to do at the end. I always thought there'd be a pause, a time for gathering up your last thoughts, and someone might want to say some words and give a sign. There'd be this hesitation like when you sit down to eat with strange people and you look this way and that because you aint sure if they're the sort who say grace. But I don't hesitate. I get out the jar from under my coat, Jack Arthur Dodds, and I don't say nothing, cradling the jar in my arm, unscrewing the cap, like there's nothing else for it, and as I do, the rain starts to ease, like a gap's opened up in it just long enough for the disposing of a man's ashes, and that's sign enough.

We're at the end. I said, 'What was he doing at the end?' Amy said, 'He was sitting up in bed listening to the radio, and then, the nurse said, he took off his headphones, all neat and careful, and said, "That's it then. That's all right then," and she went off just for a moment to do something and when she came back he was dead.' I unscrew the cap and shove it in my pocket, then I hold out the jar, turning my back to the wind, and I say, 'Come on then,' like I'm holding out a tin of sweets or doling out rations. Careful now, one at a time, there's only room for one hand at a time. Lenny dips in first and takes out a handful, sifts of it slipping through his fingers, and Vic says, 'Keep your hands as dry as you can,' wiping his own hands on a handkerchief, and I realize what he means. It's so Jack don't stick to us, it's so we don't get Jack stuck to our hands. But I haven't got no handkerchief, I aint never thought. Today of all days, I never thought about no handkerchief. Then Vic puts in his hand and takes out a scoop. Then Vince pushes up his sleeve but hesitates, like he's going to say, 'After you, Raysy,' because he's had a go already, he's dipped in already, or because he just wants me to go first. But I can see it aint going to be easy, holding the wet jar as well, so I say, 'Go on, Vincey, go on.' And he takes a scoop and they all move off to the lee edge of the parapet, holding their hands out cupped and tight like they've each got little birds to set free and we've all got to do it together, so they're waiting for me. Vic says, 'I wouldn't go too near the edge, if I was you. The wind'll take it, let the wind take it,' as if we're that daft. He'll be handing out life-belts next. And I know I've got to do it quick, like scattering seed, only having the one hand free, so I move towards the parapet, angling the jar away from the wind, then I dip into the jar and draw up a handful to the neck. It's soft and grainy at the same time, and almost white, it's like white soft sand on a beach. Then I whip out my hand and throw. They must all have thrown at the same time but I aint looking at them, I'm looking at what I've thrown. I say, 'Goodbye Jack.' I say it to the wind. And they say, 'Goodbye Jack.'

It's true what Vic said. The wind takes it, it's gone in a whirl, in a flash. Now you see it, now you don't. Then I take the jar in both hands again, giving a quick peek inside, and say, 'Come on, come on.' They all huddle round to take another scoop. There isn't much more than four men can scoop out twice over. They dip in again, one by one. Lucky dip. And I dip and we all throw again, a thin trail of white, like smoke, before it's gone, and some seagulls swoop in from nowhere and veer off again like they've been tricked. Then I know there's not enough for another share-out, another full round, so I just start scooping myself, they don't seem to mind. I scoop and scoop like some animal scratching out its burrow, and I know in the end I'm going to have to hold up the jar and bang it like you do when you get to the bottom of a box of cornflakes. One handful, two handfuls, there's only two handfuls. I say, 'Goodbye Jack.' The sky and the sea and the wind are all mixed up together but I reckon it wouldn't make no difference if they weren't because of the blur in my eyes. Vic and Vincey's faces look like white blobs but Lenny's looks like a beacon, and across the water you can see the lights of Margate. You can stand on the end of Margate Pier and look across to Dreamland. Then I throw the last handful and the seagulls come back on a second chance and I hold up the jar, shaking it, like I should chuck it out to sea too, a message in a bottle, Jack Arthur Dodds, save our souls, and the ash that I carried in my hands, which was the Jack who once walked around, is carried away by the wind, is whirled away by the wind till the ash becomes wind and the wind becomes Jack what we're made of.

PERMISSIONS ACKNOWLEDGEMENTS

Grateful acknowledgement is made to the following for permission to reprint previously published material:

Acuff-Rose Music, Inc., and Hal Leonard Corporation: Excerpts from 'Blue Bayou' by Roy Orbison and Joe Melson, copyright © 1961, copyright renewed 1989, by Acuff-Rose Music, Inc., Barbara Orbison Music Company, Orbi-Lee Music, and R-Key Darkus Music. International copyright secured. All rights reserved. Reprinted by permission of Acuff-Rose Music, Inc., and Hal Leonard Corporation on behalf of Barbara Orbison Music Company, Orbi-Lee Music, and R-Key Darkus Music.

Essex Music, Inc.: Excerpts from 'The Gipsy in My Soul' words by Moe Jaffe, music by Clay Boland, TRO-copyright © 1937 (copyright renewed) by Essex Music, Inc., and Words and Music, Inc., New York, NY. Reprinted by permission of Essex Music, Inc.

Gil Music Corp.: Excerpt from 'I Saw Her Standing There' by John Lennon and Paul McCartney, copyright © 1963, 1964 by Nothern Songs Ltd., London, copyright renewed. International copyright secured. Made in U.S.A. All rights reserved. Reprinted by permission of Gil Music Corp.

A NOTE ON THE AUTHOR

Graham Swift was born in London in 1949. He is the author of five novels: *The Sweet-Shop Owner; Shuttlecock; Waterland,* which was shortlisted for the Booker Prize and won the *Guardian* Fiction Award, the Winifred Holtby Memorial Prize, and the Italian Premio Grinzane Cavour; *Out of This World;* and *Ever After,* which won the Prix du Meilleur Livre Étranger. He has also published a collection of short stories, *Learning to Swim.* His work has been translated into more than twenty languages.